*New York Times*

# COLLEEN GLEASON

## THREE TOMES BOOKSHOP

# HEXES, EXES AND CODEXES

J acqueline Finch had the perfect life for a book-loving
librarian (a redundancy, to be sure—for had anyone ever
met a librarian who *wasn't* a book lover?).

As of three months ago, she owned a small store called
Three Tomes Bookshop in the picturesque town of Button Cove,
nestled on the upper-left corner of the Michigan "mitten," right
on Lake Michigan.

The area had been called "Land of Delight" by the indige-
nous peoples who'd lived there centuries before the European
emigration—and there could be no better phrase to describe the
lush, rolling hills, the vast, sparkling blue water, the loamy green
forests, and the sandy dunes that rose along the westernmost
coast of Michigan. Jacqueline could hardly wait to see how
gorgeous Button Cove and the area looked in the autumn, when
the leaves changed...

But for now, she had the summer season looming ahead of
her—something she both dreaded and anticipated.

"You'll have a love-hate relationship with them," her friend
Suzette Whalley had told her, speaking of the tourists that
would descend on the region beginning Memorial Day weekend

and not let up until after Fall Color Tours in mid-October. "Your sales will be off the charts, but at the same time you'll be overrun by them. Most are lovely, friendly people, and others... not so much."

Suzette would know. She owned Sweet Devotion, the bakery across the street from Three Tomes, and had lived in Button Cove most of her adult life.

"I'll batten down the hatches," said Jacqueline with a grin, wondering if she was going to need to hire extra help for the summer season.

Currently, she was the only employee at Three Tomes... unless you counted Mrs. Hudson and Mrs. Danvers, and using the term *employee* to describe either of them was laughable.

Mrs. Hudson's other position was landlady to none other than Sherlock Holmes at 221B Baker Street in London. And Mrs. Danvers was the haughty, creepy, intimidating housekeeper at Manderley, where the ill-fated Rebecca of Daphne du Maurier's famous novel had lived.

The two women, who were presumably still landlady and housekeeper in their fictional worlds, also worked at Three Tomes. Jacqueline couldn't get rid of them even if she tried (and she'd tried).

The motherly Mrs. Hudson wasn't so bad—she ran the tea room on the second floor of the bookshop—except that the word "coffee" was anathema to her. She refused to hear a word about offering the "demon bean" to any of their customers, and Jacqueline had taken to hiding the coffee she brewed safely (and secretly) in her flat on the third floor of the building, and in a large thermos in the shop's back room.

Mrs. Danvers was... Well, she was kind of scary.

Jacqueline got along with the housekeeper all right—as long as she did what she was told to do. (Jacqueline being the one who was told what to do.) And she couldn't deny that she'd be unable to run the bookshop without the help of the two literary characters who'd somehow come out of the books in which they'd been written into.

Jacqueline had stopped wondering how or why about this movement of literary characters in and out of their books; it was pointless. It simply was. Sort of like gravity. And Murphy's law. And the fact that physics tended to work against her when she was in a hurry.

But she really couldn't look a gift horse—or two—in the mouth. Mrs. Hudson and Mrs. Danvers worked for free, and, honestly, they knew more about running the bookshop than she did. Being trained on the computer system by Mrs. Danvers— who'd lived in du Maurier's fictional world in the mid-1930s— had been surreal, but by now Jacqueline was used to the fact that her life was filled with all sorts of surreal events.

Like the fact that the three old ladies down the street were witches. And that another witch—a distant cousin of hers—had recently opened a handbag boutique down the street.

And that she'd most recently had a battle between vampires and vampire hunters in this very shop—all fictional, and all sprung from novels from her own store. Thank goodness there'd been vampire *hunter* novels too.

She sighed and looked around. It was the Friday of Memorial Day weekend. This was when the summer season officially kicked off. The weekend would be busy, and there would be a parade on Monday that would draw people to the downtown area, so she would be open on Memorial Day in order to catch the business.

She really, *really* hoped there weren't going to be any vampires or witches or Cinderellas or ogres—or any crazy characters—competing with the tourists for her attention. She was going to have her hands full just with nonfictional people!

Nevertheless, Jacqueline was smiling as she turned her

attention to the front window display she'd been putting together before opening the store for the day.

Three Tomes Bookshop was housed in a blocky three-story Victorian home with high ceilings, tall, narrow windows, gleaming pine and oak floors, fireplaces in nearly every room, and nooks and crannies that went on like a labyrinth forever. Flanking the front door were two deep bay windows that were perfect for displaying eye candy for book lovers.

Today, Jacqueline was putting together a Summer Reading collection for students who were counting down the days left of school (seven and a half, apparently) before the gloriousness of summer break. She had arranged small boxes of various shapes and sizes, then covered them all with green fabric to make them look like rolling hills. One of the trio of witches—er, old ladies—down the street, Andromeda, who had the greenest thumb, had loaned Jacqueline a huge bonsai tree that was five feet tall and who knew how old. It fit perfectly in the window.

She arranged the tree to one side of the wide and deep window, and its branches swept over the top of the display as if they belonged there.

Then Jacqueline began to fill the area with books...books she'd loved as a child (*Anne of Green Gables*, *Cady Woodlawn*, Beverly Cleary, the Boxcar Children, and Trixie Belden)...books she could hardly keep in the store, they sold so quickly (*The Fourth Wing*, the latest Leigh Bardugo, the new *Captain Underpants*)...books that had been around awhile but always found new readers (Harry Potter, Percy Jackson, *Twilight*, *The Ranger's Apprentice*, Lord of the Rings)...

She strung up an empty backpack from a low branch of the tree, then arranged the books so they looked as if they'd all tumbled from the bag and spilled over the ground. Butterflies, ladybugs, dragonflies, snails, frogs, and more decorated the

woodland scene. She added a pillow and plush, cozy blanket...
because even summer nights could be chilly.

"That looks amazing, Jacqueline!" said a familiar voice
behind her as she was examining the display from the sidewalk.
"I just want to cozy up right there in the window with the new
Emily Henry and a cocktail."

Jacqueline turned, smiling. "Hey, Nadine. How's it going?"

Nadine Bachmoto owned the yoga studio above Suzette's
bakery. The three women had become very close friends—a
surprise to Jacqueline, since she'd only been in Button Cove for
a few months and hadn't been the sort to have close girlfriends...
at least before.

Back in Chicago, where she'd lived for more than forty-five
years, Jacqueline'd had acquaintances, people she would hang
out with occasionally, and a few women from work that she
called friends...but she hadn't had anyone she'd term a "best
friend" for years—and now she had *two* of them.

Instead of life ending at fifty, Jacqueline's life was just beginning. And she was only forty-eight!

"Oh, it's going," replied Nadine in a voice that clearly said it
*wasn't* going.

She was not the stereotypical image of a yoga instructor. She
wasn't slender or long or petite. She had plenty of curves and
bulges, firm biceps, pudgy hands and ankles. Her rich brown
hair, cut in layers that just brushed her shoulders (she claimed it
was a take-off on the "Rachel" from *Friends*, but Jacqueline
thought it looked more like vintage Joan Jett, which definitely
wasn't a bad thing), was pulled up into a high ponytail. Wisps of
the layers straggled down over her nape. As usual, Nadine was
wearing workout clothes that unabashedly showed every one of
her bulges and curves.

"What's going on?" Jacqueline asked, gesturing for her friend
to join her inside the shop.

"Oh, it's Noah. He's being a complete and utter dick. As usual."

Noah was Nadine's ex-husband. He was a neurosurgeon who also thought he was God (according to Nadine, and Jacqueline had no reason not to believe her—that was simple friend solidarity). Although the divorced couple's relationship was usually amicable, as was often true with exes, sometimes there was friction. Or worse.

"I've got fresh jalapeño and cheese muffins in the café if you need sustenance," Jacqueline said.

Nadine's eyes lit up. "Ohmigod...Suzette's Spicy, Sassy Corn Muffins? *Sold*." She started for the wide staircase that led to the second-floor café and reading area, then skidded to a halt. "But I've gotta have coffee."

Jacqueline nodded in understanding. "Absolutely. I'll get the muffins—you can head to my apartment and fire up the Keurig." Now it was her turn to pause. "Should I text Suzette? How bad is it?"

Nadine sighed. "Well...it's not bad enough that Suze should be called away from her quiches and muffins and—ZOMG, those new oatmeal butterscotch brownies; have you *had* them? —but bad enough that I need a corn muffin and caffeine. I just need to *vent*."

"I can handle venting. Let me just, um, check with Mrs. Danvers and make sure she can open up," Jacqueline said, looking around warily. The last she'd seen of the housekeeper, the woman was vigorously vacuuming the Science Fiction Room.

That wasn't as much of an anomaly as one might think; there had actually been Hoovers in the 1930s.

Nadine grinned at her. "Good luck with that."

The trick with Mrs. Danvers, Jacqueline had learned, was to make the woman think whatever you wanted her to do was *her* idea, or to appear so incompetent that she pushed her way in to do whatever it was herself—all the while giving you the hairy eyeball of disgust.

As Nadine made her way to the back of the store, where there was a discreet door leading to a stairway to the third-floor apartment, Jacqueline hurried up the steps to the tea shop.

She wasn't the least bit out of breath when she got to the top —something that hadn't been true when she first took over Three Tomes. Progress, she told herself.

"Good morning, Mrs. Hudson," she said.

The motherly woman—who looked exactly the way Jacqueline had always imagined Sir Arthur Conan Doyle's creation would appear—turned from where she was straightening teacups (not coffee cups) on their hooks and shelves behind the counter.

Of an indeterminate age—probably sixty-ish—Mrs. Hudson was dressed in her normal Victorian-era garb of a sober-colored dress with a white apron over it. The dress had a high collar with a bit of lace, and its sleeves were long with more lace at the cuffs. Although Jacqueline couldn't see her legs, she knew the landlady would be wearing dark stockings and sturdy shoes.

"Good morning there, now, dearie. And what is it you're wanting to nibble on today?"

"Some of the corn muffins," Jacqueline replied, even as she eyed the blueberry cream scones that were her favorite. The scones were made not by Suzette but by Pietra, another of the three crones who lived at the end of the cul-de-sac. "And a scone too."

"Of course. And will you be having a nice pot of Earl Grey, or are you wanting an oolong this morning, then, dearie?"

"Whatever you think goes best with the muffins and scone," Jacqueline said. She likely wouldn't drink the tea, but she wasn't about to tell Mrs. Hudson about that mortal sin. "Nadine and I are meeting in my flat, so I'll take a tray to go."

Mrs. Hudson paused. "Oh? In your flat? But why don't you want to have it here, then, ma'am?" She put her hands on her hips, eyeing Jacqueline a little suspiciously.

"It's...it's a private conversation," Jacqueline replied, thinking quickly. "It's about her ex-husband, and she doesn't want anyone else hearing about it. Any customers, I mean," she added hastily.

Mrs. Hudson gave an irritated sniff—there weren't any customers yet because the shop hadn't opened—and cast a little glower at Jacqueline, but continued about her business. Even so, she was mumbling and grumbling beneath her breath as she set the teacups and a pot of tea none too gently on a large silver tray.

Just then, Mrs. Danvers appeared.

Jacqueline managed to hide her jolt of surprise; she should be used to it by now. The woman tended to pop up as if she'd apparated out of thin air, but Jacqueline suspected this time she'd come out of the elevator near the pantry in the back of the second floor. Still, she moved silently as a wraith.

As usual, Mrs. Danvers gave off the appearance of a bad-tempered crow. She was dressed in blue-black from head to toe, with shiny, inky hair scraped back so hard it surely was the reason her face seemed so tight and unmoving. She was probably in constant pain from the ruthless pinning of the bun at the back of her neck, which could explain her dourness. She was about Jacqueline's age, but her face showed no sign of the wrinkles and sags that Jacqueline noticed in the mirror every morning. Probably due to the tight hair...

Mrs. Danvers wore a belt around her slender waist, and from the belt hung a large ring of keys, which one would expect to give off a warning jangle or clink, heralding her presence...but it never did. Jacqueline suspected the housekeeper clamped a tight fist over the key ring whenever she wanted to startle her—which was, obviously, as often as possible.

"Ma'am," said Mrs. Danvers in a tone that sounded more resentful than cordial. "There is something you might wish to see."

Jacqueline's heart fell. Every damned time that woman had something Jacqueline needed to see or attend to, it was bad. The first time had been a dead body in the living room of her apartment. Another time it was a woman whose husband was trying to kill her.

"What is it?" she asked, as she always did—knowing full well the housekeeper wouldn't tell her, and that she would have to go see it anyway. But it was a knee-jerk reaction. Maybe one time it would work.

Not this time.

Mrs. Danvers merely gestured for Jacqueline to follow her down the short hallway.

Unlike downstairs, the second floor of the bookshop was a large, open space in front, with the tea room, fireplace, and many tables and sofas on which to sit, eat, drink, visit, and read. (Jacqueline had learned early on that one of the most delightful quirks of Three Tomes Bookshop was that any food or drink that spilled on the books simply rolled off or disappeared without any sort of damage.) Adjacent to the sitting area and tea room was the large, open area displaying children's books.

In the rear half of the spacious second floor was storage, an elevator, and what Jacqueline privately called "the Woo-Woo Room." This area held everything from tarot cards and angel cards to candles, incense, crystals, meditation and Wicca books, to volumes of herbal remedies, spiritual biographies and directories, and so on. Its official name was the New Age Room, and Jacqueline remembered to call it that most of the time.

It turned out this was Mrs. Danvers's destination, and she

waved Jacqueline inside and pointed to the back of the room with a sarcastic flourish.

On the floor in a rear corner was an arrangement of large, colorful sitting pillows, or poufs, that appeared to have been brought from the children's area. Three of them formed a cozy circle, and in the center of the circle was what appeared to be the remnants of a small—

"Holy crap, was someone *burning* something in here?" Jacqueline was appalled for a number of obvious reasons. "When was this? And why didn't the smoke alarms go off?"

She crouched next to what seemed to have been some sort of gathering place, frowning at the scene. It appeared that someone—or several someones; three if one assumed each person had their own pouf to sit on—had used one of the metal singing bowls (which were *not* cheap!) in which to contain a small fire.

It was impossible to tell what had been burned in the heavy bowl; all that remained in the hammered-metal cup was a small pile of ashes.

"When did this happen?" Jacqueline demanded of Mrs. Danvers, who'd stood over her as she examined the scene.

"I wouldn't know. As you are certainly aware, the second floor is not *my* purview, ma'am," replied Mrs. Danvers stiffly, and cast a sardonic look in the direction of the café and Mrs. Hudson. "A person would *think* one would notice something *burning* if one were paying attention to their responsibilities. *I* certainly don't know anything about this."

Jacqueline decided not to point out that if the second floor was not Mrs. Danvers's *purview*, then what was she doing poking around the New Age Room anyway? Besides, it wasn't even remotely true that the second floor was only up to Mrs. Hudson to manage; Mrs. Danvers was quite often found dusting, vacuuming, rearranging, and more up here. And besides, Mrs.

Hudson was too busy with the tea room and its customers to be aware of everything that went on in the New Age Room.

Jacqueline looked around the room but didn't see anything else immediately out of place. When had this happened? Yesterday, when the shop was open? Overnight? A chill ran down her spine. Had someone sneaked in overnight and...done this?

The chill down her spine turned to a prickle. It seemed pretty obvious that someone had been conducting some sort of magical—or wannabe magical—spell or incantation.

Feeling very unsettled, she was just about to hurry out and ask Mrs. Hudson whether she'd noticed anything when Mrs. Danvers gave a peremptory "ahem."

The housekeeper was looking pointedly at the floor where the poufs were arranged. Despite loathing the fact that Mrs. Danvers seemed to enjoy one-upping her, Jacqueline had to investigate.

The item that caught the housekeeper's attention (and that she hadn't bothered to stoop to retrieve) was a book that appeared to have fallen behind the thick, round floor cushion. Jacqueline picked it up and was surprised to discover that it was a history book about Henry VIII and not, as she'd anticipated, a spell book or other tome that belonged in the Woo-Woo Room and might have been used for...whatever had taken place with the fire in the singing bowl.

The book was an oversized, battered casebook hardcover. She flipped through it, looking for an indication of where it had come from or to whom it belonged. Maybe it was a library book, or even a school textbook. But there was nothing inside to suggest from whence it had come. The only thing she knew for certain was that it wasn't a book that had been for sale here at Three Tomes—there was no identifying barcode sticker on the back.

Humming to herself, Jacqueline tucked the book under her

arm and went back out to the tea room, leaving Mrs. Danvers happily cleaning up the disarrangement. She knew Mrs. Danvers was never more content than when she was setting a mess to rights—especially one that had been caused by someone else and on someone else's watch. Something that she could lord over a person.

Mrs. Hudson had a tray ready for Jacqueline—a teapot, cups and saucers, and a small plate of the pastries. When Jacqueline explained what happened and showed her the history book, Mrs. Hudson was at a loss.

"Did you see anything? Someone carrying the cushions out of the room?" Jacqueline asked.

"I was quite busy yesterday, dearie," Mrs. Hudson said in a tone that was very nearly admonishing Jacqueline for even *suggesting* that she might have somehow, even obliquely, been responsible for allowing the activity to happen. "Couldn't be keeping an eye on *everyone* who's coming through here and back to That Room, could I?"

Mrs. Hudson was not a fan of the Woo-Woo Room and its contents. In fact, she'd tried more than once to convince Jacqueline that it should be moved to a different location—on the first floor, or even the unfinished cellar. Anywhere away from her, she'd said. Jacqueline found this quite ironic, since Mrs. Hudson's presence could only be described as being *woo-woo* itself.

"I just wondered if you'd noticed anything," Jacqueline said, trying not to sound meek. She'd been a people-pleaser most of her life, and old habits died hard. But since coming to Button Cove and taking over Three Tomes, she'd been working on developing a stronger backbone. And, most of the time, she was successful. "Whoever did this left the book and had to have been back there for a while. Plus they had to have brought the cushions from the children's area. If it didn't happen during opening hours, it must have happened overnight, which obviously is even worse. So I thought you might have seen—"

"Well, now you mention it, I might have seen something," said Mrs. Hudson. "There was a girl was carrying one of them big, puffy pillows. I only thought she was moving it to sit by the window, but could be she took it back to That Room, if you say they were back there. I remember her because she wanted a macky-oh-toh—or something like that—to drink, and I told her we don't have any of that demon bean here."

"Do you remember anything more about her? What she looked like? How old she was? Was she alone?" Jacqueline asked.

Mrs. Hudson gave her a Look. "I ain't Mr. Holmes, you know. *He* never expected me to be *observing* all those sorts of things, so I don't know why you would do. I'm far too busy with customers, dearie."

"Right," Jacqueline said, and realized she wasn't going to learn anything more from Mrs. Hudson. "Well, if you see her again or if anyone comes back looking for the history book, please let me know. I'll have it with me."

She wasn't going to leave the book here in the tea room. She wanted to return it to its owner herself, for obvious reasons.

Jacqueline took the tray and carried it, along with the history book tucked under her arm, down the hall to the elevator hidden inside the pantry. She'd recently installed a code to access the third floor so that customers didn't accidentally take the lift to her flat. That had only happened once, but it was enough.

"Sorry it took me so long," Jacqueline said to Nadine, breezing out from the elevator, which was located in the back of her apartment's small kitchen. There was a half wall that separated the eating area from the living room where Jacqueline's beloved blue velvet sofa sprawled in front of a large fireplace.

Nadine was sitting on the sofa and had two cups of steaming coffee on the low table in front of it. She set aside her phone. "No worries—I was just checking my email."

"You won't believe what I found in the New Age Room," Jacqueline told her as she set the tray on the table.

As she and Nadine dove into the scones and corn muffins, Jacqueline explained.

"What the hell? Do you think someone was doing some sort of...spell or something?" Nadine asked.

"I don't want to think about that," Jacqueline said, even though she of course already had. There'd been too many spell-like, curse-like, witchy-like things happening at Three Tomes, and she just wished things would settle down for more than a few days at a time. She glanced toward the fireplace above where a large, round mirror used to hang—a mirror that had been possessed by an angry witch who thought *she* should have control over the bookshop.

Now, a beautiful painting of a woodland scene at twilight, dominated by a large cedar tree, hung there. It had been a housewarming gift for Jacqueline, presented by the three old ladies who lived at the end of the court. Zwyla, Andromeda, and Pietra—also known as the ZAP Ladies—were undeniably witches.

Another thing Jacqueline tried not to think about too often.

"And you said whoever it was left that book there with the stuff?" Nadine nervously eyed the tome Jacqueline had set on the table next to the tea tray.

"It's not that kind of book," Jacqueline said hastily. "At least, I don't think it is."

She knew Nadine was wondering whether someone was going to pop out of the Henry VIII biography—just like Cinderella had emerged from the *Grimms' Fairy Tales* and the Artful Dodger had sprung from *Oliver Twist*. Usually when she found a book on the floor it portended such an event—although the book always fell and landed *open* if someone was coming out of it. This one hadn't been open.

"Anyway, this book isn't from the shop, for one, and for two, it's not fiction. So far we've only had fictional characters...uh... emerge."

Still, she couldn't help but give the volume a wary look.

"If you say so." Nadine tilted her head and gave her the side-eye.

"So tell me what's going on with Noah, the Man Who Thinks He's God but He's Really Just a Neurosurgeon," said Jacqueline, happy to change the subject.

"Oh, he's just being a dick. Danny needed new brakes on her car a few weeks ago, which he paid for—grumbled about, but paid for—and now she needs new tires and a muffler. He told her she's maxed out her budget on car repairs for this year and is refusing to help her pay for it. So now *I* have to find the cash." Nadine took a big gulp of coffee that was so laden with cream it was pale beige. "It's not as if the man's not freaking loaded. And it's not like he's paying me alimony or even child support now that Danny's over eighteen. She's in college full time and can't work more than fifteen or twenty hours a week—and that's for living expenses.

"He's being a royal jerk. Plus he's the one who told her to buy a used car—well, what happens when you have a used car? You don't have a car payment, and you've got lower insurance—but you might have to *fix* it occasionally. What a dick."

"Didn't he just get back from a big trip with the new girl-friend?" Jacqueline asked, feeling her friend's pain. Nadine's yoga studio did well financially—she owned the building, lived on the second floor, and rented out some spaces in it, including Sweet Devotion—but not well enough that she could drop a thousand dollars on tires and a muffler without feeling the pinch. And Jacqueline knew that Danny lived with Nadine when she wasn't at school, so she covered most of her daughter's living expenses anyway.

"Oh yeah. It was a month-long cruise through the Mediterranean. I happen to know they booked the Captain's Suite, too—which, seriously, one freaking night would have paid for Danny's repairs four times over. Of course I checked," Nadine said, not even a little embarrassed. "He never took me on a cruise like that—and I don't care about that, to be honest. Too fancy for me. Anyway, the guy's just being a douche. She's his daughter, and she's a poor college student, and he's making it sound like she *chose* to have car problems."

"That is definitely douche-y behavior," Jacqueline said. "Doesn't he want his daughter to be driving around in a safe and reliable vehicle?"

"Right? Exactly what I said." Nadine sighed and shook her head. "I don't know. Maybe he'll change his mind. But Danny's so mad she's not even talking to him. And she doesn't want to ask me for the money—she *hates* asking me because I pay for most everything else—but she's *got* to have new tires. Hers are practically bald. And you can hear her Jeep coming from a mile away with that raggedy muffler. Ugh." She made a face and popped a chunk of jalapeño and cheddar muffin into her mouth, then said, around the bite, "Hey...didn't you just get back from seeing *Six*? It seems kind of coincidental, that Henry VIII book showing up, if you ask me."

Jacqueline opened her mouth to pooh-pooh the idea, then closed it. She *had* just returned from a few days in Chicago to see the rock musical about Henry VIII's six wives—called, appropriately, *Six*.

Then she opened her mouth again, feeling confident. "It's just a coincidence. Like I said, the book isn't even from my shop.

But, speaking of dick-ish exes, something did happen when I was there in Chicago."

"What?" Nadine perked up, her ears seeming to quiver with interest.

"I ran into Josh Wenczel—my former fiancé."

"*No!*" Nadine's eyes popped wide. "From *years* ago? Ooooh!"

"Yep. First time I've seen him since I dumped his butt three days before the wedding. I did tell you he'd been boinking one of the bridesmaids, right?"

"That's so cliché," Nadine said, shaking her head.

"Seriously. The guy never did have a lot of imagination. Other than in the bedroom..." Jacqueline felt her face heat up.

Nadine nearly surged across the sofa. "*In bed?*" she shrieked, her eyes wide, her lips curved in surprised and delighted laughter. "Jacqueline! Was he a *tiger* in bed? A magician? A gymnast? An *artiste*? What? Tell me!"

Jacqueline's blush didn't ease, but she did manage to say, "Well...that was one thing that was quite beneficial about our relationship. I do miss that, even though it's been years." Many years.

"Mmhm," Nadine said, grinning with delight. "And why wouldn't you. So...what happened when you saw him? Was it weird? Was he with someone? Was he wearing a ring? Who were you with, anyway?"

"I was with Wendy and a couple other people from the library. We've had the tickets since January—it was at the show where I ran into him. All those people and I'm at the bar getting a glass of Prosecco, and I turn around and nearly run right into Josh."

"Did you spill your drink on him? I would've," Nadine said. "Then I'd have made him buy me a new one."

Jacqueline laughed. "Good idea. No, I saved the bubbly from spilling, and it was... Well, he didn't seem surprised to see me.

Like, I was surprised when I turned around and saw him, but he wasn't. Or didn't seem to be. He didn't stay in the drink line...he walked away with me."

"He *did*?" Nadine's brows rose in little peaks. "Girl, he *knew* you were in line and he got in behind you so he could talk to you. I bet he did. Did you look to see whether he was wearing a ring? What happened?"

"He wasn't wearing a ring. Of course I looked. And nothing really happened. We said hi, and he asked how I was, and I said I was fine and mentioned I'd moved to Button Cove, and he said he'd heard about that..." Jacqueline frowned. "I'm not sure how he would have heard about it, since it was so long ago that we broke things off that we don't even have any mutual friends anymore...but...he knew."

"He probably stalks your social media," said Nadine.

"Maybe. I don't know why he would, but...anyway, it wasn't as awkward as you might think. It was... Well, it was fine."

"*Ohmigod you still have feelings for him,*" Nadine said gleefully.

"No I don't," replied Jacqueline...not quite certain whether that was true. Josh had looked pretty good for being over fifty. "The guy cheated on me. *Right* before our wedding."

"Yeah, but he was a tiger in bed," Nadine reminded her with a lascivious grin. "You could just have revenge sex with him." She sighed. "That's the only real thing I miss from when I was dating Pete last year. He was good in bed too, damn the man. An idiot—but he knew what buttons to push, let me say." She had a faraway smile. Then it turned lascivious again. "So what's the deal with Massermey? Is he still gone?"

Jacqueline didn't know why her cheeks heated. She was with her friend who knew most everything about her very budding romance with the town police detective, Miles Massermey. "Yes. I think he's back today. We have plans for tomorrow night."

"*Plans*? I'll bet you do," crowed Nadine. "I'm betting he wants to follow up on that distracting kiss you laid on him during the vampire melee last week."

Jacqueline rolled her eyes, but couldn't control a laugh—or a blush. "Vampire melee" was the perfect way to describe the events that had happened in her shop. And even though she'd distracted Massermey the only way she could think of, he'd still seen...probably more than he should have. Definitely more than he *wanted* to see.

"He's making ribs and we're going to watch *Buffy*," Jacqueline told Nadine.

"Isn't that a little on the nose?" her friend said. "Watching a vampire hunter show after vampires invade your store? Well, at least it might make him feel better to know that there are such things as vampire slayers." Then she sobered. "I wonder how Mandy is doing."

"I'm sure he'll fill me in tomorrow. It was so nice of him to take time off to spend with her," Jacqueline said, unable to keep a fond smile from curving her lips. Mandy was Massermey's daughter and was in veterinary school at Michigan State. Her boyfriend had been killed by one of the vampires. Not that Massermey knew *that* bit of detail, but he had seen enough during the so-called vampire melee to be unable to deny the existence of the undead. "I think he took her to Chicago for a couple of days—just to get her away for a while. I probably passed them on the drive back up here."

"That's more than Noah would do for Danny," said Nadine grimly. "Bastard. Anyway, so, speaking of Chicago—let's get back to the *other* matter at hand... Do you feel okay about seeing Josh? Did it, I don't know, raise all sorts of specters or anything?"

"It was weird to see him. That's all," Jacqueline said. "Kind of brought me back, you know? And... Wow, it's been almost twenty years."

"That's a long time. A lot of things can change...and people grow up." Nadine shrugged. "They change. Not that I'm saying you should forgive the guy or anything—"

"I'm not ever going to see him again, so it doesn't matter," Jacqueline replied, reaching for a scone. "I don't need to spend any energy on him at all."

She didn't hear the Universe laughing.

## 2

When Nadine went back to her studio, Jacqueline came down to the bookshop.

She found it doing an unusually brisk business for a Friday morning, and wondered if the tourists were already starting to show up. Mrs. Danvers gave her a dark look as if to ask what had taken her so long, but Jacqueline ignored her. The woman was always giving her dark looks or side-eyes even when she *was* around working her tail off, so Jacqueline figured nothing was new.

A trio of women who appeared to be in their late thirties were standing in line, each toting a number of books by Emily Henry, Jennifer Weiner, Colleen Hoover, and Jodi Picoult. It was, after all, Beach Read Season.

Jacqueline stepped in to help Mrs. Danvers ring them up, and a few minutes later, the front of the shop was empty of customers, so the two of them could take a breather.

Mrs. Danvers gave her boss-in-name-only another withering look, then muttered, "I'll be packing up the online orders that came in overnight, ma'am," and sailed off into the depths of the shop.

That was a task Jacqueline was more than happy to relinquish. Three Tomes did extremely well with walk-ins, but their online sales were also very strong. They included orders of new titles, used or vintage books—of which the shop had a great number tucked away in various locations—and loose teas, most of which were blended and provided by Andromeda, one of the ZAP Ladies.

The shop door opened, its bell jingling. Jacqueline's mood soured a little when she saw who it was. "Good morning, Egala," she said, nevertheless managing to inject some friendliness into her words.

Egala Stone was a distant—*very* distant—cousin of Jacqueline's. She had no idea how they were related, but they were somehow from the same family tree. When Jacqueline first arrived in Button Cove and took over Three Tomes, Egala had tried everything she could to chase or frighten her away. But Jacqueline wasn't going anywhere, and once Egala realized that —and after Jacqueline helped do away with the witch living in the mirror above her fireplace, saving Egala's life in the process —the two had come to an uneasy truce.

Now Egala—who, unfortunately, was also some sort of witch —owned a little shop just down the street from the bookstore. It sold gorgeous purses—pocketbooks, handbags, wallets, totes, and so on—that were lightly charmed to do things like not get lost or dirty, or to help the owner retrieve whatever they wanted or needed from the bottom of the bag.

And, Jacqueline had to admit, the gorgeous leather tote Egala had gifted her—and its magic charm—had come in handy during the vampire melee.

"Hi," said Egala. Jacqueline wasn't certain how old she was, but estimated in her early sixties. Her skin was unlined and didn't sag, and Jacqueline couldn't help but hope that was a trait that ran rampantly in their family tree.

Egala had a strong Dolores Umbridge vibe, with the same sort of hairstyle and demeanor, but she wore flowing, colorful clothing instead of prim pink skirt suits. Her eyebrows were drawn on in slender brown arches, and her lips were a jarring fuchsia. "How are things this morning?"

"Fine," Jacqueline replied automatically.

"Everything's quiet here, then—er, just waiting for the hordes of tourists to descend, I suppose?"

"We've been steady all morning," Jaqueline said. "But not crazy." Her eyes narrowed. "Why are you asking?"

"Er...no real reason," Egala replied, trying out a smile. It appeared pained.

"I don't believe you," said Jacqueline. "What's going on?"

Egala sighed. "I just sense some sort of...disturbance. In the energy, you know, around here. Don't you?"

Jacqueline knew she was talking about the fact that Three Tomes Bookshop and Camellia Court were in a location where several powerful ley lines crisscrossed. That was supposedly the explanation for all the strange things that happened there. Sort of like the Hellmouth of *Buffy the Vampire Slayer* fame.

"I don't know what the disruption is," Egala went on. "And so I wanted to know whether anything strange has been going on... here."

Jacqueline hesitated, then said, "Nothing, except that it seems someone was burning something in a little bowl in my bookshop yesterday. Or last night."

Egala nodded almost as if she'd expected it. "Someone's messing around with something they shouldn't be," she said ominously. "That could explain it. Do you know who it was?"

"No. But they left something behind, and if they come back for it, then I'll know." For some reason Jacqueline didn't want to get any more detailed about the book being left behind. She still didn't trust Egala as far as she could throw her, and since strength training was pretty low on her list of things to do, that wouldn't be very far should she deign to try.

Egala nodded again. "Well...if you find anything out, let me know. I'm not liking this feeling I have."

Neither was Jacqueline. "I will. And if you have any other information, let me know."

Once more, Egala nodded. Then she left.

Jacqueline looked after her, her lips flat and grim. After what happened last week with the vampires, she could no longer deny that she herself had...abilities. Special abilities. She wouldn't go so far as to call herself a witch—why put a label on it?—but it was her actions that had stopped the vampire melee.

And so maybe she *should* be paying attention when Egala or someone asked her if she felt a disruption in the energy.

But, the truth was, she didn't. Not really.

But if that was so, why had the sight of that bowl of ashes sent frissons of apprehension rushing through her?

Maybe she sensed more than she realized.

Or, like Massermey, more than she *wanted*.

~

A SHORT WHILE LATER, Jacqueline was alone in the shop. She'd just begun unpacking a case of books that had recently been delivered by the UPS person when she heard a familiar *thump*. The sound came from one of the fiction rooms down the hall, away from the front area. Since no one was in the store at the moment, and neither of her two cats—Max and Sebastian— would be inelegant or interested enough to have knocked over a book, Jacqueline knew what that meant.

She left the inventory on the front counter and grimly went to investigate.

As expected, when she came into the room, she found an old

book on the floor. It was open, and a mere glance at the page—where familiar names leapt to her eyes—told her which novel it was before she even picked it up to check the front.

*Pride and Prejudice.*

Jacqueline's heart gave a funny little skip, and she looked around hopefully. Since she'd come to accept her fate of owning a bookshop where literary characters materialized out of their books, she'd harbored a secret hope that Fitzwilliam Darcy would one day be among them.

She wouldn't mind meeting Elizabeth Bennet or the charming Mr. Bingley, but having Mr. Darcy—with his "pride" and social awkwardness and romantic heart—loitering about the store would make all of the craziness worthwhile. She was *dying* to see what he looked like in real life. Colin Firth or Matthew MacFayden? Or neither?

"Hello?" she called tentatively. "Is anyone there?"

A movement, barely caught by the corner of her eye, had Jacqueline spinning eagerly. But it was only Sebastian, the fluffy, whisky-colored cat that somehow exuded an aura of sensuality. He'd sauntered in and leapt onto a shelf, and now sat there eyeing her as if she'd accused him of knocking over the book.

Other than that disturbance, the room remained quiet and still.

Jacqueline closed the tattered copy of *Pride and Prejudice* as she continued to look around for signs of a newcomer. But just because no one was there presently, that didn't mean someone wouldn't appear. In fact, that was most often how it happened—the book would fall from the shelf and then, some time later, the character would make themselves known to her.

This time, however, Jacqueline didn't feel the same sense of anxiety or stress over who might be emerging from the book. There simply wasn't any real *villain* in *Pride and Prejudice*.

The famed seducer George Wickham wasn't a nice guy—he

was a rake and a rogue, leaving broken hearts and ruined women in his wake—but in today's world, that sort of ruination was simply mean and hurtful and not lethal or scary. It certainly wouldn't make a woman unfit for marriage, if she even wanted marriage at all.

So this wasn't like when *Dracula* had fallen off the shelf and Jacqueline worried that the vampire or one of his minions or Renfield would make an appearance...or when *Grimms'* had taken a tumble, and there were *plenty* of evil characters to worry about.

Happily, Jane Austen's romance novel didn't contain anyone who concerned Jacqueline. In fact, for the first time, she was actually *eager* to see who might materialize. She'd even be able to tolerate Mrs. Bennet or Mr. Collins—both of whom were annoying but, again, not villainous.

She slipped the old book back onto the shelf where it belonged, sliding it into place next to two newer editions of *Pride and Prejudice* and an array of volumes of *Sense and Sensibility*, *Emma*, and *Persuasion*.

"Ma'am."

The stiff British tones had Jacqueline spinning again, but when she turned, she only saw Rebecca de Winter's housekeeper standing there, wearing a disapproving expression.

"What is it, Mrs. Danvers?" Jacqueline said in a cool tone. She always had to remind herself that she had better results managing the housekeeper if she adopted a "lady of the manor" tone and demeanor, rather than a "kindly boss" sort of one—just as the second Mrs. de Winter had learned to do. However, the arrogant lady-of-the-manor persona wasn't Jacqueline's normal style, and so it wasn't a natural reaction.

"I found this," said the housekeeper. She offered a long white feather, holding its calamus by the tips of her fingers as if afraid it would bite or otherwise contaminate her.

Jacqueline lifted her brows. "I see." Was there some sort of relevance to a single white feather? She couldn't immediately think of one.

"It was in the room with the burnt-out bowl, ma'am," said Danvers, not bothering to hide her impatience. "Under one of the pillows. One can presume it was left by the miscreants who were burning things."

"All right. I'll take it. Thank you, Danvers," she said, slightly mystified as to why the housekeeper was acting as if she'd found a dead body or a cache of jewels. Then, as she took the feather, Jacqueline had a sudden, sharp worry that she was missing something. Something related to witchery or crone-isms or something.

Something she should be paying attention to.

She dropped the feather onto the room's fireplace mantel, deciding that maybe Mrs. Danvers had the right idea not to touch it. Maybe she ought to go down and ask the ZAP Ladies if they had any ideas. Between the ashes in the singing bowl, Egala's strange visit, and now this singular white feather, Jacqueline was starting to feel even more anxious than usual. And this time, she couldn't blame her hormones.

Danvers, as was her habit, had vanished as soon as she delivered the feather.

The bell over the front door jangled pleasantly, announcing a new arrival. Jacqueline gave one last affectionate look at *Pride and Prejudice* and hurried out to greet the newcomer.

It was a woman by herself, and immediately Jacqueline caught an aura of tension and nerves wafting from her. The woman was probably in her late thirties, maybe forty, and was dressed in casual but expensive clothes—capri jeans, leather sandals with thick soles, and a cotton-blend shirt that stopped sort of being a tunic, but hung almost as long and loose. Her hair was in a sagging ponytail that seemed to have taken little effort, and she wasn't wearing any makeup or jewelry that Jacqueline could discern. There were shadows under her eyes, but who knew whether that was normal for the pale-faced woman.

"Good morning," Jacqueline said with a smile. "Can I help you find something, or are you just browsing?"

"Are you the owner?" There was an intensity in her expression and voice that made Jacqueline apprehensive.

"Yes. Jacqueline Finch. How can I help you?" she asked, mostly because she had to, not because she thought she'd want to. The person didn't seem to be a sales rep, and so she was either there with a complaint...or a request.

Maybe she was one of those moms who wanted to decide what books *everyone* could read—or, more accurately, *not* read—and not just her own children. A person who wanted to stop certain novels from being sold in stores or offered through library systems—stories that offered anything from erotica to magic to LGBTQ characters to history that didn't whitewash unpleasant facts.

Jacqueline knew how to deal with people like that. She'd had lots of experience during her years at the Chicago Public Library. Hardly a month went by when some group wasn't outside picketing over some title or author.

The woman, who hadn't so much as glanced at any of the books on display, came closer and looked around furtively.

When she seemed to have assured herself they were alone, she leaned even closer to Jacqueline, just stopping short of taking her by the arm, and said, "I need your help. I want to put a hex on my husband."

# 3

Jacqueline stepped back.

*Damn.*

She'd had a feeling.

"Um...a what?" she said, struggling to find a gracious way to say, *Hell no!*

"A *hex*." The woman had desperation and determination written all over her. Her brows drew together and her lips flattened. "I want to put a hex on my husband—soon to be my *ex-husband*."

"I see. So...when you say 'hex,' what exactly do you mean?" Jacqueline asked, giving the woman the chance to explain herself in a reasonable way.

"You know—a hex! Like, something that turns his life miserable. Like, uh, he breaks out in really ugly, itchy boils...or he falls down the stairs and breaks a leg and has to be laid up for six months...or, I don't know, every business deal he tries to make goes bad. Or his dick goes soft and wormy and even Viagra won't make it work. Oooh...I like that one," she said with a vicious smile. "The dick hex. Because he is a dick. So, anyway, I want to hire you to make up a hex to ruin his life."

"I see. Thank you for clarifying. But, I'm sorry to say, I don't... do that sort of thing," Jacqueline said, giving her a smile. "I don't really know anything about—"

"Yes, you do. I *know* you do. I've heard all about it. You're online, you know. It's all there. The bookstore and so on. So, what, is there a password or something I need to say? To, what, get into the club? Or—wait. I get it. Just let me know how much. I'll pay anything. I'll use *his* money while I've still got access to it," she added grimly as she plopped her purse on the counter. "It'll serve him right, the bastard."

"Look, um, Mrs....?" Jacqueline felt safe using the title based on the information the woman had given her.

"Jessie Gould," she said. "My husband owns Gould Motors. He's got *plenty* of money. Trust me."

Jacqueline nodded. There were five new-car dealerships in Button Cove, and three of them were named Gould. There were also two used-car lots owned by Gould.

"So, listen, Mrs. Gould, I don't know what you've heard, but I really don't do that sort of thing. Whatever you saw online isn't really true. I could sell you something anyway, and *tell* you it was a-a hex," she said, speaking a little louder in order to cut off the other woman's argument, "but that wouldn't be ethical, would it?"

"But—"

The shop door jolted in its jamb, then rattled a little as if someone pulled it the wrong way, then opened with a burst of energy and wildly jangling bell. In poured (that was the only word to describe the manner in which they flowed inside, all in a single movement) the three ZAP Ladies.

"Good morning, Jacqueline!" trilled Pietra, carrying, Jacqueline was pleased to see, a wicker basket over her arm. That boded well, for the basket usually had baked goods in it—special favorites of Jacqueline's that Suzette's bakery didn't offer, plus usually homemade catnip treats for Max and Sebastian.

Pietra was the shortest and roundest of the three ZAP Ladies, all three of whom were in their eighties or thereabouts. Today she wore a long, loose maxi-dress in tangerine. It was trimmed with dark red beaded fringe on the hem and a V-neck that stopped short of displaying any cleavage. Large orange hoops dangled from her ears, dancing beneath her short mop of gray-brown hair with layers that winged every which way. She looked luscious and motherly, with pink, apple-like cheeks and a variety of tiny dimples around her smiling mouth.

"Hello, Jacqueline," said Andromeda with a smile, even as she looked around for Sebastian. But today, Max was the first feline to catch her eye, and since he was within reach instead of sneering down at everyone from the top of a shelf, Andromeda gathered him up into her arms.

"Got you!" she said, looking down at him with a wicked smile. Max was long and sleek, and looked like a miniature black panther except for moody green eyes that missed nothing.

To Jacqueline's surprise, Max—normally aloof and condescending—allowed Andromeda to bury her elfin features in his satiny fur. Perhaps it was because Andromeda's hair, short and spiky as usual, today matched him in color. When Andi was hugging the cat, you couldn't tell where one ended and the other began.

"Hi, ladies," said Jacqueline as the third of the trio fixed her with a raised-eyebrow look, clearly questioning whether they were interrupting.

At this moment, Jacqueline didn't mind the interruption.

Zwyla, tall and of regal bearing, wore a brightly patterned turban over what Jacqueline knew was a shaved head. She was dressed in easy denim trousers that flowed like linen, and a loose, flax-colored top with embroidery along the edges that matched her turban. A series of bangles clattered musically on her wrist, and her long, elegant feet were shod in thin-soled, strappy sandals. Her toenails were cobalt blue.

"Good afternoon, Jacqueline," Zwyla said. "I hope you aren't too busy and that we aren't interrupting." Her eyes, dark in an equally dark face, were sharp and knowing.

"Mrs. Gould and I were just, er, chatting about ex-husbands and how we wish we could—well—I don't know—*hex* them," Jacqueline said with a casual laugh as she gave Zwyla a meaningful look.

"Ex-husbands are the worst," said Andromeda, allowing Max to slip from her arms and land lightly on the counter. "I've got three, and each of them is a piece of work. I *should* have hexed them." She gave a genteel shudder as Jacqueline stared at her. *Three* ex-husbands? "If I ever get married again, it'll be to a woman. Anyhow, what sort of revenge are you planning?" Andi's sly smile encompassed both Jacqueline and Jessie Gould. "Can I help?"

Jessie seemed a bit startled by this open discussion of hexes —and Jacqueline was horrified at the fuel being added to the fire.

But Jessie recovered quickly. "My ex *is* the worst. Or will be, once the divorce is final. So he's not technically my ex—yet— but it's only a matter of time. And once that happens, I want his life to be a complete and utter disaster. I want him to *rue* the day he crossed me. The asshole just can't keep his pants zipped."

"He stepped out on you?" Zwyla said. Her brows drew together, making her seem even more intimidating than usual. Jacqueline almost smiled at her use of such an old-fashioned term. "He deserves every bit of shit that comes his way."

"It started when I was seven months pregnant. I found out. And, well, I couldn't divorce him then, could I? When I was pregnant? I believed him when he cried and said he was sorry and that it would never happen again. After all, I was *carrying* his *child*."

"I'd've showed up in court in my seven-month-pregnant body and sued the shit out of the bastard," muttered Zwyla to Jacqueline.

"But then I caught him again a few years later," Jessie went on. Tears glistened in her eyes, and despite her sympathy for the woman, Jacqueline couldn't help but think what a cliché this was. She'd heard it all before. Over and over. It was a cycle. Once a cheater, most always a cheater.

"They were just one-night stands," Jessie went on. "He'd go out with business associates or go golfing, and stay after when they left, and then he'd...well, hook up with someone. They didn't mean anything."

"Only that he didn't respect his wife and the mother of his children," Zwyla muttered. Sparks—literal ones—shot from her eyes. Fortunately, Jessie Gould didn't seem to notice. "He's lucky he never brought home a freaking *disease*."

"How long has this been going on?" asked Pietra kindly. Her eyes brimmed with sympathy.

"F-fifteen years," said Jessie. Her own eyes glistened with tears, but there was a layer of fury in there too.

"*Fifteen years?*" Andromeda exclaimed, unable to help herself. "You let him—I mean, you kept forgiving him and working things out for fifteen years?"

"I know. I'm *so stupid*. I can't believe I let him walk all over me for fifteen years. Over and over. I guess I just believed him when he said the girls he picked up didn't mean anything—they were just, you know, a way to...relieve tension."

Zwyla snorted. "I'll say. Look, this guy's been sleeping around for a decade and a half. He's a sleaze. But why now? What was the straw that broke the camel's back?"

Jessie's face turned dark. "He found one he wants to marry."

"Ah," said Andromeda.

Jessie nodded miserably. "Fergie Valentine. Her name is *Fergie Valentine*, can you believe it? Who names their kid that? It sounds like a porn star name. She probably *is* a porn star. She's been working at the Jeep dealership for a few months now, but who knew what she did before that."

Jacqueline thought she heard a snort from Zwyla, but she didn't look over because she might lose it if she did.

Jessie continued. "Anyhow, since he's throwing me over for *Fergie freaking Valentine*, I want to make his life hell. I kept giving him chances, and forgiving him, and trying to stay together—mainly for the kids; thank God they're older now—and now he wants to trade me in for someone else. He deserves to be miserable." She looked at Jacqueline. "I want to *seriously* hex him. I need your help."

Jacqueline turned to the three ZAP Ladies for assistance. Unfortunately, they all looked back at her with bland expressions, with Zwyla's being on the verge of "well, go for it!" and Andi's "you know he deserves it!"

"I...um... Can't you just, uh, put shrimp shells and fish carcass in his curtain rods?" Jacqueline replied.

"What?" said Pietra, her face scrunching up in major confusion.

"Shrimp shells? In his what?" replied Jessie.

"It's a classic revenge story—probably an urban legend, but I don't see why it wouldn't work," said Jacqueline hastily. The gleam in Zwyla's eyes suggested the older women knew exactly what she was talking about. "You put shrimp shells and whatever else would smell horrible when it rots inside the hollow curtain rods of the house of the person you're—er—wanting to hex. About a week or so later, it'll start to smell terrible—or so the urban legend goes. And no one will be able to figure out where it's coming from. Who's gonna look in the curtain rods?"

"Someone who knows the urban legend?" murmured Andromeda, her eyes laughing.

"Anyway," Jacqueline went on, ignoring her, "it supposedly would cause lots of consternation and unpleasantness—but no one gets hurt. According to the urban legend"—which, at this point, she was beginning to think probably *was* an urban legend —"the person will be forced to move, and if they take their own curtains with them, they'll never get rid of the stink."

"It's got to be an urban legend," said Pietra. "No one takes their window treatments with them when they move."

Jacqueline sighed. "I know. But I like the idea. You could also put the fish stuff inside their shower curtain rods too. If they have shower curtains." But she guessed a house like the one the Goulds lived in probably had grand, walk-in tile showers. "Or take off the outlet plates in the house and stuff it inside there."

Jessie was looking at her with an expression of both interest and disbelief. "I want an actual hex. I want to *hurt* him like he's hurt me."

"What about plastic-wrapping his car so he can't get into it?" Jacqueline suggested desperately. "Or...or getting into his email and social media and changing his name so it reads something terrible like Horny McNastyPants or something like that?"

"Horny Mc-who?" Pietra said.

"The poor woman wants to hex her husband," said Andromeda bracingly. "I think you ought to help her, Jacqueline."

Jacqueline could have put a hex on *her* right then—especially when she saw Jessie's hopeful expression. "But I don't..."

"Please," said Jessie, her eyes wide and glittering—not with tears, but with determination and desperation. "I don't know if you have any idea what it's like to be cheated on, but it's the absolute worst sort of pain. It just messes up your whole psyche."

Jacqueline was absolutely *not* looking at any of the ZAP Ladies, because she suspected she knew what she'd see in their collective expressions. Judgment. They all knew about what had happened with Josh, and that Jacqueline actually *did* know what it was like to be cheated on...and not only with her lover, but with a friend, too.

"I kept trusting him—because that's what we're supposed to do, right?" Jessie continued. "Forgive, forget, move on."

"Yes, that's what they say—whoever *they* are," said Zwyla. "But at some point, it becomes abuse when he keeps doing it. It's no longer a mistake by then. Or a moral failure. It's conscious and emotional abuse. It seems to me that your husband knew full well what he was doing, and he kept doing it, knowing it hurt you. He didn't feel enough remorse to stop."

Jessie nodded her head vigorously. "Yes. That's it. Will you help me?" She pinned Jacqueline with her eyes.

"I..." Jacqueline's own gaze skittered around, and then, as if they planned it, the three ZAP Ladies parted, stepping away from each other as if they were a curtain opening to reveal what was behind it...and right behind them was the bookshelf built into the side of the stairs to the café.

It was the bookshelf with glass doors that Jacqueline kept locked because it was filled with old, vintage, antique, *and* antiquarian tomes.

And it was in the smallest, narrowest part of the triangular case that a large, old book—nearly the size of a cinder block—sat, wedged in among numerous other decrepit volumes.

The old book that contained recipes and instructions (Jacqueline wasn't ready to use the word "spell" even in her own mind) for such things as protection amulets and...er...ways to destroy vampires. As she well knew.

She assumed there would be directions on how to make...

not hexes, but, say, revenge tools. Vengeful incidents or accidents.

Jacqueline sighed. Maybe she could look in there and find something that wasn't really harmful, but that would upend Mr. Gould's life enough to satisfy his soon-to-be-ex-wife.

"I'll need to do some research," she said finally. "And...and see what I can come up with."

Jessie heaved a sigh of relief and clasped her hands together in excitement. "Oh, thank you so much. Thank you!"

"I'm not promising anything," Jacqueline told her sternly. "And I refuse to do anything that would physically hurt him or anyone else, do you understand?"

Jessie had to consider that, but after a moment she nodded. "I suppose that's probably for the best. He *is* the kids' father, after all, and I do want the alimony he's going to owe me after all these years. But I like the idea of the boils...and his dick turning soft and oozy," she added hopefully. "Or—can you make it turn green? Imagine Fergie Valentine's face when she sees his *green dick*."

"Right, and I don't know," said Jacqueline uncertainly, even as Pietra was murmuring in agreement. She couldn't *wait* to get the old crones alone so she could read them the riot act—egging her on to do spells and hexes!

Jessie left her contact information and promised to check in with Jacqueline in two days if she hadn't heard from her.

"Great," muttered Jacqueline as she waved goodbye to the woman. As soon as the door closed, she rounded on Zwyla, Andromeda, and Pietra. "What do you think you're doing?" she demanded.

"Why, whatever do you mean?" said Andromeda with such an air of innocence that Jacqueline nearly laughed.

But the situation wasn't a laughing matter. "Telling that

woman I should make her a hex," Jacqueline responded heatedly. "I'm not going to do that! I can't do that—"

"You can if you want to," said Zwyla.

"Well, I *don't* want to," Jacqueline said. "That's just wrong."

The three crones exchanged looks. "Is it?" said Andromeda softly. "Is it really?"

"Well, *yes!*" Jacqueline exploded. "Putting a hex—"

She caught herself, snapping her mouth closed just as the shop door opened. A pair of women came in, chattering happily.

"Good afternoon," Jacqueline said to the newcomers, giving the ZAP Ladies a dark, meaningful look that spread across the three of them equally. "Are you looking for anything in particular?"

The two women were, in fact, looking for something in particular, and Jacqueline was more than happy to help them find the latest Kristin Hannah novel, which they were reading for a book club, along with the new cookbook from a tapas restaurant in Chicago.

By the time Jacqueline finished ringing them up and then helping several other shoppers, the ZAP Ladies had disappeared. She fumed a little over that—she hadn't quite finished her rant about their roping her into doing something questionable. She even went to the front door and opened it, sending a little glare down the street to the end of the court, where their blue Victorian sat like a fancy Easter egg.

When the glare felt like more of a sizzle and spark than just a dark look, Jacqueline hastily stepped back inside. *Crap.* Did she even know her own abilities?

It seemed the crones did.

*Ugh.*

Jacqueline didn't want to be a witch or crone or whatever it was they called themselves. She didn't want to cast spells or send hexes or install charms. She just wanted to run her book-shop. She heaved a sigh.

The store was quiet for the moment. Even Danvers was absent, and although Jacqueline could hear the faintest of clinking from Mrs. Hudson upstairs, she was, for all intents and purposes, alone.

And her attention kept straying to that bookshelf under the stairs. To that large cinder-block book.

It was so old, whatever might have been embossed or imprinted on its dark leather spine was long gone. She knew from previous experience that the pages were yellowed, brittle, and musty with age.

Jacqueline had used it once to create a protection amulet for someone who'd come into her shop and asked for her help—just like Jessie had done today.

It hadn't turned out the way Jacqueline had anticipated, and that was part of the reason she was balking at doing something like that again.

And then, last week, a recipe in that book had helped her to save the shop—and her friends—from the undead.

Her feet were somehow carrying her to the bookshelf. And she found herself bending next to the shortest part of the cabinet.

Jacqueline was just about to reach for the book when *thud!*

She snapped upright and turned, hurrying back to where a book had fallen off a shelf. She was torn between thinking, *Another one?* and congratulating herself for not extricating the big spell book from its moorings.

As soon as she saw the book on the floor of the fiction room, she recognized it. And was confused.

It was the same book that had fallen earlier—*Pride and Prejudice*. The exact same copy.

Did that mean more than one person was going to come out of the book? If so, that was something new.

Or did it mean that whoever it was had gone back inside without Jacqueline even seeing them?

She picked it up, glancing at the page, and almost got sucked into reading Mr. Darcy's initial and inept—yet still romantic, because she knew what it cost him—proposal to Elizabeth Bennet. She didn't know whether the open page suggested which character would come out; it never seemed to have corre-lated before, but she couldn't help hope it was a sign that Fitzwilliam Darcy would grace Three Tomes with his presence.

Then she blushed. What would she *do* if Mr. Darcy made an appearance? It would be like having her fantasy of Jon Bon Jovi —on whom she'd had the greatest of crushes in her teen years —pulling her out of the crowd at a concert and inviting her backstage (a common daydream from her youth) actually happen.

It would be terrifying.

She'd be a mess.

She'd completely muck it up.

What would she say? Do?

Jacqueline sighed. She wasn't cut out for wildly hot and sexy men like Jon Bon Jovi or Fitzwilliam Darcy (as portrayed by Colin Firth, of course), and she knew it. They were waaaay out of her league: a forty-eight-year-old woman with wildly curling carroty hair, dead white skin, and who carried an extra ten or so pounds—and who was like a walking encyclopedia.

Just then, the jingle of the front door followed by the sound of it wedging back into place alerted her to a new customer. Jacqueline tucked *Pride and Prejudice* back into place, gave it one last narrow look, then came out to the front of the shop.

Speaking of hot and sexy men...

The man standing there in the front room might have

seemed out of place in a bookshop if she hadn't known better—
that he was quite a versatile reader.

He was a broad-shouldered man of forty-five with hair that
had once been bright strawberry blond but was now mostly
white—except for his thick beard and mustache. He had fair
skin covered with freckles that gave him a ruddy, pleasantly
weathered look. He wore slacks and a button-down shirt, but
still somehow managed to look like a Viking conqueror who'd
just stepped off his boat.

"Hi, Miles," she said, blushing a little. Definitely hot and
sexy. And probably *not* out of her league, if their past interac-
tions were any indication. Her blush deepened a little more,
damn it, and would show on her pale face like a beacon. "You're
back," she added warmly, realizing he must have *just* returned...
and had come to see her as soon as possible.

"Hi, Jacqueline," said Massermey. She loved the way he said
her name—with a soft "J" sound. Not enough to sound affected,
but enough to sound sexy as hell. The smile he gave her was one
of distinct pleasure, and yet there was a questioning look there.
"Everything all right?"

"Yes, of course," she said, ordering her red cheeks to settle
down. "What makes you think something's wrong?"

"Well, unusual things do tend to happen in and around your
shop," he said with a pained smile.

Jacqueline laughed. "True, but today, things are pretty calm."
If he only knew half of the things that happened in her shop.
"How are you?" she added. "How was your trip?"

"I'm good—but not as good as I'm going to be tomorrow
night," he said, his eyes twinkling. "We're still on, I hope? It was
the only thing getting me through lots and lots of shopping at
vintage clothing stores with Mandy. I'm looking forward to
finally seeing *Buffy*."

"Definitely," she replied, feeling a pleasant little buzz in her belly. "I've got a bottle of Cabernet ready for those ribs you've been promising me."

"They'll be marinating in my special dry rub by tonight," he said, his eyes gleaming as if the idea of a "dry rub" was something more than spices on meat. "I'll start slow-cooking them tomorrow morning."

"Really looking forward to it." She made a show of looking up at the ceiling that separated them from the tea room, then said in a low voice, "Did you want some coffee?"

"Only if it's not too much trouble," he replied, also looking up at Mrs. Hudson's domain with an exaggerated wince.

"Not at all. You know I've been keeping a stash in the back. I'll get you some, and you can tell me how Mandy is holding up." She led the way down the hall to one of the unobtrusive storage rooms tucked in the back-right side of the shop.

Unfortunately—or, in this case, fortunately—the little alcove where she put a large, thermos-like carafe of coffee every morning was small and crowded. Massermey eased in next to her, and before she'd even reached for one of the go-cups she'd taken to keeping on hand (mostly for him), he took her arm and turned her to face him.

He smelled *really* good. Spicy and fresh and manly.

"I'm glad to be back, Jacqueline," he said, looking down at her. Then he leaned in for a kiss.

She went on tiptoes to meet his mouth, feeling the gentle brush of his mustache and beard over her lips. She smiled because it was *very* nice. *Very, very* nice.

His lips moved into a smile against hers, and after a moment —not long enough—he eased back. "Yes," he said, nodding firmly, "that was just as good—no, better—than I remembered." He looked down at her, his eyes a darker blue than usual. "Now I'm *really* looking forward to tomorrow night. I'm hoping to do some further investigating."

Jacqueline's cheeks were warm with pleasure, not shyness or embarrassment. And other parts of her were *humming.* "I'm counting on it, detective. Now, let me get that coffee. And you can tell me how Mandy is doing."

"She's doing as well as can be expected. They hadn't been together very long, so I suppose that makes it slightly easier."

"Still, it has to be difficult." Jacqueline filled his cup, and since he liked his coffee black, she had only to cover it with a top and offer it to him. "There you go. Cop coffee."

"She's young and resilient," Massermey said with the confidence of a parent. "She'll be all right. I hope." The confidence faded into a bit of misery. "I just hate seeing her hurting."

"I know. I'm sure you're right—she'll be fine. Eventually—Oh, there's the front door. Someone's here. I'd better meander up there before Mrs. Danvers catches us fraternizing back here," she said with a smile.

Massermey followed her to back to the front of the shop. "Did I tell you Mandy tried to get me to go to this thing called the Bridgerton Experience while we were gone? It's based on that TV show. She showed me pictures, and it looked crazy. Everyone dressed up like they're in *Pride and Prejudice*, and they do those fancy dances, and—"

Jacqueline had stopped so suddenly that he nearly careened into her. She hardly heard what he was saying because her attention had fallen on the person who'd come into the shop.

It was a man about her age—two years and one month older, to be exact—and he was looking around with unadulterated interest, almost as if he'd never seen a bookshop before. His dark brown hair was just beginning to recede and thin, but was combed into a neat, trim style. He wore no facial hair, but did have a pair of chic, dark-framed eyeglasses.

His clothing was casual but well made: dark slacks and a light blue patterned shirt with what appeared to be forest-green tornados spiraling all over it (it looked better than it sounded when Jacqueline described it later). His loafers were leather and probably expensive.

He looked up when she came into view, stopping suddenly as she did. "Jackie," he said with a faltering smile.

"J-Josh," she stammered. "Wh-what are you doing here?"

## 4

"He called you *Jackie*?" exclaimed Suzette as Nadine squealed, "And you thought you'd never see him again! *Ha!* I told you!"

Jacqueline gave Nadine a glare. "Yeah. Famous last words, huh?"

"So *what happened*?" Suzette demanded, swiping an arm across her forehead. It left a trace of flour over her temple.

They were in Sweet Devotion's kitchen, where Suzette had just added a large clump of flour to a mixing bowl the size of a baptismal font. A massive metal paddle with large holes had been spinning through the ingredients, which were now beginning to form a pillow-sized lump of dough.

The bakery and bookshop were closed for the day, but Nadine had scooted down from her yoga studio on the floor above as soon as her six o'clock class ended. "I've only got fifteen minutes," she told Jacqueline. "So spill."

"Nothing happened—Massermey left, and I talked to Josh for a few minutes," Jacqueline told them.

Nadine slammed her hands onto her hips and cocked an eyebrow. "You texted us all freaked out that Josh showed up when Massermey was there, and now you're saying nothing happened?"

"I still can't believe he called you Jackie and you didn't murder him," muttered Suzette, giving Jacqueline the side-eye.

"It was a shock to see him," Jacqueline said, feeling stupid about raising the alarm. "I mean, he was the last person I expected to see in my store."

Nadine tsked and said, "It shouldn't have been. I told you that you hadn't seen the last of him. And I told you that he accidentally-on-purpose made certain to run into you at the theater."

"But that was in Chicago, and this is Button Cove—"

"And he knows you have a shop here, and it's only, what, four hours from Chicago?" Nadine pressed. "What did he *say* when you asked what he was doing here?"

"And did Massermey realize what was going on?"

Jacqueline decided to answer Suzette's question first. "I don't think so. He didn't seem to. He got a text from Mandy right then, and he wasn't paying much attention. I think that's probably good. As far as he knew, Josh was just another customer."

"Mmhmm," said Suzette, eyeing the contents of the gigantic metal bowl. She turned off the beater and poked at the smooth lump of dough. "Perfect," she murmured.

"So Massermey got the text, then what? Did you introduce the two of them?" Nadine asked, looking at the clock on the wall. "Hurry up—I've got to get back upstairs in seven minutes. Can't rush into a yoga class all wound up, can I?"

"No, I didn't see any need to introduce them. Miles, um, said goodbye—"

"I love that you're calling him Miles now," said Nadine with a sigh. "And precisely how did he say goodbye? A kiss?"

"No, no, he wouldn't do that in front of a customer—*any*

customer," Jacqueline replied. "He just said, 'Sorry—Mandy needs me. I'll see you tomorrow.'"

"So what happened after he left? When you and Josh were there alone?"

Jacqueline shrugged and spread her hands. "Nothing. Really, nothing. I asked him again what he was doing there, and he explained he was up for the holiday weekend and wanted to see my shop."

"And that's it." Suzette was not convinced. She'd removed the bulk of dough from the metal bowl and was using a bench knife to slice it into a dozen or more loaf-sized pieces.

"So far," said Jacqueline.

"Did he *buy* anything?" demanded Nadine with the loyalty of a fellow small business owner.

"Um...yes. Actually, he did. He bought a Baldacci and a Lee Child. Both hardcover." Jacqueline wasn't going to mention she noticed the flashy titanium credit card—clearly an elite one —he'd used to make the purchase. Obviously, Josh was doing well financially.

"How did he look?" asked Suzette. "When was the last time you saw him? Was he wearing a wedding ring?"

Jacqueline had forgotten she didn't know about the run-in with Josh at the theater, so she filled her in.

Nadine interrupted with a groan. "I've gotta run. Drinks in ninety minutes? We've got more to discuss, clearly. I think I have a bottle of vodka left over from the mules I made last week."

"Want to come over to my place?" said Jacqueline. "We can drink my booze tonight. I need to tell you some more stuff anyway. As Mr. Holmes might say, 'Something's afoot.'"

∾

JACQUELINE LEFT Suzette to finish her bread dough—which would be baked early the next morning—and darted across the street to the shop. It was after seven, and the store was dark and quiet, even though the sun hadn't set yet. Even the upstairs windows of the tea shop were dark.

She let herself in through the front door, since that was easiest, and, as she often did when she was alone, took a moment to pause and absorb.

She was the *owner of a bookshop*. Books, books, books...everywhere. All kinds. In rooms that (somehow) went on forever, with shelves that never bowed or sagged or tipped, with every sort of tome or volume one could imagine.

She smelled the scent of newly printed ones, the slight must of the older, antiquated ones, and a faint lemony scent that indicated Mrs. Danvers had been cleaning.

*This is my place.*

She felt a bump of awareness when she glanced at the locked glass doors of the bookshelf under the stairs.

*All of it.*

*And with it comes some responsibility,* she told herself. *Damn it.*

Reluctantly, she unlocked the glass case and withdrew the large cinder-block book that had come in handy when she was making a protection amulet, and when she was looking for a way to destroy the vampires. She supposed she should at least look inside for something to satisfy Jessie Gould. Female solidarity and all that.

Heavy book in hand, Jacqueline was just about to walk to the back of the shop where the stairs would take her directly to her flat when she noticed something on the steps to the tea shop.

The object was slender and white, and it almost shined in the gloaming light of the store.

She climbed two steps, and when she saw what it was, her heart gave a little lurch.

A large white feather.

After glancing around—she wasn't certain why she felt the need, but she did, and by all indication, she was alone in the shop, just as she'd believed—Jacqueline reached for the feather. When she touched it, she felt...*something*.

It wasn't bad or frightening, but it was *something*. A little sizzle of energy or awareness.

"Damn," she murmured, holding the feather gingerly by its calamus. She looked around again, just to make sure Danvers wasn't lurking.

As she climbed back down to the ground, Jacqueline wondered if maybe this was the same feather Danvers had found in the Woo-Woo Room. If it was, she wasn't certain whether that was a good thing or not, but she wanted to know. Maybe one of the cats had retrieved it and brought it here.

It took her a moment to remember she'd left the feather on the fireplace mantel in the Romance Room, where Danvers had first brought it to her. Not bothering to turn on the lights, Jacqueline hurried to that room and shined her phone light on the mantel.

*Crap.*

The original feather was still there, and it was almost identical to the one she currently held. They were from the same bird or type of bird, that was certain. Pure white with a white quill, or calamus. But which bird? Not a songbird or even a seagull—they were too small. Like a swan's feather? They were certainly big enough. What other large white bird?

Jacqueline picked up the second feather and left the room. Instead of going down the hall to the back of the shop and heading up to her flat, she returned to the front and gathered up the cinder-block book, carrying it with the two feathers. She marched up the steps to the tea room.

Something was telling her to check the New Age Room.

The café smelled pleasantly of spices and herbs in the teas that Jacqueline usually avoided. The cups and pots and plates were neatly stacked on their open shelves. The counters were clean. The large windows that graced the front wall and parts of the side walls allowed the last bit of sunlight to filter into the space, frosting the shapes and shadows with gold.

Everything was silent. It wasn't even very dark, though the light was low and edging toward dusk.

Yet...

Jacqueline hesitated, then walked through the café and children's picture book section to the short hallway that led to the New Age Room and the storage space with its elevator.

As she drew closer, she smelled something...something burning.

*Crap.*

Her heart pounding, her throat dry, and her palms slick, she walked soundlessly to the doorway of the Woo-Woo Room.

Holding her breath, she peered carefully around the edge of the jamb.

No one was in the room.

Nothing appeared disturbed.

But the smell of burning paper or wood clung to the air. It wasn't strong enough to set off the smoke detectors, but WTF?

Jacqueline stepped into the room and flipped the light switch.

The space was suddenly bathed in the soft light of numerous wall sconces and a large chandelier hanging in the center of the room.

There in the back corner, in the same place Mrs. Danvers had found the poufs and singing bowl with its fire remnants, sat a single pouf. Another singing bowl—with ashes in it—rested on the floor in front of it.

And...

Jacqueline's heart skipped a beat.

...a book. An old book was lying on the ground next to the sitting pillow and singing bowl, a.k.a. small fireplace.

Jacqueline crouched next to all of those objects, then, when her knees protested, gave up and allowed her butt to plop onto the pillow. Whatever had been burning in the small metal bowl was reduced to smoldering ashes with just a waft of smoke rising from them...

It smelled pungent. Not like paper, but like something else— a fragrant piece of wood, or a branch of some herb she couldn't quite identify.

But it was the book that captured her attention.

It was very old—so old, Jacqueline was almost afraid to touch it. The pages looked as if they might crumble into dust at the slightest pressure or movement. Even the cinder-block book she'd brought with her wasn't as aged as this one.

The tome was closed, which she was relieved to see—for no one had yet come out of a closed book—and its cover and binding was of ancient, battered red leather. If anything had been printed or painted on the cover or spine—which, despite its age, was still the color of blood—it was long gone.

Gingerly, Jacqueline lifted the cover—it was impossible to tell whether it was the front or back—and felt a little shiver of awareness skitter up her arm and across her shoulders. The hair on the back of her neck lifted even more when she made out the words on the page staring up at her.

They were hand-painted onto the paper, barely legible and fashioned with many serifs and flourishes and swirls. She could barely make out the words:

*Spellf & Hexef & Cursef*

Beneath the notation was a crude drawing of a bird—a white

or colorless bird—wearing a crown and sitting next to a cluster of red flowers. Roses, maybe.

Was it a crest? A symbol? Something signifying the author of the book?

Jacqueline stared at the drawing, feeling something niggle the back of her mind. Where had she seen something like that before? A white bird, a crown, a rosebush...

A white bird.

Now the hair on the back of her neck shot to attention.

And where had this book come from? Although old, vintage, and antiquated books often appeared randomly in her shop, Jacqueline was certain this one hadn't been in the locked cabinet below the stairs. She would have noticed the blood-red spine among the other drab and aged books.

Gathering up the old tome, Jacqueline looked around warily. She was alone; she was certain of it.

But someone had been here.

～

SHE TOOK the feathers and the two spell books upstairs with her to wait for Nadine and Suzette to arrive. She considered contacting the ZAP Ladies to see if they wanted to come over and add their two—or three—cents' worth, but decided she didn't have enough energy to deal with them. She loved them, but they were *a lot*.

Besides, she was still annoyed that they'd pressured her into agreeing to look into a hex for Jessie Gould's ex.

A hex and an ex...and a codex.

Jacqueline looked down at the old red book. It definitely qualified as a codex—a book with bound pages, sometimes handwritten, often with decorative ornamentation.

She groaned quietly and set it aside in favor of getting ready for her friends. That was much easier—and far more pleasant.

Before moving to Button Cove, Jacqueline had rarely, if ever, entertained. She'd lived alone in the same small house she'd rented for years and suddenly lost when the owner decided to sell. The place had had a tidy garden in the back next to its slab of concrete patio, and was located in a suburb of Chicago.

Jacqueline had had no pets, no housemates, and no desire to disrupt her solitude. All she wanted to do when she got home from work was read, poke around in her garden, and occasionally putter in the kitchen. Sip a glass of wine (alone, with a good book) and survey her tiny garden from a chair on the patio.

Since moving to Button Cove, Jacqueline had had society inflicted upon her daily. If it wasn't the ZAP Ladies spilling into her shop with food, advice, or cryptic warnings, it was Mrs. Danvers and Mrs. Hudson bossing her about or giving her the stink-eye—not to mention a steady flow of customers, and those, at least, she was supremely grateful for.

At first, Jacqueline had been taken aback by the boisterousness of Nadine and the calm friendliness of Suzette and their assumption that Jacqueline would become the third in a trio of close-knit friends and business owners. She'd tried to keep herself at arm's length from emotional attachments, as she'd done throughout her life, but it hadn't worked for long. Nadine and Suzette had wormed their way into her life and heart.

Now, just over two months into her ownership of Three Tomes and the move to Button Cove, Jacqueline couldn't imagine life without those two women. And she didn't want to. She was grateful to them for so many things, and only hoped that they valued her friendship as much as she'd come to value theirs.

But it still amazed her how she'd gone from being a solitary, bookish person to one surrounded by people all the time.

She moved about quickly and efficiently in the small kitchen, extracting two bottles of wine (she knew her friends) and three glasses and setting them on the table in front of her blue velvet sofa. A plate with gorgonzola, Gruyère, and cheddar, plus crackers, nuts, and olives, followed. After digging around in her fridge for other nibbles, she filled a tiny dish with a tablespoon of apricot jam and nestled an equally tiny spoon in it.

Then she really got inspired and dragged out a frozen cheese pizza and doctored it up with some of the gorgonzola, tomato slices, basil, and a tiny drizzle of spicy honey while waiting for the oven to heat.

She didn't have anything to put out for Nadine's sweet tooth except the bit of apricot jam, and she hoped Suzette would bring something, as she usually did.

The oven had just beeped, announcing that it had reached its pizza-appropriate temperature, when Jacqueline heard Nadine and Suzette's clomping up the back steps.

"Suze brought macaroons!" sang Nadine as they burst in from the back door.

"Maca*rons*, not maca*roons*," Suzette corrected her gently. "The first is light, delicate, and French—a sort of sandwich cookie. The second is a delicious blob of coconut, sugar, and egg whites."

"I'm not picky," said Nadine, setting the bakery box she'd obviously liberated from Suzette on the long, low sofa table. "'Roons or 'rons are fine with me. Anything from Sweet Devotion is going to hit the spot."

Jacqueline slid the pizza into the oven then came out from behind the half wall of the kitchen to join them in the living room. Suzette had already poured a glass of wine for each of them, and Jacqueline took hers gratefully.

"All right, we're here, there's food and drink—spill everything," said Nadine as she swiped a knifeful of soft gorgonzola onto a cracker.

Jacqueline took a healthy sip of wine. "Someone was in the Woo-Woo Room again tonight," she said, for some reason starting at the most recent events. "They were burning something again. But this time they left this codex."

"A codex?" Nadine's nose scrunched up. "Like in *The Da Vinci Code*?"

"That's a cryptex," said Jacqueline, picking up the old book that had been left behind. "*This* is a codex."

"It looks like an old book," said Suzette, popping an olive into her mouth.

"It is. A codex is technically what we think of as a book: something with its pages bound along one side, creating a spine. As opposed to a scroll or a papyrus roll. But most historians use the term codex to refer to very old books—usually handwritten —and often in Latin, which was the language of the so-called scholars. In either case, I think this"—she hefted the book— "qualifies as a codex."

As her friends made sounds of awe and wonder, Jacqueline opened the cover and pointed to the words on the first page. "This doesn't make me feel any better."

"'Spells and hexes and curses,'" read Suzette. "Is this from the cabinet under the stairs?"

"No," Jacqueline replied. "I'm pretty sure it isn't. Someone brought it here. And notice the drawing. It's a white bird with a crown over its head, near what I think is a rosebush. A white bird that might have left something like this." With a flourish, she picked up the two feathers that had been resting unnoticed on a side table. "Mrs. Danvers found one this morning when she was cleaning up after the first little fire escapade, and I just found the second one on the stairs leading to the tea shop.

Someone had just been in there burning stuff in my New Age Room, and now this feather was left behind."

"Do you think a witch came out of this book?" asked Nadine, cautiously lifting a brittle page and turning it.

"I *hope* not," Jacqueline said with feeling. "We've got enough witches floating around here."

"Maybe it was a bird that came out. From the size of those feathers, it would have to be a swan or an egret or something big," Nadine said. "Or—oh, hear me out—a shapeshifter that changes from bird to human or witch."

Jacqueline gave her friend a pained look. "I don't really like any of those ideas. So please don't say them."

"I don't blame you, but we've got to be real," replied Nadine wisely. "If something or someone came out—"

"I'll find out soon enough," Jacqueline said wearily.

"So this book was left in the New Age Room tonight, and yesterday a different book was left. A history book?" Suzette had piled two slices of Gruyère on a Triscuit, then plopped a tiny dollop of apricot jam on top.

"Yes. A biography of Henry VIII," said Jacqueline. That niggle was back again, poking in the recesses of her mind. There was something she knew that might help this make sense...but she simply knew too many things to extract it at the moment. And the wine—she'd nearly finished her first glass (she *so* deserved it)—wasn't helping keep her thoughts clear.

"But that's not all that's happened," she went on with artificial perkiness. "A woman came in today and wanted me to put a hex on her ex. And the ZAP Ladies think I ought to do it."

"Well, why not?" said Suzette, reaching for another olive. "You've obviously got the chops, based on your past experience, and he probably deserves it. What did he do? Cheat?"

"Got it in one," said Jacqueline. "Multiple times over the last fifteen years."

"Asshole."

"At least Noah never cheated on me," Nadine said. "That's one thing I can say about His Highness the Neurosurgeon and God. He might be a tightwad—unless it's to take his new babe on a luxury cruise—but he was faithful. So what kind of hex are you going to do? I think you should turn his dick green or blue."

At that moment, the timer sounded from the kitchen. Jacqueline made to rise, but Suzette was closer and waved her back to her seat. "I'll get it. You tell us about the hexing."

"Look, I just don't know if it's, well, morally right to hex a person," Jacqueline said. "I mean..."

Nadine settled back in her seat and studied her as she sipped her wine. "All right, I can see this is bothering you, even though I'm not sure why it should. So let's unpack this."

"Yes, let's do that."

"The first thing is, we already know you're *capable* of bestowing a hex on someone."

"Capable doesn't mean I *should*," Jacqueline retorted firmly.

"I get that's a problem for you, but let's just walk through it, all right?" Nadine said mildly. She'd moved from her easygoing and fun-loving persona to the calm, thoughtful yoga teacher. "So you're capable and you have the tools." She gestured to the cinder-block book and the new codex that had been found in the New Age Room. "And Mister Cheaterpants—can you give us a name or something? For simplicity."

"It's Raymond Gould of Gould Motors," Jacqueline said, only mildly concerned about sharing the information. After all, the ZAP Ladies had been present when Jessie was blathering about the hex she wanted.

"Ooh... I always got a slimy impression from him," said Suzette, walking in with the cut pizza on a platter. "I almost bought my Jeep from him, but at the last minute, I went down to

Cadillac and bought it there. He was too slick and oily. No surprise he's got it for the ladies."

"Okay, so Raymond Gould is slick and oily and a serial cheater. He's been doing it for years, you said?" Nadine asked as she drew a slice of pizza onto a small plate. "Damn, this looks really good, Jacqueline. You didn't make this?"

"No, I just doctored up a simple frozen cheese one. You know I can't compete—and don't want to—with our Pizza Queen." She smiled at Suzette, who often made pizza for the three of them on Sunday nights.

"So he's been cheating for years and the wife just found out?" said Suzette.

"No, she's known." Jacqueline gave them the details about Jessie's husband's serial cheating over the last fifteen years. By the time she was done, her friends were staring in outrage.

"A green dick isn't enough," said Nadine. "You need to make it fall off."

"I'm not going to do that—"

"No, no, it's better if he still has it but can't use it," said Suzette. "I think you ought to put huge, ugly boils on it, and—*oooh!*—can you make them disappear whenever he goes to the doctor? So no one believes him and he can't get treated?" She hooted with delight, and Nadine joined her.

Even Jacqueline had to laugh. That would be perfect...if she were inclined to do such a thing. Which she wasn't.

"So here's the thing," Nadine went on, still obviously unpacking the situation. "The guy made a vow to his wife and broke it multiple times over the years. And now he's found someone to marry—what was her name again?"

"Fergie Valentine," Jacqueline said with a very straight face.

"Right," Nadine said on a snort-laugh. "Fergie Valentine. I mean, that sounds like one of those made-up names from memes that go around on social media. You know, your porn name is the name of your first pet and the street you grew up on. In this case, it's pick your favorite celebrity name and mash it with a fun event or something. You know, Fergie the former princess—or singer—and the holiday in February. *Anyway*, I digress. There has to be some sort of comeuppance for Mr. Cheaterpants, don't you think?"

"I suggested shrimp shells in the curtain rods, but Jessie wouldn't go for that," Jacqueline said.

"I think that's an urban legend," said Suzette. "But it's still a delicious idea."

"Right. But Jacqueline can do better than that," said Nadine.

"But I don't think it's *my* place to do something to get revenge on him," Jacqueline said.

"You're doing it for Jessie Gould. She's asked you to do it. It's *her* revenge; you're just helping her. It would be like her friends helping her, I don't know, shrink-wrap his car or something like that. You're not doing it out of malice or because you're interfering—you're doing it to *help* someone who's been abused and downtrodden and taken advantage of. For years. And who's asked you for *help*."

"And don't say, 'But she could have left him,'" Suzette jumped in. "We all know it's not always as easy as that. Besides, if he apologized so prettily and emotionally every time, and if she still loved him... Who can blame her for sticking with the status quo? She had kids and a comfortable life. Do you know that divorce is one of the leading causes of financial distress and even bankruptcy for women? Honestly, I can sort of see why she stuck it out. As long as he came back home and gave her a stable life..."

"And now he's leaving her, so she's going to be on her own," said Nadine.

"She'll get alimony and child support," Jacqueline pointed out.

Nadine heaved a sigh and lifted her brows. "And I'm here to tell you that's not always as simple and consistent as it sounds. There are a lot of expenses that aren't covered by freaking child support."

"Right." Jacqueline sighed too. "I just don't know if it's right to get involved."

"Okay, let me ask you this question," Suzette said, peering at her over her glass of Pinot noir. "If you were helping a friend plan a little revenge thing for her cheating husband and it *didn't involve magic*...would you help her? Like, if Nadine here wanted to shrink wrap Noah the God-Surgeon's car because he'd cheated on her or whatever, would you help her?"

Jacqueline stilled. "Well, of course. Duh. But Nadine's my friend."

"But you'd help with the revenge."

"Yes. I would. And I see where you're going with this..." Jacqueline heaved another sigh. "And you're mostly right—it's the, uh, *hex* part of it, the—oh, hell, I guess I have to say it—the *magic*"—she winced—"part of it that gives me pause."

"It didn't give you pause when you helped make a protection amulet," Nadine reminded her.

"It certainly did," Jacqueline shot back. "But yeah, I did it anyway. And I don't need to remind you how it turned out. I guess that's part of it. I don't know this Jessie Gould person, and what if it's not what she says it is? What if she's lying—like what happened before?"

"Then you deal with it after. *Or*...maybe we do some investigation to make sure Jessie is actually telling you the truth. But based on what I know about Mr. Gould, she is. Slime bucket."

"Oh my God," said Nadine suddenly, sitting upright. Her eyes were lit with wild humor. "I just realized something *hilarious*." She was hardly able to speak over a threatening giggle. "We've got hexes...exes—and we've got a few, don't we, with your ex, and my ex being a dick, plus Jessie Gould's soon-to-be ex—and...wait for it...*codexes!*" She pointed to the old book as she snorted a laugh and snagged an olive. She was laughing so hard that Jacqueline was a little worried she might choke on the spherical olive.

"Well, technically, it's *codices*, not codexes," Jacqueline said, chuckling as she bit into a cheese-laden cracker.

"Oh, *hush*, Miss Pedantic Librarian," said Nadine, still giggling (and having successfully swallowed the olive, to Jacqueline's relief). "I'm saying codexes because it sounds better. Hexes, exes, and codexes—see? So feel free to report me to a grammar cop. If he's cute, he can put handcuffs on me." She snort-laughed again, leaning back into her seat on the sofa. "Hexes, exes, and codexes. It has a nice ring to it, doesn't it?"

"Yeah. My life has a nice ring to it," Jacqueline said, trying to be grim but unable to keep from smiling. Her friends were a trip. "And here's the other thing I haven't told you. Guess what book fell off the shelf."

"What?" Suzette and Nadine said together, leaning forward, eyes goggling.

"*Pride and Prejudice!*"

Jacqueline barely got the words out before her friends were swooning and squeeing.

"Darcy!" they moaned in unison.

"Oh, please, please let it be Darcy," said Nadine, clasping her hands to her bosom in supplication.

"I wonder what he'd look like," said Suzette. "I mean, Colin Firth is *the* Darcy in my mind—"

"I liked Matthew Macfadyen too," said Nadine. "He was more brooding...and that scene where he comes across the moors that morning to tell Keira Knightley he loves her..." Her eyes went vacant and she gave a little squeal in the back of her throat.

Jacqueline sat and listened, eating pizza and enjoying the reactions of her friends—which she of course shared, albeit less loudly.

In her experience, it was the common course of action when Jane Austen's most famous novel was mentioned. Most every woman she knew swooned over Fitzwilliam Darcy—whether the topic was the Darcy of the actual book, or either of the actors who'd most famously played the character.

She wondered what Jane Austen would think if she knew the sort of spectacle people made of themselves over her literary creation. Even more so than Rhett Butler, or even, she suspected, Roarke from the In Death series (although Roarke would have to be a close second to Darcy in generating global swooning and squeeing).

Finally, Suzette and Nadine ceased their excited chatter and sighing and turned their attention back to Jacqueline.

"Now that we've got that out of our systems," said Nadine with a laugh as she scooped up a piece of pizza.

"Well, has anyone showed up yet?" Suzette asked.

"No. Not that I'm aware of," Jacqueline said. "But here's the strange thing—the book fell *twice*."

"Twice? What does that mean?"

Jacqueline shrugged. "I have no idea. It could mean whoever it was came out and went back in. Or I suppose it could mean that two people will come out. Your guess is as good as mine."

At that moment, she looked up at the large picture that hung over the fireplace.

It was a housewarming gift from the ZAP Ladies, the painting of a large, elegant cedar tree in a small wooded area. The varied shades of blues and greens and purples created a relaxed, comfortable scene of a glen at twilight or dusk. A few bright spots of fireflies and other lights seemed to twinkle in the scene—they probably were actually twinkling, considering the source of the painting—and Jacqueline had noticed that, depending on the time of day or night, the image changed slightly. Sometimes it was a bit lighter, as if the sun had just set. Other times, it had the long shadows of twilight. Still other times, it was dark as night, except for the limning of some invisible moonlight over the very topmost leaves.

But now, just as she looked at it, Jacqueline caught sight of a white flutter. Her eyes went to the upper-right corner of the painting, where the longest limb of the cedar arched. A white bird sat on the branch.

And then, just as suddenly, it was gone.

"What is it?" Suzette poked Jacqueline.

"I...I'm not sure." She blinked. The white bird had disappeared. But obviously it meant something. "I just saw a white bird in the painting there."

"Like the feathers. What kind of bird was it?" Nadine asked, turning to look at the picture.

"It was like a crow. Or a raven— Oh *hell*," Jacqueline said as the light bulb of realization popped on over her head. "Oh, *hell*."

"What? What is it?" Nadine and Suzette wore twin looks of concern as they gaped around the room.

Jacqueline sighed. She might be wrong.

She was probably wrong.

She *hoped* she was wrong.

But...

"So..." she said slowly, "the book that was left in the New Age Room overnight was a biography of Henry VIII. And"—she had to force the words from her mouth—"who is probably the most famous—or infamous—of his six wives?"

"Anne Boleyn," said Suzette promptly.

"Exactly."

"She is?" said Nadine, scrunching up her face. "Not Catharine of Aragon? I thought she was the one he broke away from the Catholic Church to divorce—so she'd be the most famous, in my opinion. She was the cause of the big church splinter."

"It doesn't matter the label," Jacqueline said. "I shouldn't have made that statement. Both are famous for different causes. But I was thinking of Anne Boleyn for a number of reasons." She frowned at Nadine, who was murmuring something as if she was counting off a list. "What?"

"I'm trying to remember from the musical—you know, *Six*? —which one she was. They list themselves off in the first song, right? Divorced, beheaded, died...divorced, beheaded, survived —right? But I can't remember which one was Anne Boleyn."

"She was beheaded," said Jacqueline, a little more impatiently than she intended. But Nadine didn't seem to notice or mind, for she nodded.

"Okay," said Nadine. "I thought so. I feel like there's a lot out there about her being brought to the Tower of London for her execution. But was she the first one beheaded, or the second one?"

"Basically, once Henry realized how easy it was to divorce or behead a wife he didn't want, he just did it whenever he felt like it," said Suzette dryly.

Jacqueline didn't have the energy—or, to be honest, the desire—to argue about Suzette's opinion. Her friend was basically correct. But she did clarify for Nadine, "Anne Boleyn was the second wife, and the first one beheaded. She was the mother of Queen Elizabeth the First. And," she said with a sigh, "part of the reason she was condemned and put to death was that she was supposedly practicing—wait for it—*witchcraft*."

"Oh shit," said Nadine as Suzette hummed with interest.

"And that's not all," said Jacqueline, picking up the white feathers and waving them. "Guess what Anne Boleyn's royal crest was? A white raven...alighting on a rosebush."

## 5

"So...what do you think that means?" said Suzette. "That *Anne Boleyn* is here? That she came out of the Henry VIII biography?"

"I don't know," Jacqueline replied, spreading her hands. "Like I've said before, I don't make the rules, and I don't even understand the rules I think I know. But," she said, poking at the codex, "I think this book belonged to Anne. It's got her crest on the front page."

"Right below the words 'spells and hexes and curses,'" said Nadine grimly. "Hey! Wouldn't she be considered an ex too? An ex of Henry's? I mean, maybe not really, since he murdered her instead of divorcing her—but it's really the same thing, isn't it? He was her husband, then decided he wanted someone else, so he dumped her at the guillotine."

"I mean, I suppose you could look at it that way," said Jacqueline uncertainly. "But the divorced wives—that's Catharine of Aragon and Anne of Cleves—really have more of a reason to call themselves exes. Wait a second... I just remembered something. I'm pretty sure Henry *did* annul his marriage to Anne Boleyn—a few days before she was executed. So she is, technically, an ex as well!"

"I don't think we ought to get picky," said Suzette, nudging the box of macarons on the table, as if to draw attention to it. "We've got hexes and exes and a codex. Now what do we do?"

Jacqueline felt a sudden sting of tears. The use of the pronoun "we" told her once again that she wasn't alone in whatever mess this was.

She blinked rapidly and snagged a bright pink macaron. "What flavor is this?" she asked as she bit into the crusty cookie. It flaked and collapsed delicately with a rush of flavor. The inside, a more jelly-like filling, was the perfect balance to the airy, crispy exterior. "OMG, Suzette. This is the best damned macaron I've ever had! It's just... The outside is light as a feather!"

Suzette smiled modestly. "Thank you. I've been testing them for a while, but this is the first batch I felt comfortable sharing with anyone. That one is raspberry. The lighter pink is strawberry cream. And the pale ones are vanilla."

"You've been making these and you haven't shared them?" Nadine was outraged. "You know we would have been honest with you."

Suzette patted her arm. "I know. But I was embarrassed. They didn't look very pretty and they weren't as light and airy— All right, all *right*. I promise to let you taste-test everything I make from now on, no matter how bad it is."

Satisfied, Nadine settled back in her seat with a strawberry cream macaron in her hand. "Thank you. It's the BFF code, you know."

"Right. So, anyway, what are we going to do about all of this, Jacqueline? And, by the way, before we go any further, please tell me again how this Josh guy gets away with calling you Jackie and still lives," Suzette said with a pair of raised eyebrows.

Jacqueline laughed. "Well, it's simple. He always did call me Jackie, and he was the only one I allowed to do it. It was...sort of a pet name, a special thing with him. So that's why. No real secret. And no, you can't call me Jackie."

"I was thinking more about Massermey," said Suzette innocently. "Can he call you Jackie? Jacqueline is such a mouthful, and in the throes of—"

"No. Just stop right there," Jacqueline said, laughing as she waved her hands to stop her. "Besides, I love the way he says my name... It's very sexy."

Nadine and Suzette oohed and grinned but, to her relief, didn't tease her any more.

"Are you going to look through the Anne Boleyn codex?" asked Suzette. "Maybe there's a hex in there you can use for Jessie."

Jacqueline groaned. So they were back to that again. "Tomorrow. I'll look at it tomorrow." She sighed. "I suppose I can probably find something that wouldn't bother my conscience too much to inflict on the bastard. And I should probably take the codex over for Zwyla and the others to look at."

"Good plan. So, you think Anne Boleyn might be the one burning stuff in your Woo-Woo Room?" asked Nadine.

"Maybe. I wish I knew what she was burning. Whoever it is." Jacqueline sighed. "All right, enough talk about hexes, exes, and codices," she said, giving Nadine a slit-eyed look. "Let's talk about something else."

"Like Darcy maybe showing up?"

"Sounds good to me," replied Jacqueline.

∼

JACQUELINE DIDN'T SLEEP well that night.

Well, she normally didn't sleep all that well (thank you, perimenopause and anxiety and two glasses of wine), but she slept worse than usual.

At six, she gave up and climbed out of bed. Normally, she didn't rise until eight (a wonderful development since owning her own business), but there was no sense in tossing and turning for another two hours when she knew there was no chance of her falling back asleep until just before it was time to get up.

Comfy in sleep shorts and a loose tee, she padded down the back hall of her flat to the living room, and as she came around the corner, the first things her gaze fell upon were the two old tomes: the cinder-block book and the codex that had been left in the New Age Room.

Jacqueline sighed. That was why she hadn't been able to sleep—those two books.

She'd ignored them after Nadine and Suzette left and gone into her bedroom with a much newer and far more enjoyable read about Agatha Christie's housekeeper, who found a dead body in Mrs. Christie's own library and went on to play amateur detective. Despite the dead bodies, nineteen-thirties England was a far more genteel and calmer setting than Button Cove and its supernatural happenings.

And so there the two books sat on her coffee table: one like a large, squat toad and the other bright, like a slash of blood.

Even though she wanted coffee with every fiber of her being, Jacqueline found herself taking a seat on the sofa. She tucked a soft, knitted afghan around her cold toes and gave the two books an irritated look.

"Okay, fine. I'm here," she said. "You've got my full attention."

Not for a moment did she feel strange speaking to them. Books were living, breathing entities, in her mind, anyway—and her experience with literary characters coming to life had only cemented that notion.

Fortunately, despite her cross words, nothing happened (the

books didn't become animated, they didn't fly open with a breeze ruffling their pages, nor did sparks fly). She picked up the heavy one, the one she'd used twice before to create...recipes.

*Oh, all right. Spells.*

"I'm looking for a mild hex to teach a philandering man a lesson," she said as she opened the heavy cover. "I don't want to maim him or do any permanent damage, but make him uncomfortable for a while. Maybe humiliate him a little, just as he's been humiliating his wife."

The punishment—or, in this case, hex—ought to fit the crime, Jacqueline thought, nodding to herself as she flipped through the crisp, yellowed, age-spotted pages. That might help her to feel less ethically challenged about doing Jessie Gould a favor.

In the past when she looked through the cinder-block book, Jacqueline hadn't leafed through each page. Nor had she checked the table of contents, and a book this old didn't have an index. Instead, she'd relied on intuition to help her find what she needed, and this case was no different.

So when she discovered herself looking down at *For the Humiliation of a Man*, she chuckled and looked up to thank the Universe and all its wisdom.

"All right, then," she said. "Thanks." And read on.

Although it didn't precisely describe the type of "humiliation" with which the "man" would be beset, Jacqueline felt confident that whatever it was would be appropriate to the recipient, and would not cause lasting harm. In fact, there was a notation in the margin—handwritten—that suggested this was the case: *if needed, repeat once per moon.*

The recipe itself was simple. She needed something personal from the man—a lock of hair, a fingernail, a scraping of skin—and several other items easily attained.

Blueberries (*for confusion,* said another handwritten note, which intrigued her) were simple enough. Graveyard dirt, no problem—Jacqueline was very familiar with the local graveyard, thanks to the recent vampire activity. *Broken glass for pain and a shattered heart*—yes, that was easy. A jar, a string... All of that was easy. The only thing she didn't have was wormwood, and she suspected she knew where she could get some.

The cinder-block book was conveniently equipped with several old but still functional ribbons, so she marked the page of the hex and turned her attention reluctantly to the bright red codex.

How something so old could still be so vibrant was a question she couldn't answer. She picked up the slender tome and brought it to her nose, sniffing. Old, very, *very* old. Musty, earthy...and something else.

Jacqueline shivered and abruptly pushed the volume away. She didn't like the feeling of this book. Or its smell. That other scent mingling with that of age and dirt made the hair on the back of her neck prickle unpleasantly.

She looked down at the slender codex, suddenly wary. Could it be bespelled? Was she picking up something magical or malevolent attached to it?

Untangling her feet from the afghan, Jacqueline rose quickly and, after a moment of hesitation, shoved the book into the microwave. She didn't have a lead box anywhere, so she figured a microwave would be the next best thing to contain whatever might be emanating from the codex.

Of course, it had been sitting out all night in the middle of her apartment. With an annoyed curse, she pulled the book back out of the microwave.

"I suppose any damage has probably already been done," she told the tome.

It vibrated in her hand.

Jacqueline squeaked and dropped it. The book landed on

the floor by her bare toes—whose pink polish needed refreshing before her date tonight—and seemed to stare up at her balefully.

"What was that?" she said to the codex. Annoyed, she swooped down and snatched it back up (she could never leave a book on the floor). This time, the book behaved and sat, inanimate and unmoving, in her grip.

Grumbling, Jacqueline looked down at it, turned it around in her hands, fluttered through a few of the aged, rough-edged pages. She *could* not, *would* not be afraid of—or even anxious or nervous about—a book. Books were her whole life. She believed with every fiber of her being that *books* were never evil... Only people using what was in them could be evil.

But this little red codex certainly seemed to have some serious energy around it. Still holding it, Jacqueline marched back to her bedroom and dug in the little jewelry box on her dresser. The first thing she'd done after the vampire melee last week—something she should have done before that—was to create her own protection amulet.

When her fingers closed over the amulet—a small onyx wrapped in filigree gold—she felt the codex give a little lurch in her grip. As if it were startled—not hurt or offended or angry.

"So you felt that, did you?" she said to the book. "Good." She flipped the amulet's leather cord over her head and settled the little pendant beneath her tee, so that it touched her skin.

Thus armed, she returned to the living room and considered the velvet sofa...then opted for coffee instead. She had a feeling she was going to need caffeine for whatever was in store.

A few minutes later, she settled back on the couch with her coffee and the codex. With care, she opened the red leather cover.

The same *Hexef and Spellf and Cursef* title was there, and the drawing of the white bird over the rosebush.

"You belonged to Anne Boleyn, didn't you?" said Jacqueline, settling her hand over the title page. She wasn't prepared for the sudden rush of energy that blasted into her palm and fingertips and through her body. "I see," she said a moment later, when she'd regathered her wits. "Who brought you here?" she asked. The same burst of energy washed over her, but it didn't clearly answer the question. Nonetheless, Jacqueline couldn't help but look around to see whether anyone had appeared.

To her relief, she was still alone in her flat. Sipping her coffee (light with guilt-free monk fruit sweetener), she eyed the book cautiously. Then, with her beverage safely out of reach, she turned the title page.

It was all handwritten, of course, even though Anne Boleyn's husband had employed the printing press more than any previous English king. Jacqueline understood precisely why such a book wouldn't have been entrusted to a typesetter and printer.

"I don't blame you one bit," she murmured, squinting at the ancient text. She was a librarian, not a historian, and deciphering old writings or script was not one of her skills.

The prose was more like a journal or letter, rather than a recipe or spell with ingredients listed and then instructions. She was able to make out a few words—*secret, ability, wise, aged*—but the overall content was mostly lost on her.

She turned the page and found drawings that were immediately and stunningly clear.

"You had a mean streak, didn't you, Anne?" Jacqueline muttered, looking at a primitive but unambiguous sketch of a sword run through the belly of a man...who happened to be wearing a crown.

On the next page there was another drawing of a man—same crown—with his hand lopped off and blood spurting everywhere. Again, a rudimentary image, but its meaning was abundantly clear.

More pictures: a tower with flames roaring from its window and the crowned head protruding from the same opening. A man—crowned again—beneath the feet of a large black warhorse that would aptly be called a "destrier."

"So that's how you spent your time while locked away in the tower," Jacqueline muttered. "Creating a graphic novel of revenge fantasies."

There were more pictures further on in the codex—more graphic ones along the same lines, but also crude drawings of plants and berries with notations next to them.

Finally, more than halfway into the book, the recipes or spells began to appear. They had names obvious enough that Jacqueline could make them out: *Revenge Curse* (or, in this case, *Curfe*), *How to Kill a Man* (yikes), and *Spell to Tightly Bind a Lie*.

But it was the last one that caught her attention—one that was graphically illustrated.

*Caftratuf: The Beheading of a Man Bloodleffly.*

There was a drawing of a man proudly displaying an erect penis, followed by the man (it was obviously the same one, for he wore a crown and was colored in purple, with a long sword in his hand) with an ugly, blackened, shriveled-up penis. The third picture was of the man looking down at the ugly, blackened, shriveled-up penis...which was lying on the ground in front of him.

Jacqueline shivered and nodded. Apparently, women through the ages tended to have the same revenge fantasies about men who betrayed them. Although in this case... Could witchcraftery possibly make such a thing happen? She shivered again, glad (not for the first time) that she didn't possess a penis.

There were a few more pages in the book, with more illegible notes, and what could have been spatters of blood, wine, or dirt. The last few pages were blank.

"Whew," Jacqueline said, setting the codex aside in favor of caffeine. "That was intense."

She figured she'd better take the codex over to the ZAP Ladies and let them look at it. Not only because of the very graphic images and the words she couldn't make out, but because of the intense energy she'd felt from the tome itself.

Jacqueline finished her coffee then went to get dressed for the day. She could do her pre-opening work early and then nip down to visit the ZAP Ladies and be back before ten, when the shop opened.

It was the Friday of Memorial Day weekend, and she knew she was going to be busy. At least, she hoped she was going to be busy.

Jacqueline was just finishing her hair—not that she could do much with it anymore; it was Little Orphan Annie curly thanks to an annoyed witch, and only behaved when she applied certain hair products—when she heard someone pounding on the door to her apartment.

Frowning, she grabbed her cell phone and looked at it as she hurried down the hall. Whoever was pounding on the door would have had to have access to the bookshop in order to get to the door. There were no messages on her phone, which was both a relief and a surprise. So it wasn't Nadine or Suzette, both of whom had keys to the shop.

The back hall of her flat connected the living room and kitchen with the bathroom and two bedrooms, along with a small utility closet and the main door to the apartment. It was on this door that someone was pounding.

Jacqueline looked through the peephole and was surprised to see Mrs. Hudson there, with Mrs. Danvers lurking behind her.

She flung open the door, mystified and apprehensive. The two women had never bothered her up here before, and to see them together did not bode well.

"What is it? What's wrong?" Jacqueline asked.

"Sh-she's here," Mrs. Hudson managed to say. "Oh dear, my heart can't take this, now, can it?" she prattled on, clapping a hand to her apron-covered bosom.

"Who's here?" Jacqueline asked, a strong foreboding settling in the pit of her stomach.

"If you would come and see, ma'am," said Mrs. Danvers in a slightly less impertinent tone than usual, which made Jacqueline's nerves explode and every hair on her body stand on end.

She sighed. She suspected there was a very good reason the two women were in a tizzy.

The games were about to begin.

## 6

Jacqueline followed Danvers and Hudson down the stairs to the first floor of the shop, then, to her surprise, Mrs. Hudson led the way along the hall from the back of the store to the front and then *up* the steps into the café.

"Hark. Who goest there?" said a female English voice as they approached the top of the stairs. "Attend us, we sayest! We have long been awaiting."

Jacqueline had been following Hudson and Danvers, but then, all at once, she found herself in the lead. She wasn't certain how it happened, but that question became irrelevant when she discovered what was waiting for her in the café.

Seated on the largest sofa in front of the fireplace was a woman wearing the widest, most elaborate dress Jacqueline had ever seen outside of a museum. The woman was positioned in the center of the couch, and her dress completely filled it from arm to arm and billowed onto the floor in front of her. Its skirt was in two parts: an overskirt, which was made from heavy purple brocade and which was designed to be open, revealing the underskirt of rippling silk, embroidered to within an inch of its life, beneath.

The bodice of the gown was made of three parts: an under-blouse with puffed sleeves that Jacqueline knew were actually sewn on when the woman was dressed, and a frontispiece that was flat and rigid. It was formed in the shape of a shield, or a modified upside-down triangle, ending in a point just above the crotch. The frontispiece was trimmed with a sort of bric-a-brac ribbon and had the effect of squashing the woman's breasts nearly flat—except for the parts that overflowed and threatened to explode from the top of their confines. Her head was covered by a soft hood, known as a French hood, which revealed only the front part of the woman's hair and covered most of the rest of it.

Jacqueline had taken the time to sweep her attention over the absolutely authentic Tudor clothing—when else would she see such historic perfection?—before lifting her gaze to the face of the person who could only be Anne Boleyn.

She was in her late twenties, with rich blue eyes and a pale, oval face. Although Anne Boleyn had been known throughout history as a scheming husband-stealer who lured Henry to her bed with her feminine wiles, the woman in front of her wasn't what Jacqueline would consider stunningly beautiful. The queen was more striking than gorgeous, and it was the naughty tilt of her mouth and the sensual uptilt of the corners of her eyes that a man would likely find intriguing.

"Thou," said the woman, pointing an imperious finger at Jacqueline. "Art thou the one who chargest here?"

"I am," Jacqueline replied, catching herself just before she curtsied to the former Queen of England. There was no need to be subservient. This was her shop and her world. Anne Boleyn had no power here—at least, not as a queen.

Although as a witch...

"How art thou called?" Anne demanded.

Jacqueline gave a little shudder and decided that while

subservience wasn't going to happen (at least on her part), deference would certainly be prudent. "Jacqueline Finch, madam."

Anne looked at her, one pencil-thin brow lifted high and haughty. She seemed to expect something else from Jacqueline, but for once in her life, Jacqueline decided not to be a people-pleaser. Instead, she merely looked back with the same expectation she saw in the former queen's expression.

After all, she was a witch too. (She winced inside as that unwelcome but undeniable thought sank into her brain.)

"Art thou the one who hath summonest us?" demanded Anne after a moment of silence. She leaned forward stiffly, just as far as the unyielding brocade frontispiece would allow. Jacqueline felt a pang of sympathy for the poor woman. Between the farthingale—the frame of her gown that made it as wide as a doorway—and the frontispiece, the poor thing was practically in a cage.

"No," Jacqueline replied. She could feel rather than hear or see the shock from Hudson and Danvers from behind her. They were likely nearly prostrate with shame and horror that she wasn't groveling on the floor in front of an English queen. "I did not summon you, madam. But I believe I have your spell book."

Anne shifted in her seat. The flash of surprise was there, then gone in an instant. "Of what doest thou speakest?"

Jacqueline decided to change tactics. She needed to do something very quickly, for the bookstore was due to open soon. She couldn't have a Queen of England commandeering her tea shop, especially one dressed as Anne was. "Madam, if you will come with me, I believe we can find you more comfortable accommodations"—not to mention attire—"and perhaps some refreshments."

Anne hesitated, then nodded. She flung her hands out wide, and before Jacqueline could react, both Hudson and Danvers practically leapt to the queen's aid. They helped Anne to her feet

—obviously something that could not be done on her own, dressed as she was.

"This way, madam," Jacqueline said, suddenly having a brilliant idea. After all, *A Connecticut Yankee in King Arthur's Court* was one of her favorite Twain novels.

She indicated the back hall that went to the New Age Room. She watched Anne—who was assisted by Danvers and Hudson managing her train and the very broad skirt through the narrow hall—for a sign of recognition as she approached. Presumably, this room was from where she'd emerged, but whether Anne had been responsible for the burning was uncertain.

But the queen hardly glanced into the New Age Room, leaving Jacqueline to conclude that whoever had summoned the queen had been the one to burn papers in the singing bowls, not the queen herself. Who that might be was yet another mystery to solve.

She gestured Anne into the elevator, which was unobtrusively tucked next to the storage closet where a few weeks ago the Artful Dodger hid the loot he'd been pickpocketing from Jacqueline's customers. Danvers and Hudson, of necessity, remained in the hall. It was a very small elevator.

"Madam, if you will," Jacqueline said, and helped to maneuver the ridiculously complicated skirts through the narrow opening by gently turning Anne sideways in order to pass through.

"What is this?" demanded Anne, hesitating just as she stepped inside. "Doest thou put us in a prison cell?"

"Not at all. It is a magical room." Jacqueline assisted the queen to turn once more so she was facing the doors, which was instrumental to her plan. "It will take us to a new and safe location where you will be far more comfortable than a prison cell."

"Magical." Anne's eyes narrowed, and they scanned Jacqueline up and down. "What doest thou knowest about magic?"

"I know quite a bit," said Jacqueline, squeezing into the elevator with her and sliding to one side to half face her companion. She made a sweeping gesture, and the doors slid closed, seemingly on their own.

Anne's eyes widened. She'd been looking out into the corridor, and then suddenly it was gone. Jacqueline felt the other woman's body tense slightly, for they were alone in the small space. The button for the third floor was behind her, and she pressed it without turning as she murmured, "Bibbidi-boppidi-boo"—just loud enough for Anne to hear and assume she was speaking an incantation.

The queen eyed her, and Jacqueline saw a bit of nervousness in her gaze. Yet she held herself erect and still looked down her nose at Jacqueline. A queen through and through. You had to admire her for that, at least.

The elevator was smooth and quiet, and there was only the slightest jolt when it came to a halt; probably not the least bit noticeable to the other woman.

With a cool look at Anne, Jacqueline gestured to the door, and it slid open to reveal a view through the kitchen of her apartment into the living room.

The expression on the queen's face was priceless. There was shock and awe, and then, when she looked at Jacqueline, admiration and reverence. For all Anne Boleyn knew, they'd teleported to another continent instead of simply traveled up one floor in the same building.

"Thou hast a most powerful magic," said the queen in the most genuine, almost girlish voice she'd yet used.

Pleased with this development, Jacqueline assisted Anne and her gown through the doorway and the narrow passage between kitchen and living room. There was nearly an upset when the queen passed hastily by a low side table that held a porcelain vase of flowers, but Jacqueline was quick enough to save them from being knocked over by wayward brocade and silk.

She gestured to the blue velvet couch. "A most comfortable place to sit, madam."

The queen seemed to be enamored with the soft, luxurious sofa and her surroundings, for she looked around while also trying not to appear starstruck.

It was obvious why, for the large windows with clear, unwarped glass—so different from any Anne would have experienced in sixteenth-century England—allowed bright sunlight to stream inside. The space was large and open, uncluttered and well lit; again, very different from her native environment. The furnishings were modern, and they gleamed with glass, brass, polished wood, and even a bit of bling in a crystal table lamp next to the couch.

Jacqueline offered a hand to help balance Anne as she carefully lowered herself onto the sofa. Then she walked over to the gas fireplace and made a sharp gesture as she surreptitiously flipped the switch that turned it on. Anne jolted and her eyes went wide when the flames gently erupted around fake logs. It wasn't necessary to have a fire right now, it being nearly Memorial Day, but the morning was a bit cool, and Jacqueline had wanted to cement in the woman's mind that she was a very powerful witch.

"Madam, would you care for refreshment?" she asked, flicking a hand toward the floor lamp between the armchair and sofa as she stepped on its foot switch.

Anne jolted again, her eyes goggling as the light came on as if by magic. "Thou..." she said in a strangled voice. "Willst thou teach us these spells?" She gestured with a graceful hand that nonetheless shook slightly.

"Perhaps," Jacqueline said, giving the woman a haughty look. "Tea or coffee, madam?"

"Tea? Coffee? Nay, we are not ill," replied Anne, even as she did look a little ill. Her face was definitely paler than it had been. "We should be well met with ale or wine."

"Perhaps you might like some coffee, madam. To settle your insides?" Jacqueline pressed. Although coffee and tea had been introduced in England during the Tudor era, they were, as Anne's reaction reminded her, mainly used for medicinal purposes. She knew it was a better option than to offer water, for no one in Tudor England drank water.

Anne hesitated, then gave a regal nod, clearly succumbing to the will of someone she, if not feared, then at least was wary of.

Jacqueline returned to the living room after only a minute, having used the Keurig with her back to Anne in order to obstruct her view of what she was doing (she'd also used dramatic hand gestures in order to add to the effect). She found the queen sitting very still on the sofa, seemingly entranced by the fire—no, it was the painting of the cedar tree that had captured her attention.

Jacqueline noticed that the white raven that had fluttered into the picture last night was perched in the cedar tree, its bright whiteness a beacon in an otherwise twilit scene.

"A beautiful painting, isn't it?" Jacqueline said, setting a tray with the coffee and a scone on the oval glass and brass table that had a height-adjustable leaf, making it easy for the queen to reach even in her restrictive gown. She wondered what else, if anything, Anne had seen in the picture.

The queen tore her attention away from the painting, but as she did, she wore a faint smile. Then she eyed the tray in front of her with interest. After a brief hesitation, she picked up the delicate china coffee cup and examined it minutely before bringing it to her lips—and then she stopped suddenly before sipping. A bit of coffee sloshed over the rim.

"Thou drinkest this anon." She held out the cup to Jacqueline, who took it and drank, making it very obvious that she was, in fact, taking a sip and swallowing it.

"It's not poisoned, madam," she said, returning the cup to the queen. It was also very sweet and milky, due to the hazelnut cream version of coffee she'd used and the generous bit of monk fruit added for sugar.

Anne took the cup and an experimental sip. Her eyes went wide. "'Tis well delicious. Thou sayest it is coffee?"

"It's a special brew," Jacqueline told her, deliberately using that word. "It will not harm you, but make you feel more, um, comfortable in this world."

She sat down next to Anne on a chair (obviously there was no room for anyone else on the sofa).

"I believe this belongs to you." She placed the codex on the table next to the coffee tray.

Anne's graceful movements hitched slightly when she saw the book, but she continued to reach for the scone. "What is it?" She was still playing innocent, speaking of the codex, not the scone, and Jacqueline couldn't quite blame her.

The poor woman had been divorced and beheaded, and accused of many crimes there was no evidence she'd committed —including incest. Plus, she knew precisely what happened to witches during her time.

Jacqueline merely picked up the book. It was filled with energy; she could feel a sort of sizzle emanating from it. Whether that was because the codex recognized its owner or for some other reason, she didn't know.

She flipped carefully through the pages, feeling Anne's eyes on her the whole time. "Nice drawings," she said, glancing up at the queen. "Looks like you had a few plans for your husband."

The flash of malice in Anne's blue eyes was there and gone in an instant, but Jacqueline had seen it.

"The *Castratus* Curse seems pretty severe," Jacqueline

commented, turning to the two facing pages that illustrated the three-step dick-shriveling and falling-off spell. "I'll bet you wished you'd had the chance to cast it on the king."

"Such a thing," replied Anne, "wouldst be treason. To even speak of doing so wouldst be treason."

Jacqueline shrugged and set the book down carefully. "You were found guilty of treason and punished for it whether you did it or not."

Anne lifted her chin proudly. "I was *never* treasonous."

The fact that she dropped the royal "we," in combination with her determined expression, caused Jacqueline to believe her.

She could see the clock on the microwave in the kitchen and realized it was after nine already. She needed to get downstairs, so it was time to put the second part of her hastily formed plan into motion.

She rose. "Madam, I have things to which I must attend. I will leave you for a time. You are quite safe here in this...tower... but there are spells of protection around it. You may neither leave nor allow anyone entrance other than me. It is for your safety."

"We are imprisoned?" Anne said sharply.

"Thou are not a prisoner," Jacqueline said, somehow slipping into a more formal, archaic syntax. Those Philippa Gregory books were certainly coming in handy. "Thou art well protected here. But take heed—do thou not attempt to leave unless I am with you," she said firmly. "Thou hast seen the extent of my magic. I don't wish for anything to happen to you. The protections work both ways. I vow, I will return as soon as possible."

Anne gave her a measured look followed by a brief nod. Her attention trailed to the codex, but Jacqueline picked it up. She didn't think it was a good idea to leave it with the queen, especially when she was alone. Besides, she wanted the ZAP Ladies to take a look at it.

"I shall return as soon as I am able," she said, rising. She felt a little guilty leaving the poor woman by herself in a strange place, but what else was she going to do with her? Too bad Anne hadn't brought a lady-in-waiting or a lute player or someone else along with her for amusement.

"Very well," said Anne, as if granting her permission to leave.

Jacqueline hurried out of the room and used the elevator to go back to the tea room. She considered sending Mrs. Hudson up there to stay with Anne, but then who would run the tea room?

She was confident the queen wouldn't try to leave, but what if she needed to use the bathroom or something?

Jacqueline rolled her eyes and shook her head. She didn't know enough about the people who came out of books to know whether they needed to do things like eat, sleep, or pee, and she didn't have time to obsess over it. She'd just have to trust that all would be well.

"What did you do with her?" demanded Mrs. Hudson in an uncharacteristically sharp voice. Then, as if to collect herself, she added, "I mean to say, is Her Majesty quite all right?"

"She is settled in my apartment, and I've told her not to leave. I wish there was someone who could stay with her." When Mrs. Hudson opened her mouth, Jacqueline waved her off. "And who would run the tea room? I think it's best if you stay here. I'll think of something."

"Of course I should stay here. But you could send that Danvers woman up there, dearie," Mrs. Hudson said with undisguised relish. "The two of them ought to get along like peas in a pod."

"Mrs. Danvers has other things to do," Jacqueline replied. Besides, she didn't like the idea of those two manipulative, potentially malicious women left together unattended. The jury was still out on whether Danvers had set Manderley on fire or not. The woman had a vengeful streak—just like Anne Boleyn.

"I've got to speak with the ladies down the street," Jacqueline said, still holding the codex. "I'll be back as soon as I can."

Mrs. Hudson sniffed the sniff of the offended (apparently, she didn't approve of Jacqueline gallivanting off when the shop was about to open). "Very well, dearie, I'll just do my best, then. It's Memorial Day weekend, you know."

"I'm quite aware of that," Jacqueline said, and blithely started down the stairs to the main floor.

She found Mrs. Danvers standing like a sentinel behind the counter. "Is Her Majesty quite settled?" she asked, in the same suspicious tone Mrs. Hudson had used. "Ma'am."

What on earth did Danvers and Hudson think Jacqueline was going to *do* to Anne?

"Yes, she is." Jacqueline's reply was even and cool, and the look she gave Danvers was as close to quelling as she could manage. She was still a bit intimidated by the woman. "She is quite comfortable. I need you to handle the shop for a few minutes while I go down the street."

"Down the street? Why, it's Memorial Day weekend!" Mrs. Danvers was scandalized.

"I'm not going to be gone all weekend," Jacqueline said impatiently. "And it's only nine thirty. I might even be back before we open."

"But we open at nine thirty in the summer," Danvers replied as she swept to the door and flipped the sign to OPEN. "And we stay open until half past seven. It's for the tourists, you see. Ma'am," she added with unhidden condescension.

"I don't remember having that conversation," Jacqueline said, fumbling in spite of her determination not to show weakness in front of Danvers.

The austere housekeeper merely looked down her nose at her. "It is the way it's been done."

Jacqueline sighed and decided to save her breath. "Fine. I'll be back as soon as I can. I am quite certain you can handle the hordes of customers that are going to be flocking here any moment now."

She looked outside, expecting to see an empty sidewalk...but there was a cluster of women standing there.

The door swung open, the bell jangled, and five women streamed into the space.

Mrs. Danvers gave Jacqueline an arch look, then repositioned herself behind the counter.

"Good morning," Jacqueline said. "Welcome to Three Tomes Bookshop. Is there anything in particular you're looking for this morning?"

Just as she said those words, she recognized one of the five women. It was Jessie Gould.

She surged forward, flanked by the four other women, and said, "We're here for you to hex our exes."

## 7

Jacqueline's welcoming smile froze as five eager faces looked at her.

"You...what?" She looked at Jessie Gould, doing her best not to send (literal) sparks at her. She was, after all, a customer and lived in the small town.

"I want my ex-boyfriend hexed," said one of the newcomers. She was in her late twenties and had short, messy purple hair. "He's shacked up with my ex-best friend—hey, maybe you should hex her too." She squinted craftily.

"My ex-husband took all my credit cards with him when he left," said another woman, probably forty or so. She carried a large red handbag from Egala's shop and had her brown hair in a ponytail. "He ran them up, and now I'm stuck with the tab— even though *I* didn't *do* it! The legal system in this country is fucked. So I want you to hex the *shit* out of him." Her eyes flashed, and Jacqueline suspected if the woman had any magical powers, the whole room would have gone up in flames.

"I... Okay, wow," Jacqueline said, unable to form any other words. "I—um..."

"Jessie told us you were working on a hex for Raymond," said another of the women. "We want in on it too. Figured if you were doing one, you could do five, right? What's the term for that?"

"Economies of scale," Jacqueline said faintly.

"Right. That. My ex lives in Wicks Hollow—is that too far away for you to hex him? I'm sure I could figure out a way to get him here, though," the woman went on. She was very attractive, with long, butter-colored hair and bright red lipstick. "He's always up for a booty call," she said with a layer of disgust. "We've been split up for six months, but he still comes around panting whenever I crook a finger."

"Wh-why do you want to hex him, then?" Jacqueline asked. "It seems like you've, uh, already got him on a short leash."

"Because he's a *dick*, that's why," replied the blonde. "He wanted me to quit my job so much he screwed around with my email and work computer and nearly got me fired."

"Right." Jacqueline resisted the urge to swipe a hand over her face. "Okay, look... I'm still in the process of researching these, er, hexes, Jessie. But"—her voice rose to overpower the mutterings from her small audience—"I do know that I will need something personal from each of your...exes..."

"Like a lock of hair?" asked the fifth woman eagerly. She was older than the rest, a wizened little woman with apple cheeks and unnaturally blue-black hair.

"Yes. Or a nail clipping, or even a scraping of the skin."

"A scraping of the skin?" The woman with the red handbag narrowed her eyes as her lips curled with delight. "I'm going for that. It's not skinning him alive, but it's close enough."

Jacqueline decided right then and there that none of these women—especially the handbag lady—was going to get anywhere near Anne Boleyn.

"All right, then, fine. Go off and do that and...and I'll be in touch," she said to Jessie.

"When?"

"Later today or tomorrow," Jacqueline said rashly.

"Great. That gives me time to set up that booty call," said the blonde, her smile crooked and wicked. "I'll make it *so* worth his while."

"While you're here," Jacqueline said meaningfully, "maybe you'll want to look around? There are lots of books about, um, witches. *A Discovery of Witches*, *Jonathan Strange and Mr. Norrell*, *The Mayfair Witches*, and many more. And other things. Books about other things."

The women seemed to appreciate this suggestion, and Jacqueline watched as they dispersed into the back rooms of the shop, glad that she hadn't mentioned all the Wicca books and plant witchery books up in the New Age Room. She didn't really want them trying things out on their own.

Jacqueline was waffling over whether it was safe to leave— surely Mrs. Danvers could handle the group—when the back door opened and three more people came into the shop.

Jacqueline tucked the codex under the counter and set about doing what she loved best: helping people find their next great read.

There was a steady stream of customers all morning, and normally, she would be ecstatic about the hundreds of dollars of sales being rung up (she *was* ecstatic, actually), but she also really needed to talk to the ZAP Ladies. Not for the first time, she regretted the fact that she had no way to contact them—no phone number to call or text. In the past, they always just showed up whether she wanted them to or not, or she went to them.

"And there you go," she said, handing off the bright blue shopping bag with the Three Tomes Bookshop logo on it to a woman who'd purchased five beautiful picture books, including two of the fairy tales gorgeously illustrated by Darby Wright. "Have a wonderful afternoon."

To her shock, she realized it already *was* afternoon. Just after, but still. She'd been swamped and busy and talking books for more than three hours.

"Is it going to be like this all summer?" she said to herself, finally able to catch her breath. There was only one customer, and he was back in the Science Fiction Room.

But Danvers heard her. "One would expect. And hope." Her comment was more of a chastisement than anything. "Ma'am."

"I need to go upstairs and check on Anne—er, the queen," Jacqueline said.

She was just reaching for the codex to take it with her when the bell jangled over the door once more. She looked up and saw the ZAP Ladies filling the entrance. Not for the first time did she notice that they looked uncomfortably like the picture of the Witches Three from *Macbeth*, which hung just above the door.

"Jacqueline! How are you today? You've been so busy," trilled Pietra with a smile. "We wanted to come down sooner, but there didn't seem to be a good time." Her sky-blue caftan dipped and shifted as she trotted into the front room. She was not, to Jacqueline's disappointment, carrying a basket of goodies today.

"Where are the cats?" said Andromeda, looking around expectantly. Today, her hair was done in shocking pink spikes. She wore black capris and a loose, *Flashdance*-style, off-the-shoulder tunic of dusky blue. Her toenails—on pretty good-looking feet for a woman of eightyish—matched her hair.

"I haven't seen them all morning," Jacqueline said, realizing it was true. This was not a cause for concern, however. Max and Sebastian were cats, after all. "I've been a little busy. I'm really glad you're here. I wanted to come down and see you—"

"We know," said Zwyla with a smile. Today, perhaps in honor of summer's imminence, she wore an unusually flowery, frilly maxi dress. It was splashed with blooms of cherry, tangerine, cotton candy, and Granny Smith. Her shaved head was covered by a bright red wrap, and two huge earrings—suns—dangled from beneath it. "Would you like to go up to the tea room, where we can talk?"

"How about up to my flat?" Jacqueline said, giving her a meaningful look. "There's someone you need to meet."

Zwyla's brows rose to the edges of her turban, but she nodded. And, without speaking, Zwyla and her companions followed Jacqueline down the hall to the back of the shop, then up two flights of stairs to the apartment.

But when they walked down the hall past the bedroom and came into the living room, it was empty.

"*No.*" Jacqueline frantically began to look around—in the bedroom, bathroom, even the pantry and the elevator next to it, but it was clear Anne Boleyn was gone. "Crap. Crap. *Crap.*"

"Do you want to tell us what's happened?" said Andromeda.

"Oh, I see you've been looking up hexes," Pietra commented sunnily, picking up the cinder-block book. "Oooh. This *is* a good one—the humiliation one. I've used that myself a few times."

"Petey, now is not the time," Zwyla said when Jacqueline only gaped at them, looking back and forth as she tried to collect her thoughts. It was like herding cats, dealing with these three women. It really was.

Jacqueline found her voice. "Anne Boleyn is gone. She was here. I told her to stay here. Someone must have—"

"What's this?" Zwyla picked up a small metal mixing bowl that had been sitting on the coffee table. Inside were the remnants of several burned pieces of paper.

"Dammit!" Jacqueline exploded. "What the hell is going on here?" This outburst captured the full attention of the three crones. She launched into a detailed explanation of everything that had happened, and her current suspicion that whoever had conjured or called Anne from out of her book had recently been in Jacqueline's apartment, once again, burning papers.

"There's a bit of writing on this one," said Pietra, squinting at a charred paper scrap. "I need my glasses to see it."

"Join the club," muttered Jacqueline as Pietra fished out a pair of bright red-framed cheaters from somewhere in the depths of her bodice.

When she put them on, her eyes became magnified as large as goggles. "I can't make out much... A B...maybe 'am'... The paper is smudged with ash. A J or a T—it's so difficult to tell with script and old writing."

"Remember sometimes S's are written as F's," Jacqueline said, feeling otherwise helpless. Not only had someone been doing conjuring or summoning spells in her shop, but somehow they'd gotten into her private living space and were doing it here too!

"Take a look, Andi," Pietra said, dropping the scrap of paper into her friend's palm. "You have better eyes than I do."

"Definitely a J... Oh, maybe it's a T. I can't tell if that's a smudge there. And a B for sure," said Andromeda as Jacqueline fumed silently.

She didn't really care what was on the papers. She wanted to know who kept coming into her space and doing spells.

"Jacqueline, dear," said Pietra suddenly. She was standing at one of the windows. "You might want to see this."

Feeling ready to pull out her hair, Jacqueline joined her at the window. "Good grief," she muttered when she saw what was happening below. Anne Boleyn was walking down the middle of Camellia Street. Her gown took up the entirety of one lane of traffic, causing a backup of cars who couldn't get around her. The louder they honked, the slower she walked.

"This is a disaster," Jacqueline grumbled. "What are people going to think about a woman in Tudor clothing marching down the street?" She was already dashing for the stairs. The steps were in the back, and Anne was in the front, but climbing down was faster than taking the elevator.

"I wouldn't worry about it too much," Zwyla said, pounding down on the steps behind Jacqueline. "People will just think she's an escapee from the Renaissance Festival."

"There's a Renaissance Festival?" Jacqueline panted as she clomped onto the ground floor. How did she not know this?

"Of course. It opens Memorial Day weekend and goes every weekend all summer. It's out in the hills at an old farm."

"Well, there's that at least," Jacqueline muttered as she rushed down the hall to the front of the shop.

Danvers tsked as she blew past, but continued ringing up a man at the counter.

By the time Jacqueline got outside, there was a small crowd around Anne. The queen was holding court, as one would expect—responding to every comment with regal condescension. The fact that she was infallible in playing Anne Boleyn only added to the crowd's interest. Nothing they said or did could shake her from her character.

"Madam," said Jacqueline, pushing her way through the people. "Your Majesty," she added, louder and against her better judgment, but she thought it best if she played along for the sake of the audience.

Anne turned at the sound of her voice. Jacqueline thought she saw a moment of relief before the haughty expression returned.

"Take us to our chamber," commanded the queen, her elegant nose high in the air. "There are far too many serfs and riffraff about." She thrust out her arm imperiously, assuming Jacqueline would take it.

"If you had *stayed* in your chamber, this wouldn't have happened," she told the queen from between her teeth.

"We were summoned," Anne replied flatly. "Didst thou not call for us?"

"I did not," Jacqueline said, maneuvering her to the bookshop. "How were you summoned?"

She resisted the urge to shove the queen through the doorway into Three Tomes. Instead, she gathered her thoughts and composure and gestured Anne to precede her inside.

Fortunately, the customer Mrs. Danvers had been ringing up had already left and the front room was empty—leaving just enough room for Anne and her obnoxious clothing. If she brushed too close to a table, her dress would knock everything askew or onto the ground.

The three crones were standing on the steps leading to the tea room, and Jacqueline gave them a look that said, *We need to talk*. Then she took Anne to the elevator's location on the first floor. Jacqueline herself rarely used it, but having such access to the tea room was important for those with mobility challenges. She also didn't want to have to fuss with Anne's skirts climbing up a flight of stairs.

She did the whole magic thing with the elevator again, and Anne was properly astonished a second time. Still, Jacqueline wondered why, if the queen was so taken by her magic skill, she had risked leaving the apartment.

By the time Jacqueline got Anne settled on the blue velvet sofa, the ZAP Ladies were clomping down the hallway from the back door.

"Who art thou?" Anne said imperiously, and gave Jacqueline a look.

"They're friends. They have much more powerful magic than I do," Jacqueline said truthfully. "Now, I would like to know why and how you left this place after I told you it wasn't safe to do so."

Anne looked at her with narrow eyes, and for a moment,

Jacqueline thought she would refuse to answer. But then she said, "We were summoned, as *we* hadst told *thou*. One moment we were here, and next she appeared. And then—'twas like the magic room—we were somewhere else."

"On the street?"

Anne shook her head. "Nay. 'Twas a garden. We were sat in a garden, and there were many strange metal monsters around me. They had large eyes. They weren't moving, but we did not like them. And so we left."

"You said someone was here? A woman? Who was she?" Jacqueline pressed.

"We knowest not," replied Anne haughtily. "She appeared from somewhere—we did not see. And she started a fire—not as thou didst"—she gestured to the fireplace—"but 'twas only a small one."

"She started a fire in this bowl?" Jacqueline showed Anne the small bowl that held the ashes.

"Aye. And then we werest disappeared, and found in the garden with the metal monsters."

"And the woman who appeared—she wasn't with you in the garden?"

"Nay. We have toldest thou—we were there alone."

Jacqueline exchanged glances with the ZAP Ladies, who'd (shockingly) remained quiet during this exchange. "All right, just so I understand it—you were sitting here, and suddenly this woman appeared. She started a little fire in the bowl, and then you apparated—I mean, you disappeared and then you were in the garden?" This all sounded very strange and illogical. "Did the woman say anything to you?"

But here, Anne clammed up. She lifted her chin and shook her head. Jacqueline didn't believe her. Surely the woman had said something; otherwise, why would Anne believe she'd been "summoned" by someone working with Jacqueline?

Jacqueline threw up her hands and looked at the ZAP Ladies. "I don't know what to make of this."

"Let us sit with her a bit, dear," said Pietra. "Perhaps she'll be more inclined to speak frankly to us."

"Be my guest," Jacqueline said with great feeling. And then she suddenly remembered. "The codex! I left it downstairs."

"Codex?" Zwyla's brows lifted. "You have many codices, Jacqueline. Which one do you mean?"

Jacqueline explained, then said, "I was just about to get it from under the counter when you three arrived, and then I forgot to get it. I'll be right back."

She hurried to the elevator and took it to the first floor, which was clustered with customers. Mrs. Danvers seemed to be holding her own, however (Jacqueline couldn't deny the woman was just as capable—but much scarier—than Agatha Christie's own crime-solving housekeeper), and so she ducked behind the counter to grab the codex, with the intention of heading back upstairs with it.

But the shelf was empty.

The codex was gone.

## 8

Jacqueline searched frantically under the counter, ignoring Mrs. Danvers's irritated mutterings as she got in the way of her helping customers. But the codex was not there.

"Hi," Jacqueline said as she rose from behind the counter to see what felt like a sea of customers. She knew her fair cheeks were flushed dark pink with exertion, frustration, and horror, but she couldn't ignore the people waiting in line. "I can help the next person here." She mustered up a smile.

Jacqueline efficiently rang up three customers before she had the chance to murmur to Mrs. Danvers, "I put an old book with a bright red cover under the counter here, and it's gone. Do you know what happened to it? Hello there, I can ring you up here," she said, pivoting back into shopkeeper mode. "Did you find everything you were looking for?"

"I was hoping to find the new Nora Roberts," said a woman wearing the most fabulous sunglasses Jacqueline had ever seen. They were tangerine, with crystals at the cat-eye corners. "I think it's been out a few weeks, but it's perfect for a holiday weekend read."

"Oh, of course. It's back in Romance. Let me show you. By

the way, I love your glasses." Jacqueline smiled and led the way
back to the room with one bright red wall and a lush, thick rug
on the floor. The fireplace in this room had a frame made from
rose-colored marble tiles, and the mantel was painted with
pearlescent paint. Two velvet armchairs in pink flanked the fireplace. It was Jacqueline's favorite genre section.

But as she came into the room, she stumbled to a halt. *Pride
and Prejudice* was on the floor again. Open.

She glanced around—no one was there—before swooping
up the book, then tucked it back on the shelf. "Um...let me see...
Ah. Here it is." She regrouped quickly and pulled out the hardcover book for her customer, then stepped back when she
noticed the woman plucking a second Nora book off the shelf to
peruse.

She loved it when people found more books than they'd
intended!

But that rush of gratitude and delight faded quickly, for she
grimaced then glared at the Austen collection on the shelf. If
someone was going to come out of *Pride and Prejudice*, she really
wished they'd show themselves sooner rather than later. What
was all of this "falling off the shelf"—multiple times—business?
It didn't make any sense.

Assured that the customer would be busy for a few minutes,
Jacqueline slipped out of the room. She glanced into the
Mystery/Thriller area and saw a stack of books customers had
probably left on the table next to a bench by that room's fireplace. (Jacqueline loved that almost every room had a fireplace,
but she was also aware that they took up vertical real estate that
could have housed bookshelves. Still, every book she needed to
shelve somehow seemed to have a space, so she didn't quibble
with whatever energy in the Universe made it so.)

She ducked into the room and began to re-shelve those
books. A Dan Brown, a David Baldacci, two Ian Fleming novels,

a Catherine Coulter thriller. As she came around the back of the last shelf, she discovered a book on the floor. Open.

A little prickle whipped over the back of her neck as she stooped to pick it up. *Diamonds Are Forever.*

James Bond?

Jacqueline looked around, but she was alone in the room. Had this merely been a careless customer, or was this a Book Falling Sign, and she would soon have someone from Ian Fleming's spy thriller world lurking about her shop? Who was the villain in *Diamonds Are Forever*? She needed to know right away so she knew what to worry about.

Maybe it would be M who showed up. That would be interesting. Or Q—the tech guru. Although the tech in this book, which was published in—she checked the copyright page—1956 wouldn't be nearly as interesting as the tech in a Daniel Craig movie.

Jacqueline shook her head. Even in her mind, she digressed.

Maybe someone had just accidentally knocked the book off the shelf and it meant nothing. After all, it was a relatively new book compared to every other one that had previously fallen off the shelf and portended a literary creation visitation.

She clicked her tongue, but instead of putting the book back, Jacqueline took it with her from the room. She'd ask Mrs. Danvers what she thought. The woman would probably love to condescend to her and explain why she was wrong.

Back out in the front room, Jacqueline discovered that the flurry of customers had ebbed to a single person browsing the gardening and grilling books display in one of the front windows.

Danvers lurked behind the desk. She gave Jacqueline a dark look when she spotted her.

Before the disgruntled housekeeper could speak, Jacqueline showed her *Diamonds Are Forever*. "I found this on the floor in the Mystery/Thriller Room. Is it one of those, you know, special books?"

Danvers gave her a haughty look. "I have no idea what you mean, ma'am. Special books? However, I did find a different title from that particular author on the floor yesterday morning."

"You did?" Jacqueline didn't know whether to be relieved or freaked out. "Which book?"

"Something about letting die, I believe it was, ma'am." She sniffed with disdain, her dark eyes glittering with malice. "Is something wrong, ma'am?"

"Oh, you know very well what's wrong," Jacqueline said crossly. "And since you're absolutely no help—when it comes to random books falling off the shelf," she amended quickly when Danvers drew herself up into a furious stance, "I guess I'll just have to wait and see what happens. But," she added in a firm, lady-of-the-manor voice, "in the future, when you find a book on the floor, I want you to tell me immediately. Just in case." She was pretty certain she'd had this conversation with Danvers before, dammit.

"You want me to tell you *every* time I find a book on the floor," Danvers said in a deadpan voice that was somehow laced with disbelief. "As you wish, ma'am."

Jacqueline had a feeling she'd just dumped herself into a hot mess, but what else could she do? She tried one more time. "I want you to tell me every time you find a book on the floor that could portend a character coming out of it, and *you know very well what I mean*," she added in a low, furious voice as the Nora Roberts-reading lady emerged from the back of the store. "Don't play games with me, or I'll turn you over to Dr. No."

Danvers gave her a look that indicated she didn't know who Dr. No was, and that even so, she wasn't the least bit worried about it.

"Did you find everything you were looking for?" Jacqueline

said to the woman as she put a stack of six books on the counter. Three were hardcovers—yay!—and the rest were trade-size paperbacks.

"And then some," she replied with a smile. "My husband's going to kill me, but I know how to get around him." She gave Jacqueline a woman-to-woman smile, which had the effect of reminding Jacqueline that—ZOMG—she had a date tonight with Massermey!

Her cheeks rushed warm as she thought about how things might go tonight. In—she looked at the clock—*less than six hours.*

*Holy shit.* What was she going to wear?

"There you go. I hope you enjoy," she said, handing the heavy shopping bag to the customer.

"Thank you."

No sooner had the customer left than Jacqueline refocused her mind from Massermey tonight back to the problem upstairs. She turned to Danvers once more. "I put a very slender, very old red bound book under the counter early this morning. It's not there. Did you see it?"

"I might recall having seen it," replied the housekeeper. She moved her shoulders like a crow grumpy because its feathers were ruffled.

"It's not there now. Did you move it? Sell it? Give it to someone?" Why was it always like pulling teeth to get any information from this person?

"I did not touch it, ma'am. Perhaps someone else took it."

"That someone would have had to come behind the counter and take it," Jacqueline said from between clenched teeth. "As I'm certain you are aware. Was there any time when someone might have been able to get behind the counter?"

Danvers drew herself up. "It was quite busy in here, ma'am, as you have surely noticed. I was required to leave my station a number of times to assist customers." At face value, her words were polite and even, but the tone dripped with sarcasm and disdain.

Maybe Jacqueline *would* sic Dr. No on her. (Which one was he? The underground-lair-on-an-island one? She was going to have to refresh her James Bond memory, especially since she mixed up the books with the movies, which were usually very different.)

"So someone could have slipped back behind here and taken it," Jacqueline said, more to herself than to Danvers.

She was annoyed by the other woman's attitude, but there was nothing she could—or would—do about it. She and Danvers were both aware that she'd be lost without the housekeeper (and Sherlock's landlady) running the shop. But Jacqueline bore a probably futile hope that Danvers needed her just as much as Jacqueline needed Danvers—after all, without her, who would Danvers sneer at and condescend to and lord herself over? Back in du Maurier's *Rebecca*, she was merely a housekeeper who had to hold her tongue and be deferent. Here, she could be as snarky as she liked.

Jacqueline huffed a breath of frustration, then looked one more time around behind the counter. The codex was definitely gone.

Now what?

"I have to go upstairs and take care of Her Majesty," she told Danvers, fairly assured that the housekeeper wouldn't argue when it came to seeing a Queen of England being served. "She's probably hungry." Jacqueline realized with a start that *she* was hungry too.

And she had to figure out what in the world she was going to wear on her date with Massermey tonight.

That thought had her reaching for her phone. She sent a quick text to her thread with Suzette and Nadine: *Have no idea*

*what to wear tonight. Also, Anne Boleyn is here, P&P fell again AND*
*so did "Diamonds Are Forever." WTF?*

She figured that would get a response from her friends.

Sure enough. She'd just started up the steps to the apartment when her phone began blowing up with texts from Nadine and Suzette.

It was good to have friends.

∼

To JACQUELINE'S surprise and pleasure, she discovered that not only was Anne Boleyn still ensconced in the apartment, but that Pietra had been messing around in the kitchen and there was lunch to be had.

Tuna melts with avocado and tomato slices, topped with sprouts (Jacqueline had no idea where the sprouts had come from—or the avocado, as the only one she'd had was hard and green and nowhere near ripe, but she wasn't asking). This, along with iced tea—which was the only way Jacqueline actually *liked* to drink the brew.

Zwyla sat at the small dining table between the half wall of the kitchen and the living room area. She was drinking tea and appeared to be watching while Pietra made lunch and Andromeda talked with Anne. Somehow, Sebastian had made his way into the apartment (Jacqueline was not sure how that happened, but he was a cat, after all), and the queen seemed surprisingly taken with the fluffy, amber-colored cat. She was even reaching out to scratch the flirtatious feline under his chin.

"Oh, Jacqueline, there you are," said Zwyla, as if she hadn't been gone for over an hour.

"Yes. I'm back. Pietra, that looks wonderful. Is there enough for me?" Jacqueline asked, mainly to be polite.

"Of course there is." Pietra sidled up to Jacqueline and

murmured, "I'm not certain whether Her Majesty will deign to eat it, but if she doesn't, it's her loss."

Jacqueline nodded. She was fairly certain they hadn't had tuna melts in Tudor England.

She was hungry, but there were other things on her mind as well. She sat at the table with Zwyla as Pietra brought a tray out to the queen, setting it on the same raised leaf of the coffee table as Jacqueline had placed the tray this morning.

"So where's the codex?" Zwyla asked.

"It's gone." Jacqueline explained the situation. "So someone had to have gone behind the counter and taken it."

"That means someone knew it was there," said Andromeda. She'd released Sebastian, but he had perched himself on the back of an armchair. He was very interested in the tuna.

"Exactly." Jacqueline, who'd managed two delicious bites of her lunch, turned her attention to Anne. The queen's expression was going through a litany of emotions: curiosity, anxiousness, and, finally, delight after she worked up the nerve to taste the unfamiliar food.

Jacqueline kindly waited until she swallowed before saying, "Your codex is missing, madam. Your spell book," she said to clarify. "The red one? And don't pretend you don't know what I'm talking about. No one here is going to persecute you for—er —having it. Although some of those curses were pretty violent, and I certainly would object if you attempted to put them into practice."

"Our book," Anne said after a moment. "What sayest thou? It hast gone?"

"Someone stole it. I suspect it was the person who's summoned you here. We need to know who that is, ma'am."

"But we knowest not who it is," replied the queen. "We knowest not the name nor the face of her who summoned me."

"Is the person who summoned you here, to this land, the

same person who came here in this chamber to you today?" asked Jacqueline.

"Aye, we trow she is the same."

"But you don't know who she is? And yet she summoned you." Jacqueline was confused.

"Was she from your time?" asked Andromeda. "This witch who summoned you?"

Anne shook her head. "Verily, that she was not. She spake most strange—as dost thou. And her raiment was also strange."

Jacqueline felt a strange prickle down her spine. Someone here, from Button Cove, had been burning the papers, summoning Anne Boleyn from her history book. But who would have had such easy access to the bookshop after hours—*and* here, in her apartment? It simply didn't make any sense.

Then, suddenly... *Egala.*

Could it have been Egala, who thought *she* should have inherited Three Tomes? Egala, who was a member of the same widely flung family tree as Jacqueline and therefore had witchy abilities? Egala, who'd come mincing into the bookshop yesterday, asking if anything strange had happened?

The sudden rush of fury took Jacqueline by surprise. Her fingertips went hot and something sparked off her longest nail and snapped a black, burned hole in her napkin. The edges glowed, then faded away.

Zwyla looked at her in surprise and admonishment. "You need to learn to control that, Jacqueline."

"Ya think?" Jacqueline muttered. "Egala," she said, standing so suddenly that the table jolted. "It could be Egala."

She turned back to Anne. "What did she look like? Is she my age? Their age?" She pointed to the crones.

To her surprise, Anne shook her head. "Nay. The woman is very young. Like me."

"You mean she was *your* age?" Jacqueline was flummoxed. Egala could not pass for forty, let alone her late twenties.

"Aye."

Jacqueline sat back down, and, speaking of age, reminded herself not to furrow her brow. She didn't need any more lines on her face. "A young person who spake—er, speaks like us."

"Aye. And with garb so very strange. A very flimsy gown. 'Twas bereft of much fabric, and there was only one skirt. No embroidery, no jewels." Anne preened a little, smoothing her hands over the very detailed and very ornamented gown she wore.

Clothing in Tudor times was meant to be an expression of the wealth of the person wearing it. The more cloth—the more flounces and laces and embroidery, the more varied types of fabric—the wealthier the person was.

Suddenly, it was as if a light bulb went off in Jacqueline's head. *Pride and Prejudice!* Was it someone from *Pride and Prejudice* who'd been summoning Anne Boleyn?

Jacqueline straightened up and said, "Okay. So, her gown. It was very long, like so? Very slim-fitting and light of fabric?" She skimmed her hands from below her breasts straight to the floor, mimicking a Jane Austen-era gown. "And her hair hung like so?" She used her fingers to demonstrate a spiral curl from each temple.

But Anne shook her head. "Nay. 'Twas a very short gown." She demonstrated, cutting off the imaginary dress at the knees. "Methinks she wore only her under-raiment! And long boots, like that of a man." She gestured from the knee down, as well as she was able, confined as she was in such restrictive clothing. "And her hair! 'Twas short, like boy's!"

Jacqueline shook her head. "I got nothing," she said to the ZAP Ladies, who'd been watching with interest. "It must be someone from Button Cove, but I just don't know who would have the ability to come and go from here. I suppose I'm going to have to increase the security here." Her cheeks heated a little, since she knew someone in law enforcement that she could ask for help.

"We can help you with that, dear Jacqueline," said Pietra kindly. "We would have offered before, but didn't want to overstep."

"I see. How would that, um, work? I wouldn't want it to keep customers away or—or anyone else I wanted to see," Jacqueline said uneasily. "But I would like a way to keep, um, Her Majesty here from being summoned again."

"Of course," replied Zwyla. "That last is the simplest. Andi can take care of that with a bit of sage and salt."

"On it," said Andromeda, turning from where she'd been stroking Sebastian's undulating, arching back. "Consider Her Majesty duly protected and gently imprisoned."

"As for the other, Jacqueline, we can simply put on a protection that repels anyone or anything that intends malice on the building or those within."

"That would be nice," Jacqueline replied.

"Consider it done," said Zwyla, smiling calmly.

"Although," Jacqueline said, "how will we catch this summoning person if they are repelled? I need to know who is screwing around with my place and summoning people and everything. And what if they're already here? Would that keep them trapped here so they can't leave? And what if, you know, it was maybe a family coming in with two kids who are bickering —one might be showing malice toward the other...in a sibling sort of way...? Would it keep them out?"

"Ah, well, yes that could be problematic," replied Zwyla gravely. "What I mean to say is, this sort of protection is absolute. It doesn't, if you will, understand gray areas or things that might be chance or extenuating circumstances. Malice can be as simple as a brother tripping his sister, or as complex as someone trying to murder someone else. It isn't, as I said, absolute."

Jacqueline sighed. While she liked the idea of extra safety protections, she didn't want it to backfire. That was the thing about magic. One just couldn't be quite sure about it. "Right. Well, for now, I suppose the best thing to do is to just keep Anne here and make it so she can't leave."

"That is done," said Andromeda, reappearing from where she'd been in the back hall.

"Thank you. But we're no closer to figuring out who's been summoning HRH here," Jacqueline said.

"HRH? Oh, right. Her Royal Highness," said Pietra with a giggle.

Jacqueline leaned closer to Zwyla and Pietra so she could speak in a murmur. "The curses in her spell book are pretty violent." She described them, including the Castratus Curse.

"You're right—we don't want that sort of thing going on around here," said Zwyla, giving Anne the side-eye. "As crappy as men can be sometimes. Speaking of which, what are you going to do about the hexing of the ex for Mrs. Gould?"

"You were looking at hexes in the big book, weren't you?" Pietra said. "That humiliation one?"

"Yes," Jacqueline admitted. "And not only did Mrs. Gould come back today, all ready for me to turn over a hex for her, but she brought *friends*! It seems like there's an epidemic of people wanting their exes hexed."

Zwyla quirked a brow. "And here we have one of the most famous 'exes' in history, summoned to your shop. A woman done very wrong, as a country song might say." She glanced again at Anne Boleyn, the divorced and beheaded.

"I'm very well aware of that, but I can't figure out the connection," Jacqueline said. "And *Pride and Prejudice* has fallen off the shelf at least three times now."

"Really?" Andromeda slid into the fourth seat at the small dining table. Anne seemed to be occupied by her fascination with a copy of *Real Simple* magazine that Jacqueline had brought up from the bookshop in hopes of some inspiration for organizing her office. "*Pride and Prejudice*, hmm? You're hoping for Darcy, I'm assuming," she said to Pietra, who'd given a quiet squeal of excitement.

"Who isn't?" retorted her friend, her eyes starry.

"Actually, I'd really like to meet Georgiana," said Andromeda. "She seemed like a character who needed her own book. Sadly, Jane never pursued that—as far as we know, anyway."

"Wouldn't that be an interesting plot for a book? The Lost Austen, a novel about Georgiana Darcy," said Pietra thoughtfully.

"All right, anyway," Jacqueline said, firmly corralling the conversation. "It doesn't seem as if a character from *Pride and Prejudice* is the person who's summoned Anne Boleyn. *And* I have a hex problem—"

"Oh, just do the humiliation hex and be done with it," Andromeda said, waving her hand. "It doesn't cause any permanent damage, and it will satisfy the ex. Exes, I mean," she added with a grin. "It's simple and difficult to screw up—not that I think you'd screw it up."

"Fine," said Jacqueline. She'd already pretty much decided to do that. "And just as important, and far more pressing, is—"

A loud crash from the back hall—followed by clomping footsteps and urgent cries of "Jacqueline!"—interrupted her.

Her friends had arrived.

## 9

It took a few minutes to introduce Suzette and Nadine to Anne, and for them to regroup after meeting a Queen of England.

Then Jacqueline took another few minutes to catch them up on everything.

"All right, so the super-scary spell book is missing," Nadine said. "And whoever has it is probably the person who summoned *her* here"—she indicated Anne with her gaze—"and so should we assume the person who has it is planning to use it? And if she just wanted the spell book, why is *she*"—another side eye at Anne—"still here?"

"Excellent questions, to which we have no clue what the answers are," said Jacqueline.

"And who is coming out of the Austen book?" said Suzette. "There's been no sign of anyone in Regency-era clothing?"

"Not a one," said Jacqueline.

"And you said a James Bond book fell too," Nadine reminded her.

"Two," said Jacqueline, remembering that Danvers said she'd picked one up. And then she sat straight up. "Wait. Maybe four..." She told them about the stack of books she'd found in the Mystery/Thriller Room. "It's possible those two had fallen as well, and a customer just picked them up and added them to the stack."

"Holy crap," said Nadine. "That's a lot of characters."

"Well, I haven't seen any of them yet," said Jacqueline briskly. "Maybe they've come and gone back in and we didn't even realize it."

The pitying looks the ZAP Ladies gave her didn't make her feel any better.

She threw up her hands. "I don't know. And right now, I don't care. I've got to figure out what I'm wearing tonight."

"What's happening tonight, dear?" asked Pietra.

"She's got a hot date with Detective Put-His-Massive-Hands-On-Me," said Nadine in a singsong voice.

"Oh...I see-ee-ee," replied Pietra in the same singsong voice. She gave Jacqueline a knowing smile. "Well, you certainly want to wear something sexy underneath, don't you? What's on over it won't matter that much, because I'm betting it won't be on very long."

"Good *grief*!" Jacqueline's face burst into hot, blooming red as the rest of them burst into laughter. "Petey!"

"I have a question," Suzette said after everyone calmed down.

"Please don't ask whether I have a condom in my purse," Jacqueline said.

"No, it's not that," her friend replied. "I'm just trying to figure out how Josh figures in all of this."

"Josh?" Jacqueline stared at her. "What do you mean? Why — What does he have to do with anything? He *doesn't* have to do with anything."

Suzette lifted her brow. "Are you sure about that? You've got all this...this...*energy* happening around exes, and *your* ex just suddenly waltzes back into your life out of the blue after twenty years?"

Jacqueline stared at her, opened her mouth to speak, then closed it. She swallowed and looked around at all the expectant, thoughtful faces looking at her. "Of course he has nothing to do with any of this."

"If you say so," Suzette said. But she clearly didn't buy it.

And from the looks on the others' faces, they didn't either.

"That's ridiculous," Jacqueline said firmly. "Now, I've *got* to figure out what to wear tonight, and I really should go back down and see whether Danvers needs help. I have to get ready to leave in—good grief, three hours. Where has the day *gone*?"

She was glad to leave them—all of them and their contemplative looks—in the apartment and head back down to the relative safety of the bookshop.

She'd figure out what to wear in a little while. Now, she just wanted to put all of this out of her mind and sell some books.

∾

FORTUNATELY, the rest of the day in the shop was so busy that she hardly noticed the time fly by. She certainly didn't have much chance to worry about who was coming out of books and when and why.

She was more worried about tonight.

But Jacqueline was able to keep even that thought at bay as she helped the steady stream of people find the books they wanted, or directed them upstairs for tea and pastries. She did pay careful attention to anyone who purchased anything that had come from the New Age Room. After all, whoever was summoning Anne Boleyn had obviously spent some time in there.

A pair of young women both wearing Michigan State

University sweatshirts piqued her interest when she rang them up, for along with *Fourth Wing* and *Six of Crows*, they had a packet of incense, a book about Wiccan customs, a set of tarot cards, and a little goddess statue.

"I see you found the New Age Room," she said with a smile, trying to figure out how to probe without being nosy. Even though she *would* be nosy.

"It's *so* fabulous in there," bubbled the taller one. "We have a friend who's really into this sort of stuff, and her birthday is tomorrow. So we thought we'd go a little crazy."

"I was trying to decide between this deck of tarot cards," said her companion, who wore perfectly round John Lennon glasses with rose-pink lenses, "and an angel deck. What do you think would be better? Do you use them for, you know, guidance and stuff?"

Jacqueline looked down at the tarot deck in question, a gorgeous rendition depicting Grimm fairy tale characters as the Major Arcana, and other fairy tale elements for the Minor. "I think this deck is stunning," she said. "As for how I use them, or how *someone* might use them," she went on carefully, "I find that any cards—angel cards, goddess cards, tarot cards—are really only tools to help open the subconscious and to guide us into things we already know but perhaps aren't quite ready to acknowledge yet. And so, in this case, I think you can't go wrong with either."

"Oh, wow," said the girl with the rose-pink glasses. Her eyes lit up behind them. "Thank you."

"Then I'm going up to get the angel deck for me!" exclaimed the taller one. "I could really use something to open up my subconscious."

"Yeah," said her friend to Jacqueline as the girl bounded off and up the stairs, "she really needs to dump the asshole she's dating, but she just can't see it. He's broken up with her about three times, and Sierra keeps taking him back. Lily—that's our other friend whose birthday it is—and I wish there was a way to make Jason suffer for all the hell he's put her through. I wish it was like Harry Potter and we could put, you know, like, a hex on him or something, you know?"

Jacqueline kept her expression bland. "Well, you do know what they say. Karma is a bitch. What you put out there comes back to bite you in the butt...eventually. Unfortunately, sometimes not quite as quickly as we would like. But he'll get his."

Sierra returned at that moment, carrying the angel deck, and Jacqueline finished ringing them up. "Good luck with your friend's birthday. And everything else," she said.

She looked at the clock and saw that it was a quarter to seven. Normally, she closed at six thirty, but according to Danvers they had to have summer hours and stay open until seven. (Eye-roll.)

*But* Danvers wasn't around, and Jacqueline checked the back rooms. No one was here. The genre rooms were empty (no books on the floor! Yay!), and so she quickly sneaked to the end of the main hall and locked the rear door, flipping the sign to CLOSED.

Then she hurried back to the front and tiptoed up the stairs to the tea room. She went up only as far as she needed to look around.

It was empty. Silent. Everything was wiped down and cleaned up. Mrs. Hudson was gone.

*Yes!*

Jacqueline dashed back downstairs and peeked out the front door—no one was in sight, so she closed the door, flipped the sign to CLOSED, and locked it.

She turned around and choked off a scream.

Danvers was standing there.

"What are you doing?" said the housekeeper. She looked even more forbidding than usual. "Ma'am."

"I'm locking up," Jacqueline told her firmly, absolutely *forbidding* her voice to wobble. It didn't. Very much. "There's no one around, and I have somewhere I have to be in a half-hour."

"But we are open until seven o'clock for the summer," said Danvers. She brushed past Jacqueline and flipped the sign to OPEN. "We can't disappoint our customers. Ma'am."

Jacqueline elbowed past her—and she swore she felt a rush of arctic chill, as if a ghost was present—and flipped the sign back to CLOSED. "There's *no one* around," she said. "No one to disappoint. No one is waiting to get in. There isn't even anyone on the *street*. It's *fine* to close fifteen minutes early on the first day of summer, since no one is here."

And then someone rapped at the door.

Jacqueline swore under her breath as Mrs. Danvers lifted her nose in *the most* supercilious smirk she'd seen in her life—and Jacqueline had been the recipient of many of Danvers's smirks.

She turned to the door, intending to tell the person they were closed...

It was Josh.

Jacqueline's heart stuttered weirdly, and she gaped for a moment. He smiled through the window—damn, it reminded her of that stupid scene in *Friends* where Rachel had just closed up at the coffee shop and Ross was knocking on the window for her to let him in. But one thing was sure—there wasn't going to be any wildly crazy, sexy, pent-up-energy kiss between them.

Even though she was going to let him in.

"Hi, Josh," she said. "I—We're closed," she went on weakly.

"But the sign..." He gestured just as weakly to the door, where the painted-on numbers clearly stated the times of opening and closing.

Except that they now read *9:30 am to 7 pm, Tuesday through Saturday.*

Which was *not* the schedule that had been on there before. She gritted her teeth. *Danvers.*

Jacqueline stepped back and let him inside. What else was she going to do? "Sorry—I thought it was later than it is. I've got somewhere to be in a little while." *And I need a lot of time to prepare for it.* A little squiggle of nerves zipped through her belly. "Is there something you're looking for?"

"Well, yeah. Yes. I thought I'd see—you know, since it's closing time—whether I could, uh, take you for a drink. Or something."

Jacqueline stared at him. "You...what?"

He shrugged, appearing a little abashed. "I thought maybe we could talk."

"You want to talk? It's been twenty years," she said in a voice that was far more tremulous than she liked. She was screeching at him in her head, but the words didn't come out that way.

He heaved a sigh. "Look. I know it's been a while. I know it sounds stupid. But I... Well, I never got over you, and what I did to you and me... It's past time I apologized. I mean *really* apologized. And *really* meant it. And *really* made it clear how much I fucked up and ruined my life."

Jacqueline simply could not form words. She probably looked like a fish out of water, gaping helplessly, her eyes bulging as she struggled to make sense of things.

"Okay," she finally managed to say. He looked at her hopefully, but she collected herself and went on, "I accept your apology. Yeah, you screwed up, badly, and I've moved on. And I do have to be somewhere in about a half-hour, so, uh, now is not a good time for us to have this conversation."

"So you're willing to talk to me? Not now, I understand, but maybe tomorrow?"

"What are you doing here, Josh?" she said, frustrated and confused.

"I want to talk to you, Jackie. I'd *like* to talk to you, I mean."

"All right, all right... Maybe tomorrow. Um...I really have to go."

"Okay. I'll check back in then."

Before she had the chance to tell him it was going to be very busy here tomorrow, the Sunday of Memorial Day weekend, he gave her a sort of sad-eyed, hopeful salute and slipped back out the door.

Jacqueline heaved a sigh of relief and realized with a start that her knees felt funny. She rolled her eyes. *Don't be stupid,* she told herself. *Josh is nothing to you but a bad memory.* She closed and locked the door firmly. It was seven o'clock, and the shop was *closed.*

She turned to find Danvers standing there, watching her with an appraising look. A judgy, appraising look.

Jacqueline didn't have time for the woman's attitude, so she just rolled her eyes and stalked up the steps to the tea room because they were closer. It wasn't until she got into the elevator to go to her flat that she remembered what would be waiting for her in her apartment.

Jacqueline banged her forehead lightly against the wall of the elevator. All she wanted, *all she wanted*, was to go over to Massermey's house, have ribs, wine, watch *Buffy*, and maybe even have sex, and not have to worry about rogue English queens and falling books and cursed codices and ex-fiancés and hexes.

To her absolute shock, when the elevator doors opened and revealed her kitchen and living space, Jacqueline found it empty of people: no queens, no crones, no one.

She gave a low, gurgling scream in the back of her throat, and then she saw the note.

*Took Anne with us. Thought you'd want time to get ready without distraction. Have fun tonight. Don't do anything we wouldn't do.*

It was signed with a heart that had to be from Pietra.

Then at the bottom, in different handwriting (Andi?), someone had written: *We picked out some clothes for you.*

Jacqueline chuckled nervously, heaved a great sigh of relief, then headed to the bathroom to figure out how to make herself look presentable.

But she made a detour into her bedroom, for she saw a bunch of clothing laid out neatly on the bed.

Jacqueline took one look and began to laugh.

There were three sets of outfits—clearly, each one had been put together by a different one of the crones. And none of them —*none*—were items Jacqueline had had in her closet!

Her eyes misted a little, even as she continued to laugh. Apparently, the ZAP Ladies didn't think she was able to dress herself.

"All right," she said aloud, looking at the three sets of clothing. "What's it gonna be?"

It was immediately obvious to her who'd selected or arranged or created or conjured—whatever—each ensemble, and that made her tear up even more.

One was a pair of capri pants in black, and it would be topped by a pink tank top with fancy beading and a little bit of sequin on its straps and just along the neckline. The straps would peek out from beneath the loose, gauzy, flowing topper of pale pink. *Cute.* Maybe a little too blingy for Jacqueline, but maybe not. The pink would look great with her dark red hair. Andromeda had an excellent eye.

With the capris and fancy tank was a bottle of nail polish (perfectly matching the pink tank), a pair of espadrille sandals that she would probably kill herself wearing, and... *Oh my God...*

Jacqueline blushed as she realized the frothy pile of pink was undies and a matching bra *completely made of lace.*

"If I put these on, there'd be *nothing* left to the imagination," she said, feeling the heat of her face...as she actually considered it.

"All right," she murmured. "Next."

She turned her attention to the second ensemble. It was a maxi dress with a very low-cut neckline. The fabric was a gorgeous sky blue printed and embroidered with gold and silver organic patterns. The hem, neckline, and cap sleeves were all edged in a tasteful beaded lace. Loose, easy, and sleeveless, the dress would hide all of Jacqueline's imperfections while giving... *whoever*...a good look at the ladies—who, by the way, looked pretty damn good for forty-eight years old.

Pietra had also included shoes and undergarments for the dress. "A *push-up bra*?" Jacqueline exclaimed, laughing and outraged at the same time. At least the matching black—also lace—panties weren't a thong. The shoes were sandals, but these were low-heeled and had pretty beads on the straps, matching the dress's trim. The nail polish that she was somehow supposed to have time to apply to her toes (ha!) was gold.

"All right, Zwyla...what do you have for me?" Jacqueline said, almost afraid to look. There was no way she could pull off wearing the types of clothing the long, lean, regal woman preferred.

Zwyla's selection was laid out on the leather storage bench at the foot of the bed that Jacqueline used for extra blankets. The outfit was...not what she'd expected.

A just-above-knee-length sundress—something Zwyla would probably never wear—of a light and airy floral material of mauve. Next to it was a short, crocheted vest thing that presumably Jacqueline would wear over the top of the sundress, which had an empire waist and would be great for camouflaging the persistent tummy she'd acquired since turning forty-five. The crocheted vest was fashioned of neutral-colored yarn but with a tiny bit of gold shot through it—to give just a little bit of glint. It would tie in the front, right over her bust, and it ended just about at the bottom of her ribcage. The footwear was the biggest surprise: cowboy boots! Made from rich, coffee-brown leather with a bit of mauve detailed stitching on the sides. Not too fancy, but just enough to be feminine.

It wasn't until Jacqueline picked up the dress and held it to herself in front of the mirror that she realized there were no undergarments or lingerie with this ensemble. Did Zwyla really think she'd *go commando*?

She looked around in case a bra and panties had fallen to the floor...but there were none to be found. Holy crap. No *way* was she going commando.

Giving the outfit—which was the one she'd been leaning toward—a skeptical look, she hummed thoughtfully to herself. She could wear the pink bra from Andromeda's outfit and... Well, why not mix and match and honor all three ladies and their choices? She could wear the black, lacy panties Pietra had picked out (they weren't sheer like the ones Andi had selected) and the espadrille sandals.

With this settled, Jacqueline headed to the bathroom to figure out how to fix her hair and face, and, of course, to shower.

In the bathroom, she found more surprises from her crone friends: earrings, bangles, perfumes, and even what looked like an ankle bracelet.

She picked big, dangly earrings that look like something Andromeda would have designed—gold hearts within hearts within hearts that looked like those garden wind-spinners. And a choker that screamed Pietra: woven of thick gold cord with a single long piece that hung down from the center—down into the vee of Zwyla's sundress—with a large flower pendant nestling *right there.*

Jacqueline smirked to herself. Massermey wouldn't know where to look.

She glanced at her phone for the time and shrieked. OMG. She had to leave in fifteen minutes!

She fairly leapt into the shower and washed and buffed and *shaved* as quickly and carefully as possible and managed not to nick herself anywhere important. She was just stepping out of the shower when she heard a text notification on her phone.

A quick glance told her it was from Massermey.

Her heart plummeted. Crap. Was he canceling? Had someone died? Was there an emergency? He was a cop, after all. Eve Dallas was always getting called away from social events for murders.

She dried her hand then fumbled for the phone, dreading looking at the text—and was surprised at how disappointed she would be if he was canceling.

The text was a photo. When she saw what it was, she laughed.

It was a pic of a slab of ribs glistening on the grill. After that, he'd sent a text that read: *We can't wait. Get here soon.*

She resisted the urge to reply: *Nice rack.* Instead, she texted back: *On my way in 10.*

Still smiling, she scrunched her hair with product that was supposed to make the curls look good while not being crunchy. She didn't fuss too much with makeup—just mascara to cover and lengthen her redhead's pale lashes and a swipe of mauve eye shadow. At her ripe and mature age of forty-eight, she figured if a guy couldn't see past a full face of makeup (she'd die before she ever did anything like *contouring*), he wasn't worth the trouble. Besides, she never wore a full face of makeup, and Massermey seemed attracted to her anyway.

She *did*, however, dab on some perfume that had mysteriously appeared with her other beauty aids, putting it behind her ears and knees (why not?) and in the vee of her décolletage. It smelled divine, and she mentally thanked whichever of the ZAP Ladies had prepared it for her.

There really wasn't time to do her toes with the pretty nail polish, but they definitely needed to be done. She wasn't going to Massermey's wearing sandals with ratty, chipped toe polish. Not that he would probably notice—he was a man, after all. But to her surprise, the nail polish dried immediately. She grinned. The crones sure knew how to take care of things.

Not only was the perfume gorgeous and the nail polish insta-drying, but the clothing she'd chosen fit perfectly.

"Not bad," Jacqueline said, looking at herself in the full-length mirror. "Not bad at all." She grinned, added lipstick, then hurried out of the apartment.

As she drove out of the parking lot in the back of the shop and onto Camellia Avenue, she blew a kiss toward the robin's-egg-blue Victorian where the ZAP Ladies lived.

*Thank you!* she said mentally. She knew they'd get the message. They were a lot of work, her crone friends, but they were worth every bit of it.

---

## 10

Jacqueline hadn't been to Massermey's house before. She had to use GPS to find it—it was twenty minutes away, out of town and in the forested hillocks of the area—and she wasn't at all sure what to expect.

As she drove, she alternated between freaking out (was she going to have sex with a new guy for the first time in years? OMG) and being excited (about maybe having sex with a new guy for the first time in years). Or not having sex, but having a wonderful evening with a good guy who loved his daughter enough to consider going to the Bridgerton Experience with her.

Jacqueline blasted happy music in an effort to keep her mind from darting down all those anxious warrens of worry. "Walking on Sunshine" always put her in a happy mood.

Her first impression of Massermey's place was tempered curiosity as she drove down a bumpy, unpaved drive that led through the woods (she wasn't sure she'd ever want to drive down this lane in the winter, even though she had an Outback). And then she came into a small clearing ringed by more trees, with a compact parking area next to a patch of grass.

It was definitely a guy's house—a one-and-a-half-story log

cabin with a detached garage and a long, covered porch along the front of it. There were simple shutters on the windows (no heart cutouts or even complementary colors; just stained wood), and not much in the way of landscaping or flower pots. But the lawn was neatly mowed, and she caught sight of a glint of blue sparkle through the trees. He was on a lake or pond? That was unexpected...and nice.

The door opened as soon as she pulled into the parking area, and that made her heart leap a little. He'd been watching for her.

"Jacqueline," he said, coming out to greet her and saying her name in that low, rumbly voice with a soft, sexy J. "And...wow," he added as he looked her over.

She smiled up at him, and suddenly the tiny bit of nerves she'd harbored leached away. She had nothing to be nervous about. Everything was going to be okay.

"Back at ya," she said, feeling surprisingly sassy and comfortable as she gave him a once-over too. His shirt was a button-down, crisp and smooth, with an understated pattern in dark colors. He wore *shorts*, and she definitely approved of his legs. They were muscular and still hairy (Jacqueline was extremely aware of how men tended to lose their leg hair as they got older). She reached into the car to grab her purse and the Merlot she'd brought.

When she turned back, he said, "I hate to mess up that pretty lipstick, but..." He looked down at her, a hand on her arm, a wicked grin behind his strawberry-blond mustache and beard. "Welcome."

"It's easy to reapply," she said, lifting herself on tiptoes so they could kiss.

His lips were soft, and the edges of his mustache and beard were gently prickly.

Delicious. Absolutely delicious.

"You have a great mouth," she said, stepping back.

His cheeks—always a bit ruddy due to the sprinkling of freckles over them—turned a little pinker, and he seemed a bit flustered when he said, "I trimmed my mustache today."

"I can tell." She lifted herself up again to get another kiss. Very nice. Her friend with benefits, the accountant Lester, hadn't had any facial hair, and neither had Josh. She realized she liked it. "I'm starving," she said when she finished another sampling of his mouth.

"That makes two of us," he replied, but there was a second layer of meaning in his words.

Now it was Jacqueline's turn to flush a little. Oh yes, she was pretty sure she was going to have sex tonight.

"Want to see the inside?" he said. "It's not much, but it's comfy." He took the wine from her, then took her hand with his other and walked her into the house.

He was right—it was comfy. The inside of the log walls was textured plaster, while the rest of the interior walls were smooth drywall painted an easy, warm taupe. There was a real, wood-burning fireplace made of brick at one end of a compact living room that flowed into a kitchen, with a bar counter separating it from the living room.

The floor was dark hardwood with rugs strewn about—they didn't exactly match, but they all had the same feel to them: rustic and simple. His seating area was a long and large sectional, positioned in front of a huge television mounted on the wall perpendicular to the fireplace and far enough away that the heat wouldn't melt it. There was a single throw pillow on the couch that looked more like a sleeping pillow than anything decorative, and a blanket was folded up over the back of the sofa. She pictured him dozing while watching TV and enjoying the fire. The low table in front of the sectional held a compli-cated-looking remote, a computer tablet, and the Michael

Connelly book he'd purchased from Three Tomes a week or so ago.

A row of windows revealed the backyard of woods and a glimpse of whatever body of water was out there. A path led from the back door into the forest and presumably to the water. There was very little grass in the back; it went almost right from the house to woods. But there was a small patio with a grill and an outdoor dining table.

"Very comfy," she said, looking around.

"I've only been here three—no, four years," he said apologetically. "Haven't had the chance to do much to it. Work can be crazy."

"And Mandy stays here too sometimes?"

"Yes, she and Cullen. She's back in East Lansing right now." Cullen was Mandy's very, very large and furry black dog. "Uh, the guest room—her room—is upstairs. It's just a little loft sort of place. Mine is, uh, that way." He gestured down a hall ending in a room with a large bed visible through the open doorway. "Um, bathroom is the second door on the right," he said quickly, as if to take her attention from the fact that he'd just pointed her toward his bedroom.

"Mind if I take a look at the rest of the house?" Jacqueline said, and they both knew she meant she wanted to see where they might end up tonight.

"Sure." Did his voice squeak a little? Was he as nervous as she was?

Nervous but anticipatory.

He didn't follow her as she went down the hall and peeked into each room. A bathroom, a small office, and the main bedroom at the very end. The bed was *big*. Had to be a king. And it was neatly made with a quilt-like coverlet and two sleeping pillows—but, again, not a decorative throw pillow to be found.

Jacqueline smiled to herself. She, Nadine, and Suzette had

agreed that most straight men they knew found throw pillows and decorative hand towels to be mysterious, annoying, and unnecessary female accoutrements. It was no surprise that this bachelor pad supported that belief.

The bedroom had its own bathroom attached, and she peeked inside. The place was neat and clean and smelled like Massermey's grooming products. The shower still had water droplets, and a faintly damp towel hung neatly on a rack.

When she came back down the hall, she found Massermey keeping himself very busy in the kitchen making a salad. He glanced up at her. "All good?"

"Very good," she replied with a smile. He smiled back, and she felt a little buzz of heat in her belly. "Can I help with anything?"

"No—I'm just about finished with the salad. Do you want to eat inside or outside? I don't have a table in here; it'd just be at the counter. Or we can sit at the table outside. The bugs shouldn't be too bad this early in the year."

"Outside is perfect. Is that a lake down there?"

"Half swamp, half lake. I own about a third of it, and two other houses the other parts. It's only about eight acres, and maybe fifteen feet deep in the middle. We—the three owners—have talked about maybe getting it dredged so it's at least swimmable, and maybe stocking it with fish. But it's pretty to look at as it is, and there's a lot of wildlife that hang out there. So I go back and forth on it. You know?"

"Yes. It is a conundrum." She smiled at him, ridiculously pleased that he thought about the wildlife as well as his own pleasure. "I'll help carry everything out. Where did I put the wine?"

"It's here." He gestured to where it was sitting there, open to breathe, next to two glasses.

She poured, and they finally settled at the table. Out here, the pond/lake/swamp was much more visible, and she could see cattails and fronds of tall grass edging the body of water.

"It's so pretty," she said. "I'm sure it's very relaxing out here."

"I could sit out here every night," he replied. "Though sometimes it's a little lonely. You know?"

She smiled and nodded. "Yes, I do. By the way, I purposely didn't wear white." She gestured to the rack of glistening, caramelized ribs. They smelled *divine*.

"Even so, you look fantastic," he said with great sincerity. She felt his eyes linger on the long part of the choker, which settled like a little arrow between the valley of her breasts. *Go, Petey!*

Dinner was easy and comfortable, as she'd expected it would be. They talked about everything—his trip to Chicago and what she'd enjoyed about the city, Memorial Day and how it was the kickoff for summer, and that meant things would get crazy, how Mandy was doing, what he wanted to do to the cabin inside and outside, and more. It wasn't until she'd begun picking at a second section of ribs that Massermey said, "So, I've gotta ask..." He trailed off, looking at her with a pensive expression.

"Ask what?" Despite not wearing white, Jacqueline had prudently tucked a large kitchen towel into her neckline to protect the mauve sundress and its crocheted vest topper. After he'd had the chance to check out her necklace and its neon sign into her cleavage, of course.

"Yesterday, the guy that came into the store when I was there. I got the impression he wasn't just a random customer." He looked at her over the slab of ribs on which he'd been nibbling.

Jacqueline's belly did a funny thing. So Massermey *had* noticed. She shouldn't be surprised. He *was* a cop. "No. Not a random customer. That was Josh Wenczel. My former fiancé."

Massermey's thick brows rose, but he didn't say anything else.

Jacqueline guessed he was leaving it up to her whether to fill in the blanks or not. That was the mature, adult thing to do—not to pry, not to ask, certainly not to demand. Especially since they weren't really actually *dating*. They were just at the beginning of whatever this might be.

And the mature, adult thing for her to do was to tell him about Josh.

It was just that she didn't want to admit that she'd been cheated on.

It was so humiliating.

Mortifying.

She was ashamed.

Even though it happened twenty years ago, she still felt the sting of knowing she hadn't been enough for Josh. The humiliation of knowing he'd been sneaking around and she hadn't had a clue. The shame of knowing he and her best friend had surely laughed and joked and talked about how dumb she was, how they were putting one over on her, how clueless she was... Probably they even exchanged sexy looks—or text messages—when she was with them, completely ignorant that they were screwing each other behind her back.

"Look! An egret," Massermey said, pointing toward the pond. "Through the trees—you can just make out its white ruff. Do you see?"

She turned, grateful for the distraction and the fact that he'd surely done it purposely to let her off the hook and to alleviate any awkwardness if she decided not to elaborate. "It's beautiful. It's a smaller bird than I thought it would be," she said.

"It is. The blue heron is larger, but they're both so elegant and graceful. I like to watch them fish or dig for frogs or whatever they like to eat, there at the edge of the lake."

When she turned back, he was smiling and she felt better. He wasn't upset that she hadn't told him about Josh.

And so she did.

"We were engaged twenty years ago. I haven't seen him since we broke it off—three days before the wedding. Actually, I hadn't seen him since then, except I ran into him when I went down to Chicago to see *Six* last week."

"So...once in Chicago a few days ago, and now he's suddenly here in Button Cove, showing up at your shop?" When she gave him a look, he shrugged. "I'm a cop, Jacqueline."

"Right." She couldn't hold it against him. "Anyhow, I was surprised to see him both times."

"Did he, uh, know that was your shop when he came in?"

"Yes." Jacqueline turned her attention to smashing sour cream and butter into her baked potato. (It was a small one, so she didn't feel bad about the carbs.)

Massermey remained silent, and she looked back up, shrugging as she forked up a bite of potato. "I don't know why he came in. I told him I had to leave because I didn't want to be late tonight..." She realized as she spoke that she was giving him more information than she'd intended.

"So he came back today?" Of course Massermey jumped on it right away. He *was* a cop. "Three times in a week?"

She shrugged again. "Yeah. I guess he wants to talk. And to apologize." Again she'd said more than she intended. She hadn't wanted to get into the details of what happened.

"The guy's obviously an idiot," Massermey said.

She flushed. "Well, I don't disagree—which is why we aren't together—but you don't know him."

"Well, he's not with you now, is he? Either you broke up with him or he broke up with you. Either way, he's on the losing end of the stick." Massermey said it so easily and sincerely that Jacqueline thought she might jump his bones right then and there.

He must have read her expression, because his eyes widened, then narrowed on her speculatively. And his lips quirked. "You keep looking at me like that and we might not get to dessert, Jacqueline."

"Sometimes dessert is overrated...but whatcha got?" She grinned.

"Oh, it's just ice cream. With, um, caramel sauce or hot fudge to, uh, drizzle over it."

Good grief, was he blushing?

Jacqueline started blushing too, because she thought she might have read his mind. There were things other than ice cream that caramel sauce and hot fudge could be drizzled over...

"Sounds delicious." Jacqueline's voice was a throaty purr, surprising even herself. What had gotten into her?

Maybe just the confidence of knowing she looked good, and that she'd put herself together—dressed, coiffed—with the intention (in the back of her mind, anyway) of moving their relationship forward.

Suddenly, a horrified thought struck her. She looked down at her clothing. She looked good. No, she looked *great*. And why did she look so good? Why was her confidence off the charts tonight?

*No way.*

They *wouldn't*.

Would they?

Had the crones put a charm on her clothes to help her...be sexy or flirtatious? To help her get laid? She didn't know whether to laugh or cry.

"Everything okay?" he asked, folding his napkin and setting it on his plate, which was empty except for rib bones.

"Yes. Everything is just fine." So what would happen after she took *off* the clothes? Would the charm still work? Would she still be Miss Seductress?

She rolled her eyes mentally. Why was she worrying about that? She didn't need a charm to have sex with a hot guy.

*Crap.* Did she?

She was, after all, forty-eight, carrying a few extra pounds, and, well, it wasn't as if she'd had *that* much practice having sex.

Suddenly she felt a little wobbly.

Then, just as suddenly, she thrust it away. She was who she was, and Massermey could take her or leave her.

Or *take her.*

Her belly did a hot little flip, and she fortified herself by taking a big sip of wine.

"Will you show me the lake-swamp?" she asked.

"I'd love to." He seemed genuinely pleased she'd asked.

Thank goodness he couldn't hear the conversation going on in her mind.

They brought the dishes inside and refilled their wine glasses, then he took her hand in his large, callused, warm one. It was an easy, casual movement, and she gave his fingers a little squeeze to let him know she liked it.

The walkway to the lake was just a worn footpath through the woods. It ran at a long, low angle, and the uneven ground wouldn't have been difficult to traverse, except she was wearing those darned wedge espadrille sandals.

"These shoes aren't the greatest for off-road walking," she said ruefully, and gave his hand another little squeeze as a thank you for him steadying her. "I might have to hold on to you."

"I hope you do." He flashed her a smile.

At the end of the path, they were at the small lake. It could hardly be called a lake; it really was a pond.

"Green heron," he said, pointing to a funny-looking bird the size of a duck, but with longer legs. It wasn't the least bit green, but more of a maroon, with black streaks and a little yellow. It had bright yellow-orange legs and feet. The bird was prowling along an edge of the pond where the reeds weren't growing, eyeing the water.

"I love to watch him hunt for fish—he walks like such a dork, but then when he goes for a fish, his neck snaps out so long and — See! Did you see that?"

Jacqueline *had* seen that, and she was laughing. "He's cute."

"So are you." He gently turned her to face him. "I know that's not a great word for a woman our age, and I can think of other words to describe you—smart, funny, kind, sexy—but it also fits."

She looked up at him, feeling her insides shift in an oh-so-pleasant way. "I feel the same about you, cutie," she replied, resting her free hand on his chest. His heart thudded beneath her palm, and the tips of her fingers were just brushing the hair peeking through the vee of his shirt.

He twined a finger through one of her curls. "Your hair was different the first time I met you. You had it all pinned up, like a" —he laughed—"like a prim and proper librarian—"

"I *was* a prim and proper librarian." She laughed too. She wasn't feeling very prim and proper right now.

"And I was thinking what it would be like to let it all down."

She blushed. She had no idea he'd had that sort of thought the first time they met. After all, it was sort of over a dead body in her apartment.

"I like it now too, but I have to admit, I wanted to see it all come falling down."

They were pressed very close together, and she could feel things happening, and she pressed a little closer, so that his eyes went a little wide...then narrowed as he drew in a rough breath.

"So, uh..." He was fumbling for words, and Jacqueline liked knowing she was the cause of it. "I do have to ask before...well... before we head back to the house."

Because she suspected they both knew what was going to happen when they got back to the house.

Ice cream was gonna have to wait.

"Don't worry, I brought condoms," she said, and felt the little leap of his heartbeat—and elsewhere—at the bluntness.

He gave a heartfelt laugh. "I...uh...am covered there too, er, so to speak."

She laughed and he laughed, and the tiny bit of awkwardness eased. His chest still felt warm and right beneath her hand. So solid.

But he eased back a little. "Look, I just have to ask because... well, I need to know." His attention flickered to the lake, then back to her again. "Look, I'm not trying to be nosy or to push or anything, but I just need to know if, uh, you and this Josh have unfinished business. Because I don't... I won't..." He shrugged, and she knew what he couldn't quite say. "You know?"

"As far as I'm concerned, there's absolutely no unfinished business. *He's* got an issue, but it's not mine. I've hardly given him a thought for twenty years, Miles, and that's the truth."

Except when she was reminded that she'd been cheated on and wasn't good enough for the man she'd loved and was going to marry. Which explained her dearth of experience with men over the last two decades—*thank you, Josh.*

"Okay." He smiled and pulled her back into his arms for a very thorough kiss and then some.

After a while, she said, "Are the bugs coming out?" She eased back, trying to catch her breath, fighting a smile as she looked up at him and moved her hands from around his neck to the front of his shoulders. "I thought I felt something nibbling at my neck."

His eyes gleamed with delight. "That was me, my dear."

"Are you sure? Because if the bugs are coming out, I think we ought to go back to the house. I don't want to get...eaten. Up." She barely got the last word out because her voice went all husky and her throat went dry.

The look in his eyes sent a sharp, hot dart through her belly

—and lower. He muttered something she didn't quite get, but his tone was unmistakable.

"Definitely, we need to get back to the house," he said, starting to propel her (gently) along the path. "If, uh, there's any eating to be done, it should be done inside."

"In comfort," she replied, trotting along with him, confident that his steady grip would keep her from tripping or falling on the rough ground.

"Definitely."

They made their way into the cabin and were just starting down the hall when a very annoying sound came from Massermey's pocket.

He swore, sharp and hard, and stepped back from Jacqueline as he fumbled the phone out of his pocket.

"Massermey." He gave her a pained look, then his eyes went slightly unfocused as he listened to whoever was on the other end. "All right. I'll get there as soon as I can." He disconnected the phone and heaved a sigh. "And *this* is part of the reason Rachel and I are no longer together." He gestured with the phone, then shoved it back in his pocket. "In case you were wondering."

Rachel, Jacqueline assumed, was his ex-wife. But for all she knew, it could be an ex-girlfriend that he'd had *since* his divorce.

Which made her realize she didn't know that much about his past relationships.

"That was dispatch, in case you didn't guess. And, yes, they have their own very annoying ringtone so I don't ever miss a call. So, yeah, I've got to go," he said with a sigh.

"Is...is someone dead?" Jacqueline asked.

To her relief, he shook his head. "No. I do other police work besides homicides, especially over a holiday weekend. There aren't that many murders in Button Cove, thank goodness. But I do have to go. And I'm sorry. I'm *really* sorry. You have *no idea* how sorry I am."

"I'm not going to hold it against you, Miles. It's your job and it's important, and that's part of what attracts me to you."

He shook his head. "You've been reading too many cozy mysteries and romances, haven't you? The heroine always falls for the cop." Even though his words were wry, his eyes danced with warmth. Then the humor ebbed. "It's not like in the books, Jacqueline. Just so you know. It's just not that easy."

"I know. Life never is like in the books, is it?"

*Except when characters decide to pop out of books.*

He shook his head, gave her one last very regretful look, then kissed her. "I'll be in touch as soon as I can."

"That's good enough for me."

## 11

By the time Jacqueline got back to the shop, it was nearly nine thirty.

It was Saturday night of a holiday weekend, and the streets were still busy with people. Families, couples, dog walkers, a few bicyclists, and one teen on a scooter. Most of them were probably heading back to wherever they were staying, for the shops were closed. Only restaurants and bars were open.

Jacqueline parked her car behind the store and decided she might just as well make a visit to the ZAP Ladies. She could thank them for their help with her wardrobe, and then read them the riot act about putting a charm on her clothing.

And then...

She sighed. She still had to deal with Anne Boleyn and whoever had been summoning her from the depths of a history book.

*Can't I have just have one night where I don't have to think about all of this stuff?*

The ZAP Ladies lived in a pretty Painted Lady Victorian at the end of the cul-de-sac of Camellia Court. It was robin's-egg blue, and its ornate trim and shutters had recently been painted a vibrant purple. There were several gables, a wraparound porch, and sharp-peaked roofs.

The front yard was a beautiful tangle of gardens set apart from the sidewalk by a wrought-iron fence. The gardens exploded around a walkway that led into the backyard, where even more flora and fauna flourished—thanks to Andromeda's green thumb. There were plants not the least bit native to Northern Michigan, nor compatible with its weather zone, that grew back there. Jacqueline knew better than to ask how or why.

She knocked on the front door, and it was flung open almost right away by Pietra.

"Jacqueline! What's wrong? What are you doing here?" Her round, dimpled face was blank with shock and horror. "Is everything all right?"

"Massermey got called into work," Jacqueline explained as she stepped inside. "So our evening got cut short."

"Oh dear, I'm so sorry to hear that," Pietra said, closing the door. Then she took a look at what Jacqueline was wearing. "Oh."

"Oh?" Jacqueline looked down. Nope, her boobs were still safely confined behind the mauve sundress and crocheted bolero-style vest. Nothing was torn, stained, or otherwise a mess.

"Who's— Oh, crone's bones, Jacqueline, what are you doing here?" Andromeda had come from behind the tapestry that covered the doorway (and was possibly meant to hide it) to the herbary and kitchen. "Is everything all right?"

"Massermey got called into work," Jacqueline explained again. "So—"

"Well, how did everything go before... *Oh.*" Andromeda's slender nose crinkled up a little as she, too, skimmed over Jacqueline's attire.

Then she and Pietra exchanged disgruntled looks, and that was when Jacqueline realized what was going on. It was the outfit Zwyla had left for her that she'd chosen to wear, not the ones designed by Petey or Andi.

"I love the shoes," Jacqueline said quickly, showing Andromeda that she'd chosen her footwear. "And Massermey *really* liked the necklace, Pietra...if you know what I mean. Too bad he didn't get to check out what's underneath. The bra really gave the girls a lift."

The two crones gave her a dual set of "whatever" looks, and before Jacqueline could try to mollify them further, the tapestry swished again and, ducking her head so she didn't bump it on the doorframe, Zwyla swept into the living room.

"Jacqueline! What are you doing here? Oh, you look *fantastic*, doesn't she, girls?" Zwyla beamed slyly at Andromeda and Pietra. "I knew our girl had excellent taste."

A vase on the coffee table exploded into shards of glass, with water and pink Gerbera daisies spilling everywhere. Jacqueline didn't know whether Pietra or Andi had expressed their opinion, but it didn't matter. She decided she needed to change the subject, and fast.

"So, uh, how did everything go?" she asked, realizing she sounded like she was asking a baby- or dog-sitter how the evening had gone with their charge. Really, it wasn't much different—they'd had to babysit a Queen of England. "Where's Anne?"

Jacqueline looked around the living room, as if there was a chance she'd missed seeing the royal and her behemoth gown. No, Anne wasn't here in this space that was a comfortable cross between shabby chic, earth mother, and flower child.

Lava lamps, bean bags, beaded curtains, and macrame plant hangers laden with ferns shared space with an overstuffed gray sofa piled with beaded decorative pillows. Plants sat along every windowsill, dried herbs and flowers filled a large bowl like potpourri, silk and woven tapestries covered the walls, and a sleek bookshelf held countless novels, gardening books, and other volumes Jacqueline hadn't identified. There were small sculptures of stone, carved wooden décor, and a metal singing bowl, along with a collection of beautiful watercolors of birds. A thick shag rug of dark blue covered the weathered wooden floor.

But no Anne Boleyn.

"She's...mm...not here," said Andromeda quickly. "But how *did* everything go until Massermey got called away? That's why she's back here so early, Z," she added. "Honestly, we didn't expect you until tomorrow morning, Jacqueline. But I suppose your choices might have had something to do with *that*." She had the slightest sneer in her voice as she gave Jacqueline another once-over.

"Where is she?" Jacqueline tamped down the sort of terror a parent might feel if they'd been told by the babysitter that their child wasn't there.

"She's not here," said Pietra earnestly.

"I can see that. Where is she?" Jacqueline was beginning to panic. She couldn't have Anne Boleyn marching through downtown Button Cove, ordering people around and causing problems.

And then it occurred to her... Why was it even *her* problem, anyway? Why was *she* responsible for the Queen of England? *She* hadn't done anything to cause the problem. She couldn't even send the woman back into her book if she wanted to. She hadn't called her out, she had no control over the woman...

*Not my circus, not my clowns,* she told herself.

"Okay," Jacqueline said, deciding to just *let it go*. Idina Menzel's clear, powerful voice sprang into her mind, filling her head, making her want to spin around and sing the anthem at the top of her lungs (which would be a bad idea—she couldn't sing very well, and she'd probably cause something else to break). "I'm just going to go home, then. All's good. See you tomorrow—or whenever."

She waved goodbye to the crones and left them staring after her as she slipped out the front door.

They hadn't told her where Anne was—did they even know? —and frankly, Jacqueline didn't care. She was not going to *allow* herself to care.

It wasn't her problem.

She had as much control over the former Queen of England as she did over the current King of England: less than zero.

No. Instead of worrying over things, Jacqueline was going to go home, curl up with a glass of wine and a good book, and look forward to tomorrow.

She was stalking purposely down Camellia when a battered black hearse pulled up next to her.

Jacqueline looked over and smiled as the window rolled down. "Hi, Gerry. How's it going?"

Gerry Dawdle drove the town's only regular rideshare vehicle, and it happened to be a hearse. There were a few random Lyft or Uber drivers who made their way up to and around Button Cove on occasion, but Gerry was the only one who was there all the time.

He was a retired emergency room physician, and, as he'd once explained, he thought it was fitting to drive a hearse around "since I spent the last forty years trying to keep people *out* of hearses."

He was also sort of, kind of, maybe, seeing Nadine. Which Jacqueline was *all for.* Talk about an upgrade from Noah the Surgeon and God's Gift to the World.

"I was going to ask you the same question," he said, leaning his head out the window. His hair, thinning on top and brown mostly gone gray, was pulled into a short ponytail that brushed the collar of his pale blue polo. "I, uh... Nadine mentioned you had a date with Massermey tonight."

Jacqueline felt her cheeks warm. Did *everyone* in Button Cove know about her personal and sex life? "He got called into work."

"That's a bummer. Everything else good?" he said, looking at her closely.

"Well, yes," Jacqueline told him. "It was really busy in the shop today, and yesterday, but that's to be expected."

"Right." He hung a long, lanky arm out of the window and said, "It— Well, it feels like something's...*off*. You know? Like something's in the air. And I don't just mean the tourists descending like locusts."

"What *do* you mean?"

He scratched his chin thoughtfully with long, knobby fingers and took his time answering. "Well, I don't really know, but my co-pilots are kind of squirrelly right now. Tells me that something's off, even if I don't know exactly what."

Since he drove a hearse, Gerry had become accustomed to ghostly stowaways and restless spirits who'd decided to hang in and around the long, vintage car. He called them his co-pilots.

"Reminds me of when it was a full moon and I was still working. The ER was full of crazies, and even crazier things happening. You wouldn't believe the stories... Anyway, you sure nothing's going on at that bookshop of yours?"

Gerry Dawdle was basically the only male in Button Cove—as far as Jacqueline knew, anyway—who was aware of the strange happenings along Camellia Court. The man not only believed in ghosts but he coexisted easily with them in his car, so he wasn't one to be skeptical of supernatural and just plain weird happenings.

Massermey probably had an inkling that sometimes odd

things happened in Button Cove—especially on Camellia Court—but he didn't know the details.

And he probably didn't want to.

Jacqueline heaved a sigh. "Well, yes, there is something going on. Isn't there always? But right now, Anne Boleyn—yes, *the* Anne Boleyn—is running amok here in Button Cove—"

"Headless or headed?"

"Headed," Jacqueline replied, choking on a giggle. "It seems as if someone has sort of, well...summoned her out of the book." She briefly explained about the burned papers in the singing bowls. "I think it might be someone playing with conjuring or spells or hexes or something like that. Anyway, Anne's missing now—I left the ZAP Ladies in charge of her. Should I be surprised that they lost her?"

Gerry chuckled. "Probably not. Of course, they might just as easily have set her free as lost her."

"I'm guessing—hoping—people will think Anne's just an escapee from the Renaissance Faire."

"Oh, *that* explains it," he replied. "I did hear about a disturbance up there at the faire."

"A disturbance? What kind of disturbance? How did you hear about a disturbance?"

He flapped a hand vaguely toward his dashboard. "Police scanner. I like to keep an eye—I mean ear—on what's going on around here. Can affect my business, you know? There've been a few things tonight—a domestic disturbance over south of town, a coupla car accidents, a fight at Jilted. Anyway, the one that caught my ear was an altercation that broke out up at the faire when two of the queens—I'm talking women dressed as monarchs, not the other kind of queen—got into an argument over which of them was the *real* queen."

"That's *got* to be Anne." Jacqueline grimaced. Also, "police scanner" made her think of Massermey, and she wondered which of those incidents he had been called to. "I can see how Anne would take exception to someone else claiming they were *the* queen. How long ago did you hear about that?"

"Oh, within the last hour or so. Want me to drive you up there? Take a look around?"

"Do you mind?" Jacqueline said gratefully. Even though Anne wasn't really her problem, she did feel sort of responsible for her. Besides, if the queen didn't return to Three Tomes, she couldn't go back into her book (assuming it worked the same way for nonfiction people as it did for fiction) and *go away*.

The good thing was, if Gerry had only heard about the disturbance within the last hour, that probably *wasn't* the one to which Massermey had been called.

"I don't mind in the least. Business is slow tonight, believe it or not. The faire is closed for the day, I think, so I'm not sure what we'll find, but it's worth checking out. Hop in right here in front— Oh, hold on. I've got to clear these guys out of the way. In the back, the lot of you, now," he said, ducking back into the car and waving his hand vigorously at the empty front seat. "All the way in the back."

Jacqueline shook her head. Her life was utterly, ridiculously strange. This moment in particular reminded her of the end of Disney's Haunted Mansion ride, where ghosts hitchhiked in the ride vehicle—except that this was *real*.

"There you go," Gerry said, gesturing for her to climb in next to him. "Millie, I said *all* the way in the back, now. Wendell, you too. I'm not going to say it again. If I need to get a priest, I'll get one. That rosary isn't just for looks, you know."

"A priest?" Jacqueline said, noticing said rosary dangling from his rearview mirror. Then she laughed. "Oh, ha, to exorcise them from the hearse."

"I wouldn't *actually* do it," Gerry said in a low voice, "but it's a good threat."

He pulled the hearse back into the street and maneuvered it expertly between wandering pedestrians, strollers, leashed dogs, and parked cars—all of which seemed to think they had equal right to the road.

"Do you have to, uh, send them to the back every time someone rides?" Jacqueline asked.

"Not always. Sometimes. Right now they're all freaked out, practically clinging to me up here. It makes it a little challenging to drive, you know, and it's a little creepy with them breathing in my face. Nothing like death breath. But normally, they hover in the back or on the roof when I've got someone riding. Sometimes Victoria will hold on to that front ornament on the hood and make like Rose from *Titanic*."

Jacqueline grinned. "Sounds like you've got quite a crew." Then she realized what he'd said. If even ghosts were freaked out, should she be more worried?

"What happens if someone sits, you know, on one of them?" she asked, looking around even though she couldn't see ghosts. Yet. With her luck, it was probably only a matter of time.

"I did that once when I first started driving this thing. Muriel has never forgiven me—apparently, I crushed her favorite hat." His brows rose in droll skepticism. "Anyway, if you touch one of them or pass through them, you feel like you're being doused in ice water. Yesterday I was taking a couple over to their hotel. They were sitting in the back seat, and they kept asking me to turn off the air conditioning."

"Well, I'm not cold, so I guess they moved," Jacqueline said. "How many—uh—co-pilots do you have?"

By now, the hearse was traveling along Front Street, the road that curved around the bay of Lake Michigan that created Button Cove, and heading north-northwest. John Denver blared from the speakers, singing about his country roads.

Gerry shrugged. "A dozen or two. It's amorphous—ha. Some

days there are more than others, and they seem to change out whenever I drive by the graveyard. But I've got a few regulars."

Once again, Jacqueline shook her head. She could hardly believe they were so casually discussing ghost riders.

"So...Anne Boleyn is visiting," he went on. "And Nadine mentioned *Pride and Prejudice*."

"Did she swoon or squeal when she did?" Jacqueline asked.

"Yes, she did." He glanced at her, a smile quirking his lips. "I'm used to it. I have two daughters and three sisters. Plus I worked with a lot of nurses and PAs, many of whom were female."

"Well, the strange thing is, no one has made an appearance yet. And the book has fallen several times. So I don't know what that means. And quite a few Ian Fleming books have dropped as well. If there's a theme, I sure as hell can't figure it out."

"Hmm. James Bond novels," Gerry said thoughtfully. "Which ones?"

Jacqueline had to think for a sec, then she rattled them off: "*Live and Let Die, Diamonds Are Forever, Moonraker, Dr. No...* There was another one, but I can't remember the title."

"I sure as hell hope the villains aren't coming out of all of them," Gerry said grimly. "All right, you guys, settle down back there," he called when Jacqueline shivered as a gust of ice cold chilled her. "There's no need to worry about Dr. No. He's not *that* bad. I bet you could haunt the heck out of him and send him crying back to his lair."

"Is that the one under the ocean?" asked Jacqueline. "Or is that *Moonraker*?"

"Nope, right the first time. It's *Dr. No*," he said.

By now they were several miles out of town and had turned onto a narrow dirt road that led up into the hills. There were a few signs stuck in the ground that directed them to the faire, but there was no other suggestion of life or activity. It was dark, and if Jacqueline had been with anyone other than Gerry Dawdle—or Massermey—she would have been nervous about being taken to such a remote area.

"Brr," she said, rubbing her arms.

"That's Wendell. He's refusing to go in the back with the others. Said all they're doing is cooing over James Bond," Gerry said in disgust. "And some of them even think Pierce Brosnan was the best." He tsked.

"I'm a fan of Sean Connery and Daniel Craig myself. Anyhow, you're probably a fan of the Bond Girls, I'm guessing," Jacqueline said.

"Don't most straight men appreciate them?" he said, grinning. Suddenly his grin faded. "Did you say *Live and Let Die*?"

"Yes. Danvers said she'd picked it up from the floor the other day. Of course, she hadn't bothered to mention it to me, so I had no idea. I'm not even sure when that was. Why?"

"So that could have been the first book that fell," he mused. "Which means that whoever came out of that one could be engineering all of this."

"Who's the villain in that one?" asked Jacqueline. She was only vaguely familiar with the movies, and had read only *Casino Royale*.

"It's not the villain who's interesting me," Gerry went on. "It's the fact that that book—and movie—is the only one that I know of with anything like witchcraft or conjuring in it. That was one of Jane Seymour's first movies, by the way."

Jacqueline hadn't known that. "Was she the Bond Girl in that one?"

"Yes. Her character's name was Solitaire—and here's the interesting thing. Solitaire read tarot cards, but the whole backdrop of the book and movie was voodoo."

Jacqueline's skin suddenly erupted in prickles. "Voodoo. Conjuring. Witchcraft. Oh shit. I suddenly see a pattern."

"Yeah." He glanced at her.

"So you think Solitaire might have come out of the book?"

"Or someone else who can do conjuring or voodoo."

Jacqueline suddenly felt as if a bucket of ice water had been dumped over her. "Oh my God!" she shrieked, breathless from the frigid cold.

"Get in the back," Gerry ordered the spirits. "All of you. *Now.* Or I'll send this vehicle to the dump. Do you know what they do to cars at the dump? They smash them *flat.* I can get another car, I want you all to know, and you won't ever find it. And you're really tempting me to do it."

The iciness faded as suddenly as it had come, and Jacqueline was finally able to feel her fingers again.

"Here we are," said Gerry as they rounded a corner and came upon a wide-open expanse that appeared to be a field used for event parking. "Used to be a cherry farm, or so I hear."

Beyond the field was a fence enclosing the fairgrounds, and Jacqueline could see the tops of little peaked buildings—market stalls and food carts and things like that. She hadn't been to a Renaissance Faire in a while, but that was how she remembered them being. There were two cars still parked there, but no other signs of life other than a few pieces of garbage that hadn't made the trash cans. The moon wasn't full, but it was more than half and there was a large swath of stars, so plenty of light. There was also a glow emanating from within the fenced-in area.

Gerry turned off the hearse, and Jacqueline climbed out, eager to be away from the anxious ghosts. She found herself stepping in mud, and she swore. Her espadrilles would be ruined, and then Andromeda would have yet another reason to be offended.

"Well, what do you think?" said Gerry as he came around from the other side of the hearse. "Should we see if there's anything to see?"

"It doesn't seem like anyone's around—"

A shout in the distance cut off the rest of her comment, and she and Gerry exchanged looks. The call had come from the direction of the faire-grounds.

Maybe someone was still inside the gates. Maybe it was Anne Boleyn and the queen she'd been arguing with.

Fortunately for Jacqueline's sandals and her ankles, Gerry had parked near the entrance gates, so she didn't have far to navigate through rough, uneven, and muddy ground. She skirted the remains of a tree trunk, likely left over from the cherry orchard, and avoided a little dip in the ground.

As they approached the gates, she heard another shout. It sounded like someone calling for help. She and Gerry picked up their pace.

"The gate's open," Gerry said in a mildly surprised voice.

Jacqueline followed him inside and found herself suddenly catapulted back into Elizabethan, or thereabouts, times—at least, Elizabethan times with the modern conveniences of porta-johns, Wi-Fi, and Bunsen burners.

The place was set up like an English village, with many rustic stalls and stands and food carts, offering places to purchase food, clothing, jewelry, garden décor, essential oils, blended teas and honey, and opportunities to demonstrate one's prowess: walking on a high beam, archery, lifting a heavy mallet and swinging it down to send a weight catapulting up to clang a bell, slingshot abilities, and more. There were small stages and larger stages where, presumably, dancing, lute playing, juggling, stage plays, and other Renaissance types of entertainment occurred.

But now, everything was closed up with tarps or roll-down curtains. No one was about shouting, "Huzzah!" or "Where be the privies?" or "Hail, and well met, my lady!"

"Be careful; ground's uneven," Gerry warned, close on her heels due to his long legs.

They didn't have to go far before they came to what seemed to be the center of the faire—and the center of the presumed village and its square.

And right in the center of the square was a very common sight in medieval and Renaissance villages: a row of stocks, where criminals or the accused would be positioned, head and wrists inside wooden frames, so that they could be seen and ridiculed by their fellow residents.

One of the stocks was occupied.

Jacqueline gasped when she recognized who it was.

"Josh?"

---

## 12

J osh lifted his head as much as he was able. "Oh thank God! *Jackie?* What are you doing here? Can you get me out of this thing?"

Gerry was already there, and it was just as well, as he was almost a foot taller than Jacqueline and could reach the latches on the stocks much more easily.

"Oh thank God," Josh said again as one wrist was loosened, and he let his arm fall to his side. He groaned with relief. His neck was released next, and then the other arm. He groaned and began flapping his limbs and craning his neck in order to get the blood flowing again.

"What happened? Who did this?" Jacqueline asked, looking around. There didn't seem to be anyone else here.

"Some crazy woman locked me in there," Josh said, rubbing a wrist vigorously. "What are *you* doing here? And thank you," he added, looking at Gerry.

"No prob," replied the hearse driver.

"I, uh, heard about a disturbance up here and came to check it out. This is Dr. Gerry Dawdle," Jacqueline said, believing it was always correct to include a person's title if there was one, even if he was no longer practicing medicine.

Josh eyed Gerry as he rubbed his other wrist. "That was nice of you."

"A crazy woman locked you up here?" said Gerry. "Do you know who she was or why she would do such a thing?"

"That b—that crazy lady thought she was the Queen of England! All I did was offer to drive her up here—I saw her not long after I, uh, left your shop, Jackie, and she looked like she belonged here, you know, at the Ren Fest. I figured she needed a ride, and I didn't have anything else to do. And my car was big enough to hold her and that stupid dress she was wearing. That turned out to be a big mistake, because as soon as we got here, she started marching around ordering people about.

"I was trying to calm her down, but then she saw another person pretending to be the queen, and she went nuts, shouting and putting up a fuss. She even called to have the other woman beheaded! It's a damned good thing there isn't a guillotine around here. I think she might actually have done it." He glanced around as if to be certain there wasn't.

"What happened? Did someone call security?" Jacqueline asked.

"Yes, but by then the faire was closed and most everyone was on their way out. I got her to calm down when she realized the other queen was going too. She—she kept telling me to call her Your Majesty, but I think her name was Anne. I think she thought she was Anne *freaking* Boleyn," said Josh, his voice high with emotion. "That's the last time I try to do someone a favor."

"How did you get her to agree to go with you?" Jacqueline asked.

"Well, I don't know—I guess I just said something like 'You look like you're lost. Would you like me to take you to your people?' That kind of thing. She was really in character, because she freaked out when I tried to get her into the car. I finally told her it was a magic carriage."

"That must be your magic carriage in the parking lot," said Jacqueline. "There was only one left when we arrived."

"I'm glad it's still there. I was afraid that crazy woman would take off with it."

Jacqueline thought that was unlikely, considering the fact that Anne Boleyn wouldn't have the first clue how to drive one.

Without discussion, the three of them had begun to walk back toward the gates.

"So how did you end up in the stocks?" asked Gerry.

"I'm not quite sure. I mean, I *know* how I ended up there—there was another woman who was kind of loitering around as everyone was leaving. All of sudden, the two of them were talking, then we three got chatting and it was all friendly and fine, and I was going to drive them back into town. The queen lady had calmed down a little and things seemed normal.

"I was explaining what I was doing in Button Cove—and the next thing I knew, they started freaking out and suddenly ganged up on me. I didn't even realize what happened, but suddenly I was standing there by the stocks—I don't even remember going up there, but there I was, standing there with my head and arms in the stupid things. And they locked me in!"

"Why did they lock you up?" Jacqueline asked. "And who was the other woman?"

"I don't know! We were just talking, and everything was fine, and then I mentioned I'd been to the bookshop, and that I'd come up to Button Cove to…uh…" His voice trailed off.

"Go on," Jacqueline said firmly. She'd like to know exactly why he was up here.

"Well, I mentioned I was up here to see an ex and to apologize for messing things up with her…and then all of a sudden, that queen person got really angry and started yelling at me.

"And the other woman wasn't doing anything to stop her—in fact, I think she must have helped her, because there was no way that queen person could have gotten me up by those stocks, especially with her wearing that stupid dress. She would have tripped all over everything. I don't know... Maybe she forced me. I really don't remember; it was kind of a blur. Maybe the queen person was a man in drag and that's how she did it—she was strong. I don't know. I just... It's weird. It's like I blanked out. And I haven't been drinking!"

Jacqueline exchanged glances with Gerry. None of this made sense...yet she felt as if it *should*.

"I just can't understand how they got me up to those stocks. I don't even remember going near them, and then all of a sudden, *boom*, there I was." His voice faded, and she could almost hear the frown that accompanied it. "Wait a minute, there was something— Yes, I remember now. There were bubbles. Like, I was surrounded by bubbles...?" He sounded as if he didn't believe it. "I think? But I don't know what that has to do with anything."

"Bubbles?" Gerry asked. They'd reached the gates by now, and he held one open for Jacqueline.

"Yeah...you know, like little kids blowing bubbles? It was like a bubble machine or something, all at once. Maybe it was part of the fair. I don't know. Or the other woman...was *she* blowing the bubbles at me? Or using a machine? Damn...I don't know. I really don't know. My brain seems to be filled with more bubbles."

Jacqueline wasn't watching where she was going. How could she? It was semi-dark, and she was intent on listening to Josh. And so of course she stepped on uneven ground. Her foot landed wrong, at an angle, on the high espadrille heels.

She cried out as she fell, with the sharp pain telling her she'd done a number on her ankle. Twisted it, turned it, hopefully didn't break it.

Gerry turned back and crouched next to her. "You all right?"

"I think so." Jacqueline tried to pull to her feet, but the pain was too sharp and strong, and she couldn't put any weight on her ankle.

"Hold on, let me take a look here. Make sure you didn't break anything." The doctor took off her sandal, muttering, "Not the smartest thing to wear traipsing around on uneven ground."

"I didn't realize I'd be traipsing around on uneven ground in them," she retorted. "Ow!" she said when his fingers—gentle, firm, and expert—pressed on a tender area.

He gently rotated her foot in every direction. "Tell me if it hurts." It didn't, mostly, and after a thorough examination, he said, "You'll live. Ice and elevate and some ibuprofen. We'll wrap it up good—of course I've got a first-aid kit in the car."

She was able to put a little weight on her foot, and with the help of Gerry on one side and Josh on the other (even though she didn't need both of them), they got her back to the hearse. Josh was relieved to see that his car was, in fact, still there.

"I'll come back to your place and help you out, Jackie," he offered. "Um...if you want."

Gerry gave her a quirked eyebrow look as he stuffed her into the hearse—and, apparently, onto Millie or Wendell or someone, because she felt like she'd just been shoved into an ice bath. She clamped her lips closed instead of shrieking, and managed to say, "Could you get your friends to move off my seat and wrap themselves around my ankle instead?"

"Great idea," Gerry said. "Why didn't I think of that? Better than ice. You heard the lady, guys—give her ankle a good, long hug." He was rummaging in the back seat, presumably for the first-aid kit.

"Jackie?" Josh said. "Want me to come back and help you? I'm...uh...not doing anything else tonight."

Jacqueline was on the verge of declining when she realized

she had a lot more questions for him. Much as she didn't like the idea, she suspected Josh might know something that could help her figure out what was going on. She was very curious about the second woman who'd shown up.

"All right, that's fine. Back to the bookshop. We can talk there," she said with a sigh. She ignored Gerry Dawdle's second quizzical eyebrow lift as he deftly wrapped her ankle with an Ace bandage.

But once they were in the hearse, this time with John Prine coming through the stereo speakers, Gerry looked over. "What's the deal with that guy?"

"He's my former fiancé." She explained the situation. "I definitely don't want to hang out with him, but he might know something. Such as, who was that other woman with Anne? I mean, we know someone's been summoning Anne—we just don't know who. Maybe that's who it was."

"Seems pretty random if it *is* the person who's been summoning her that she shows up at the Renaissance Faire when Anne is there. How would she even know?"

"Well, whoever it is somehow knew Anne was in my flat and helped her get out. So maybe there's some kind of, you know, magical connection. Or maybe I'm way off. I just feel like there might be something Josh knows that could help." She glanced in the side mirror and saw Josh's headlights following behind.

"You want to see if Nadine and Suzette want to come over too?" Gerry suggested casually.

Jacqueline realized with a start...was he trying to protect her?

Protect her from Josh?

Or protect her from, maybe, Massermey finding out that she had Josh in her apartment? Which, by the way, was definitely *not* her plan. She was going to talk with him in the tea room. Definitely not in her flat.

"That's a good idea," she said. "I'll text them now."

Gerry seemed to visibly relax, and Jacqueline couldn't help smiling to herself. He was acting like a protective older brother.

"How's the ankle feeling?" he asked a moment later.

"Wendell and Muriel and Millie or whoever are wrapped around it, and it's not throbbing so much, thanks to the wrap and their icy chill," Jacqueline said as she texted her friends: *Meet me at the shop?*

Before she could explain further, her phone started blowing up with multiple texts coming in on top of the other from both women in various forms of: *You're at the shop???? What happened??? Why aren't you with M????*

Jacqueline simultaneously laughed and rolled her eyes, then gave a succinct explanation: *M called into work. Josh was in the stocks up at Ren Faire. Sprained my ankle. Gerry with me. Want more deets, be at shop ASAP.*

The reaction emojis and GIFs that came pouring in made Jacqueline laugh so hard she dislodged the ghosts and their chilly grip from her ankle.

When they got to Three Tomes, Nadine and Suzette were pacing outside the front door. Gerry pulled the hearse up into a parallel parking spot, and the women hurried over to open Jacqueline's door.

She was working herself out of the hearse when Josh's car slid into the spot behind them. Jacqueline did quick introductions between everyone (she noticed Gerry and Nadine greeted each other with a real kiss on the lips, so yay!) and urged all of them inside the bookshop.

She had to hobble, and Josh was immediately at her side to give her a hand. Ignoring the speculative look from Suzette—which she didn't bother trying to hide—Jacqueline gestured everyone to go up to the tea room. She didn't even try to take the steps; she used the elevator, shuffling to it with Josh's assistance.

"So what's with all the people?" he asked as the elevator door closed.

"My friends, you mean? They're here because we're trying to figure out what happened up at the Renaissance Faire. And because I don't want to give you any impression that I'm interested in being alone with you." She leveled a look at him, and he glanced away.

"Geez. It's not like I'm going to attack you or anything." He sounded hurt.

"Of course not. But I need to be clear: there's absolutely no chance of anything happening between us. *No chance*," she repeated as the elevator doors slid open. "Zero."

He strode out quickly, not waiting to assist her.

Clearly, her point had been made.

And just as clearly, his expectations were destroyed and his male ego battered.

Jacqueline wasted no time once everyone was settled on sofas and at tea tables in the café. Nadine opened her mouth to speak, but Jacqueline shook her head. She'd get to her friends' questions later.

"All right, Josh, I have a few questions for you about what happened tonight," she said, settling her injured ankle so it was on the arm of the sofa, slightly raised but not enough to give everyone a free show up her sundress skirt. "Obviously, there was something weird going on."

"No shit," Josh said, not trying to hide his irritation. Whether it was at Jacqueline or Anne Boleyn, it was difficult to say.

"You mentioned that the woman named Anne was talking to another woman. Did they seem to know each other? Was she dressed, you know, in Ren Faire costume, like Anne?" Or like Jane Austen—but she didn't want to lead the witness, so to speak.

"I don't know! How am I supposed to know if they knew each

other?" he griped. "It was weird. The whole damned thing was weird. I don't— No, she wasn't dressed in costume. She was just wearing, you know, a dress or a skirt or something. A little fancy, though, for a Ren Fest. Not a sundress." He gestured vaguely at Jacqueline.

"Was it a long dress?" she asked, thinking of Jane Austen. Her skin prickled hopefully. "Kind of loose? And what did her hair look like?"

"No. The dress was... Well, it was kind of, you know..." He flushed a little, spreading his hands. "Tight. And...uh...sexy. Low-cut."

"Like a Bond Girl," said Gerry.

Jacqueline's eyes popped wide. "Oh my God. That could make sense!" She saw Nadine's and Suzette's comprehension— after all, they knew that a few Ian Fleming books had fallen off the shelf. "Did you hear *anything* they were talking about? Anything at all, Josh?"

"I don't know. Not really. I think I heard one of them say something about a summons? And then another thing about planning something, and a book, but then the new person—her name was Kitty, I think she said—looked at me and asked who I was and what I was doing there. And so I was telling her about it, and..."

Just then, Jacqueline's phone dinged with a text alert. She glanced at it and felt her face flame hot. It was Massermey.

Ignoring the knowing looks from Nadine and Suzette, she tapped and read the message.

*You around?*

She absolutely didn't look up, even though she felt the very heavy weight of her friends' gazes on her. That was the bad thing about having two really close friends—they knew *everything* that was going on with her. Maybe even too much.

She ignored them, ignored Josh's rambling word salad, and typed back to Massermey: *Yes.*

He responded almost immediately: *Want company?*

*Yes, please,* she replied.

His response was a smiling emoji.

"Massermey's on his way here," she said, because there was no chance Nadine and Suzette were going to let her keep that to herself.

Gerry nodded in satisfaction, and her two friends grinned. Josh said, "Who's that?"

"He's a cop, and he and Jacqueline are dating," said Suzette brightly.

Josh looked as if he'd just swallowed a lemon.

"So the other woman's name was Kitty?" said Gerry, doggedly returning to the conversation. "I can't think of a Bond Girl with the name Kitty. I mean, there was Pussy Galore, but..." His cheeks flushed a tiny bit.

"*Such* a terrible, horrible name! So misogynistic," said Suzette with disgust. "I can't believe it. And Holly Goodhead is just as bad. Ian Fleming obviously didn't think very highly of women—or at least the women James Bond screwed. It's just awful."

Jacqueline's phone dinged again. *Are you in your apt? Tea room has lights on...*

Always the cop, she thought, smiling as she texted, *Sitting in tea room with the girls and Gerry. Come on up. Door's open.*

The bell on the front door jangled, and Massermey's solid footsteps sounded as he climbed to the second floor. When he saw Josh there, the smile he was wearing faltered a little. But when he saw Jacqueline's bound foot, elevated as per doctor's orders, his expression flashed to one of concern.

"I turned my ankle," Jacqueline told him right away. "Gerry helped me take care of it. He says I'll live."

"She shouldn't have been wearing those shoes," Gerry commented, gesturing to the one that was still on her uninjured foot. "But, yes, she'll live."

"I'm glad to hear it." Massermey didn't seem certain what to do next—he just stood there.

Nadine caught on first. "Well, it's time for us to get going," she said, standing abruptly. "I've got an early class, and I'm sure you got baking to do, right, Suze?"

"Sure do," agreed Suzette, bouncing to her feet.

Gerry rose too, and to Jacqueline's surprise and relief, Josh did as well.

"Thanks for your help tonight," Jacqueline told Gerry. "Josh, let me know if you think of anything else. It's important." She felt Massermey's curious look on her and started scrambling internally to figure out how to explain all of that to him.

"Miles, do you mind going down after them and locking the door? I..." She gestured to her foot.

"Of course." He gestured to the others to lead the way.

The last thing Jacqueline saw was Nadine's expression when she looked back as she disappeared down the stairs. It was a combination of salacious excitement and *oopsie!*

## 13

M assermey returned quickly, and Jacqueline gestured for
him to sit next to her on the sofa.

"I'm sorry I had to cut our evening short," he said, sliding
down next to her. He took her hand and looked down as he
rubbed his finger over her knuckles. It was a sweet gesture, and
Jacqueline melted a little inside.

"I completely understand. It's your job."

"So, do you want to tell me about the rest of your evening,
and how that happened?" he asked, gesturing to her ankle. "Or
should we pick up where we left off?" His eyes glinted with heat
that sent a pleasant little shiver through her belly.

"Either way, we should go upstairs," she said, curling her
fingers in his grip. "It's much more comfortable up there."

The glint went a little hotter, and he stood, helping her to
her feet. "Should I carry you?"

"*No!*" She was appalled at the thought of him hoisting her up
and realizing belatedly how much she weighed. Good God, she
could put the man's back out. Even though she thought he was
in very good shape for his age. "No, I'm fine to take the elevator.

And believe it or not, Gerry said it's okay to walk on my ankle—and that I actually should, as long as it doesn't hurt too much. It helps keep the muscles from atrophying. I can take the elevator."

"If you say so," Massermey replied. He took her hand, steadying her as she hobbled to the lift.

"So, everything was all right? Whatever scene you were called to?" she asked as the elevator doors closed.

"For now it is," he said. "Domestic disturbance. No one was hurt, but there were some serious tempers flaring, and it's ripe for something to happen in the future." His expression was grim.

The doors opened, and they stepped out into the tiny hallway behind the kitchen. Jacqueline moved slowly to the sofa, but once she got there, she settled in comfortably.

Massermey found a couple of pillows to help elevate her ankle on the coffee table—and took a leisurely look at her bare legs—then, at her suggestion, he turned on the gas fireplace and turned off all the lights but one small lamp.

"Much, much better," he said, settling next to her, nice and close. He picked up her hand again, his strong fingers darker and larger over hers. "So, uh...how *did* that happen?"

By now, Jacqueline had formulated her response to that logical and reasonable question. "When I got back from your place, I ran into Gerry. He mentioned that there'd been a disturbance up at the Renaissance Faire—I guess he listens to the police scanner sometimes—and I, uh, sort of wondered if that was the scene you'd been called to. Plus I haven't been to a Renaissance Faire for a long time," she added quickly. "And I thought it would be fun to check it out."

"And so Gerry took you up there?"

Jacqueline shrugged. "He was in between rides, and you know how those rideshares work—you need to be close by the venue to pick up customers. I guess he figured someone might want a ride back, since the festival was closing soon." There were a lot of holes in that theory—including, if that were the case, what was Gerry going to do with Jacqueline while he drove a paying customer back?—but she hurried on, hoping to keep Massermey from thinking too hard about it.

She'd rather he believe she was up there scoping things out because she thought *he* might be up there than tell him the truth about why she'd gone: to find Anne Boleyn.

"Anyway, we got up there and the faire was closed. But there was a car in the parking lot, and we could hear someone shouting from inside. They seemed like they were in distress, so we went to investigate. And...it was Josh," she said, allowing the shock and surprise she'd felt then to color her voice now. "Someone had locked him up in the stocks—as a joke, maybe? —and left him."

Massermey's fingers were very still over hers. She sensed he had a lot of questions and maybe even some suspicions.

"Gerry got him out, and when we were coming back out to the cars, I stepped wrong—the parking lot is in an old cherry orchard with lots of uneven ground—and *voilà!*" She gestured grandly to her ankle.

"Someone locked up your ex-fiancé—who happens to live in Chicago—at the Ren Fest and left him, and you just happened to be the one to find him?"

"Yeah. It was very weird. So random. And, Miles, I *told* you, there is *nothing* going on between me and Josh. He cheated on me, *okay*? He cheated on me with my best friend before our wedding. *He* is *never* going to happen for me ever again.

"I told him that very bluntly tonight, after we got back here. He thought he could worm his way up here into my apartment, and I invited Nadine and Suzette over instead." She gave Massermey a pleased smile. "Talk about a cockblock."

His mouth had gone flat. "With your best friend? Before the wedding?"

Her smile faded and she looked down. The humiliation was still as sharp as it had been twenty years ago. "Yes."

His fingers squeezed hers. "I'm sorry. But I'm more sorry he's not still here. I'd have a few things to say to the bastard."

Her eyes stung a little, but she kept her gaze downward. She didn't want him to see. "Yeah. So I've been a little gun-shy of men ever since."

"Very understandable." He squeezed her fingers again, then gently released them. "Well, uh... While we're having such a serious conversation, I need to talk to you about something else."

His tone made her stomach do an unpleasant flip. "Yes?" She forced herself to look up and was caught by his sober blue gaze.

"I, uh, mentioned I was called to a domestic disturbance tonight. It was at the Jessie and Raymond Gould residence."

This was not at all what Jacqueline was expecting (she was expecting something much worse, like his confession that *he'd* cheated on his wife or something equally as bad), but she still reacted with a catch of her breath. Enough that he noticed.

"You know them." It wasn't a question.

"I've met Jessie—Mrs. Gould. She's a customer here." That was the truth.

His expression changed a little. "Yes. She...uh...mentioned that."

"What do you mean?"

"She was ranting and raving about Raymond and Valentine and other things—I got the impression the two are headed for a split," Massermey went on. "And she said something about how she was going to show him, that the lady at the bookshop was going to put a hex on him."

Jacqueline's throat dried up. She managed a confused, innocent smile. "A *hex*?"

"That's what she said." Massermey heaved a sigh and settled back against the sofa. Even in the low light, she could see the consternation in his expression. He rubbed a hand over his forehead. "Look, Jacqueline, I...uh... I know that there are some... er...interesting things that have happened here at your bookshop. Things that I can't explain. That I don't *want* to explain. I mean, just last week..."

He gave a little shudder, and she knew he was remembering the vampire melee that had been fought in the main area of the bookshop. She'd done her best to distract him from it, but when it was all over, there was still a vampire on the floor who'd needed to be properly dispatched.

"Miles." She took a deep breath, hesitated...and that was when she made a really important decision. "The truth is, there are a lot more strange things that go on here than you realize. I'm sorry to tell you. It's the truth. And I understand if you don't want to know about it—or *can't* allow yourself to know about it all."

He groaned. "I was afraid you'd say something like that."

"I'm sorry to, uh, burst your bubble. It's true. And I—I don't have much control over the things that happen here."

"What is this place? Like some sort of...Narnia wardrobe or something?"

She chuckled sadly. "Or something. I think it's more like the Hellmouth in *Buffy the Vampire Slayer* than the Narnia wardrobe, but either way...yes. Weird shit happens."

"I still haven't watched *Buffy*," he said mournfully. "We were supposed to do that tonight, remember? So I have no idea what a Hellmouth is...but I'm pretty sure I don't like it."

"Well, let's just say in Buffy, the Hellmouth is not good. Here on Camellia Court, it's just...complicated, and sometimes extremely inconvenient."

He heaved a sigh. "Look, Jacqueline. I don't want to have to arrest my...uh, you...for assault and battery, or—or for *any* crime. Please tell me what Mrs. Gould said isn't true. You're not going to put a hex on her husband." He shuddered, more violently this time, as if the fact that he'd actually had to say those words, *think* that thought, was impossible to handle. "That you're not even *capable* of doing something like that. Hexes aren't real. This isn't Harry Potter. Right?"

*Oh boy.*

Jacqueline did not know how to respond to that. And she knew the longer she hesitated, the worse it would be. So she started talking, trusting that she would somehow say the right thing...or deal with losing an opportunity to develop something with him.

"Miles, you're not going to have to arrest me for anything. I *promise* you that. I'd never do anything to hurt someone or steal anything or—or even do anything to vandalize or ruin someone else's property. And the fact that you might think so—"

"I *don't* think so," he exploded. "I don't *want* to think so! It's just that *I've* seen weird things with my own eyes, and when Jessie Gould started saying those things...I had to tell you, Jacqueline. I had to ask. You understand?"

"I do, yes, I suppose. You have to follow up."

"Look, I wouldn't have even entertained the thought of saying anything about it if there hadn't been weird things that happen here anyway. And don't think I've forgotten about your breaking into the zoo and climbing into the crocodile pen." The way he looked at her was a combination of frustration and affection, and that eased her own anger.

"Miles. I would never do anything to injure someone. Or their property." She didn't think that humiliating someone counted as an injury, especially since it would be something the person brought on themselves. That was what the humiliation hex she'd read about, and planned to use, did. It wasn't permanent or injurious.

"So where did Jessie Gould get the impression you'd be hexing her husband?" Massermey asked in a milder voice.

Jacqueline sighed then looked directly at him and said, "Apparently the bookshop has a reputation."

One of his thick strawberry-blond brows rose. "A reputation."

"Online, even. It's on some website. *I* didn't have anything to do with it. People started showing up here right after I reopened, expecting...things. Me to do things."

"You? Do things? What sort of— Wait. Maybe I don't want to know." He shook his head, wearing a pained expression. "Okay, at least tell me this: are any of these things you've—uh—been asked to do—are any of them illegal?"

Jacqueline thought about the protection amulet she'd made for a woman whose husband was trying to kill her, and about the concoction she'd made to fend off the vampires, and the brew she'd made with a crocodile tooth in order to save the ZAP Ladies from a curse. "Not in the least. Nothing I've...uh...done has been illegal."

"Except for climbing into the crocodile pen," he reminded her dryly.

"But was that *technically* illegal? Or just foolhardy?"

He shook his head. "I want to believe you, Jacqueline. And so far... Well, I've seen nothing to indicate otherwise. Except that foolhardy trespass at the zoo."

"See?" she said, giving him a very warm smile. "I promise you. You won't have to arrest me."

He looked at her soberly. "I'm very relieved to hear that,

Jacqueline." He sounded utterly sincere, as if the problem had truly been worrying him.

"Although," she said, making her smile even warmer, "you might need to put me in handcuffs sometime."

The expression on his face was...perfect.

And so was what followed.

## 14

Jacqueline awoke the next morning with a big smile on her face. A very big smile.

It had been a long time—maybe never—since she'd been so well satisfied, so very relaxed and *sated*. And so comfortable.

Massermey didn't appear to be lacking either, if the slow, easy grin he gave her when he opened his eyes was any indication.

"And we didn't even get to the handcuffs," he said, tracing a finger down her cheek.

"We'll get to them," she said, surprising herself with the bold flirtation.

Actually, she'd surprised herself quite a bit last night in many ways. *I guess the old lady bits haven't dried up—and nor has my imagination.* They'd had to be careful of her ankle, but that hadn't hampered the experience in the least.

"I'll make the coffee," Massermey said, sliding out from under the covers. He had a pretty nice butt for a guy his age— not flat and saggy like many men in their late forties or early fifties. "You should still be resting that ankle as often—"

"Yoo-hoo!" came an extremely *un*expected, very perky—and unfortunately very familiar—voice. "Jacqueline?"

"Oh my God! *Shit!* That's Petey!" Jacqueline grabbed a robe and dragged it on as she bounded from the bed—heedless of her ankle, and thus causing herself to stifle a shriek of pain.

"Jacqueline? We brought tea and scones!" called another voice. Andromeda.

Jacqueline was going to *kill* them. Both of them. Even if she got arrested for it.

Massermey was flinging sheets and pillows around, trying to find his pants and socks, when Jacqueline limped out of the bedroom door and closed it firmly behind her.

"What are you two—three," she amended when she saw that Zwyla was there too, "doing here? You can't just barge in!"

"We didn't barge in," Pietra told her brightly. "We're still standing in the doorway, waiting for you to invite us in."

Jacqueline gave her a dark look, despite the fact that Petey was carrying her bakery basket—which probably meant blueberry cream scones. Petey wasn't lying, but just barely. The three had opened the door, but hadn't actually stepped inside.

"You know exactly what I mean, you nosy trio. To the living room, all of you. I'll put some clothes on and—"

"What on earth happened to you?" Zwyla said.

"I turned my ankle."

"I do hope it didn't—er—handicap any of your activities last night, dear," said Pietra earnestly.

"My activities?" Jacqueline said faintly.

"He's still here, isn't he?" Andromeda said calmly. "We brought enough tea and scones for both of you—and some quiche as well. Massermey *is* a man, you know, and probably needs to refortify himself after all of that—"

"Oh. My. God." Jacqueline's face was beet red as she thrust a finger down the hall, gesturing for them to head to the living room. She knew better than to try to get them to leave. They simply wouldn't. They'd be just *too* kind and helpful, and maybe a bit confused, and they'd pretend to misunderstand—and they would stay. It would be like moving three thorny mountains to get them to leave. It was infuriating.

"Let me take care of it for you, Jacqueline," said Andromeda kindly. "After all, it was my shoes that did that for you, wasn't it?" She seemed pleased about that fact, rather than shame-faced.

Before Jacqueline could ask what she meant, Andromeda crouched next to her.

"You mean you didn't put a stability charm on those sandals, Andi?" Pietra said archly. "I *always* put a stability charm on heels."

"I meant to," Andromeda responded a little sharply as she wrapped both hands firmly around Jacqueline's injured ankle. "But *someone* was rushing me."

Jacqueline felt a rush of heat, and the faint scents of lavender and wintergreen along with something else, and suddenly the pain seemed to fade away. The bandage fell off, and she could put all of her weight on it without flinching.

"Thanks," she said grudgingly, picking up the long ribbon of bandage that had piled on the floor.

"Of course, my dear," said Andi, giving her a motherly pat on the arm.

"Speaking of which, what other—er—charms did you put on my things?" Jacqueline demanded, remembering her suspicion about how her clothing might have inspired her to be more...forward.

"Why, none," said Pietra.

"You didn't put a little something on those clothes to 'help'" —she did air quotes—"things along? Or in the perfume or nail polish?"

"*Absolutely not,*" said Zwyla firmly. "We wouldn't do that."

"It's not as if you would *need* the boost anyway," said Andromeda, patting her on the arm. "It appears you did just fine on your own."

The three older women beamed at Jacqueline as if she were a toddler who'd just taken her first steps.

She gave them a skeptical look, then herded the trio to the living room. She wondered whether Massermey was going to join them or make a break for it. She wouldn't blame him in the least if he sneaked out down the hall and fled. She'd probably do the same if she was in his shoes.

She was still wearing her robe, and she wanted to get dressed, but she wasn't certain it was safe to leave the ZAP Ladies alone with Massermey here. Maybe she should usher him out the door herself before they got their hooks into him, so to speak.

But when she heard a quiet scuff from the hall, Jacqueline looked over to see him walking toward them. He looked like a man going to his execution, yet he was staying and taking on the situation instead of fleeing. She guessed that was partly the cop in him, and it made her like and appreciate him even more than she already did.

"Well, good morning, Detective Massermey," purred Zwyla. Jacqueline had never heard that sort of voice from her before, and she blushed at the obvious double entendre hidden in the tone.

"It is a very good morning," Massermey said. He wrapped an arm around Jacqueline's waist and pressed a light kiss to her temple. He smelled like her toothpaste and himself. "I hear there are scones and quiche?"

"Oh, yes, plenty of offerings to rebuild your stamina," said Pietra in that bright, innocent, but oh-so-cunning way of hers.

He turned to Jacqueline. "Let me help you get settled—I can make coffee. Do you need a new bandage?"

"Oh, that's okay. My ankle is—is fine now," Jacqueline said.

"What do you mean, fine? I know Gerry said to walk on it, but—"

"She means that Andromeda fixed it," Pietra said. "As well she should have. If she'd put a stability charm—"

"I'm feeling just fine," Jacqueline said a little more loudly than necessary. "It, uh, doesn't hurt anymore."

Massermey's gaze bounced from one to the other of them, then sudden, shocked comprehension flooded his face. He sighed. "I should have known you three were involved."

"Involved in what?" asked Andromeda very innocently.

"Never mind. Just... Oh, never mind."

Jacqueline took the opportunity to slip off to her bedroom so she could put on something other than a robe. She didn't feel bad leaving Massermey to the ZAP Ladies. He seemed to be able to handle himself just fine.

She felt better when she came out, fully clothed and having brushed her teeth and spritzed her sleep- (and sex-) tossed curls with a bit of water. Her four guests—and she used the term "guest" loosely on the ZAP Ladies—were sitting around her tiny dining table, eating and talking.

"Detective Massermey was just filling us in on all the details from last night," said Andromeda.

Jacqueline faltered...then realized Andi wasn't talking about the details of what had happened in her bedroom, but what had happened up the at Ren Faire. But since he didn't know *everything* that had happened—including that Anne Boleyn was wandering around Button Cove—she merely nodded and gave Zwyla a look that said, *There's much more.*

Then Jacqueline glanced at the clock on her microwave and gave a squeak. "Oh hell," she said. "I've got to get downstairs. It's time to open the shop."

Andromeda looked at her in surprise. "But I thought you didn't open until ten."

Jacqueline gave her a weak smile. "Summer hours. Not my idea—trust me. But I've got to run. Sorry!" She grabbed a scone and a piece of quiche, put them on a plate, and dashed off.

Unfortunately, she didn't realize until she got downstairs that she'd forgotten coffee. How was she going to make it through the day without caffeine?

Even so, not for the first time was Jacqueline appreciative of the fact that she lived above her place of work. If she hadn't, she would never have made it on time. As it was, when she got to the main floor—having bounded down two flights of steps without a hint of pain, and, in fact, she might have even been more agile than before—she found Danvers waiting for her wearing an extremely sour expression, even for her.

"Ma'am," said the housekeeper as she flipped the sign from CLOSED to OPEN with the same sort of attitude a snarky teen might have. "I do hope your business isn't keeping you from *other* activities."

Jacqueline wasn't going to take any shit from Danvers this morning (no caffeine), and besides, she had questions for her. "I need to know when you picked up *Live and Let Die* from where it was on the floor. When was it?"

Danvers drew herself up as if offended by such a blunt tone and question. However, she was a product of her time and class, and in the end, she knew her place. (Not that Jacqueline was a supporter of inflexible class distinction and the strict mistress/servant dynamic, but in this case, she was perfectly fine taking advantage of the situation. After all, Danvers was a *fictional character.*)

"Yes, ma'am. I do believe it was two evenings ago. The shop had just closed. You had gone across the street to fraternize with those other two women"—apparently Danvers wasn't completely above making snarky comments, servant or no— "and left me to sweep up. I was cleaning out the fireplace in the Mystery and Thriller Room, and there it was, on the floor."

"Two evenings ago? That would have been Wednesday—the night before you found the remnants of the fire in the New Age Room. Isn't that correct? The first time."

"I do believe that is correct, ma'am." Danvers lifted her nose. "Is there anything else, ma'am? The back rooms need to be dusted, and there are *several* cases of books to be unpacked."

"There's nothing else," Jacqueline replied, just as the front door rattled then opened as a couple and two school-aged kids flowed into the shop.

It was Sunday and Memorial Day weekend, and all at once, things were *busy*. The customers flowed in nonstop, with many enjoying tea and pastries upstairs as they perused the books they eventually would buy. And wow, did they *buy*.

She did get a text from Massermey shortly after she came downstairs. *Last night was perfect. Let's do it again soon? Plus: Buffy. I need to find out about this Hellmouth thing.*

She didn't have time to respond other than to send back a heart emoji. One of the things she appreciated about Massermey (and there were becoming *many* things she appreciated about him) was that he actually typed out his texts and most of the time had very good grammar. As a librarian and self-identified pedant, Jacqueline found that very attractive in a man.

She wasn't certain when he left the building; she was too busy to notice, and he might have gone out the back when she was in the front, or vice versa. Nor did she see the ZAP Ladies take their leave, and to be honest, that bothered her more. Were they still upstairs in her apartment, whipping up new outfits and putting charms on her clothing? Jacqueline wasn't certain how she felt about that, and she certainly didn't believe they were completely innocent of "boosting" her chances with her clothing last night.

She also had a slew of texts from Nadine and Suzette, who obviously needed all of the details about how things had gone after they left last night. Jacqueline's only response was the sly, sunglasses-wearing emoji and the flames emoji.

She was even too busy to wonder where Anne Boleyn and her companion—Kitty something—had gotten off to. She didn't *want* to wonder about it.

She'd just finished a big rush of customers (in between sneaking bites of scone and quiche) when the front door opened...and there was Massermey.

He gave her a *look*, and Jacqueline's stomach flipped as she blushed.

"I noticed you raced off this morning without coffee," he said, and gestured with one of the two go-cups he was carrying from her favorite coffee place. He set one down on the counter for her. "And since you didn't get much sleep last night..."

Her mouth had gone dry, but she was still grinning at him like an idiot. The best thing was, he was grinning back at her like the same sort of idiot. "That is so thoughtful of you," she said, mindful of the fact that there *were* customers browsing within earshot. "Thank you, Miles."

"My pleasure." His voice was a low purr, just loud enough for her to hear. Then he stepped back a little and said, in a normal, casual, just-another-random-customer voice, "Hey, is there a Bridgerton thing going on in town? I usually know about things like that, but I haven't heard. There's the Renaissance Faire up off Leland Pines Trail, but I haven't heard anything about a Bridgerton Experience or a Jane Austen con. If so, I'm sure Mandy's going to want to go." He grimaced a little, but Jacqueline knew it was mostly for show. He was a softie when it came to his daughter.

"I haven't heard anything about it," she said, and then her belly dropped—and not in a good way. "Um...what makes you ask?"

"Well, I saw a bunch of women walking down the street, and they were dressed like, you know, Jane Austen or *Bridgerton*."

"A *bunch* of women? Like, how many?"

He shrugged. "A dozen? Not sure."

*A dozen?* "Where did you see them?"

His gaze sharpened a little, as if he suddenly realized she had *reasons* for asking those questions. His expression turned wary. "Down the block. Why?"

Before she could respond, a man came to the counter with a stack of gorgeous grilling and gardening books, and she rang him up. And then another customer—this one a woman with half a dozen historical romance novels, including a Caroline Linden, an Eloisa James, and a Sarah MacLean—approached.

"Did you say something about the Bridgerton Experience?" she asked as Jacqueline rang her up. "Oh my God, is there one *here*? I *need* to know," she went on with a little chuckle. "I'm such a sucker for Regency romances."

"I'm not sure," said Jacqueline, not meeting Massermey's eye. "There is a Renaissance Faire, I know for sure."

The woman seemed disappointed. "Well," she said, pulling a business card out of her wallet, "will you do me a favor and let me know if you find out about one? I just moved here, and I expect to be in your shop *a lot*."

"I certainly will, um, Ms. Frenley," Jacqueline said with a glance at the business card. "And if you like, I can sign you up for our loyal buyer program."

"I would *love* that. And it's Cindy," she went on. "Mrs. Frenley is my mother-in-law. *Former* mother-in-law, I should say," she added with a grimace. "I lost two hundred pounds three months ago, and his name was Dave."

"I will definitely add you to the program, Cindy," Jacqueline said, noting that the woman's card indicated she was the assistant manager at Button Cove Bank. Nice to have friends—or, at least, fellow booklovers—in high places, she thought.

The stream of customers was so steady, Jacqueline barely noticed when Massermey slipped out. She caught a glimpse of his little wave as he left, holding the door open for a small cluster of older teen girls who flowed in.

They required some assistance from Jacqueline, as they wanted something "like *Fourth Wing* but with a lot more sex," and she'd had to dig around in the romance section to find Thea Harrison's Elder Races series and a few other titles by Shelly Laurenston and Angela Knight. The girls split up the purchase, each one buying two books so they could share, and then left, chatting giddily about their "summer book club."

Jacqueline was just slipping a few World War II nonfiction books into a shopping bag for a customer when she glanced up toward the two bow windows that flanked the front door.

*There was Anne Boleyn.*

The queen was standing in the middle of the street as if she owned it. She seemed to be surrounded, or at least accompanied, by a number of other women. Almost like ladies-in-waiting. They were too far away for Jacqueline to see whether she recognized any of them; the only reason she knew it was Anne at all was because of the ridiculous gown she wore.

"Thank you for shopping small business," she told the man, and hastily handed him the bag with his books.

"It's my pleasure," he said, and turned to leave.

"I've got to check on something," Jacqueline said to Danvers, who'd, thankfully, just emerged from the back of the shop. "I'll be back."

She didn't wait for Danvers's response and hurried out from

behind the counter. She rushed out through the front doorway and nearly collided with a customer coming inside.

"So sorry! I'll be right back, but Mrs. Danvers can help you," Jacqueline said, hurrying out onto the street.

When she got outside and caught a full glimpse of Anne and her entourage, Jacqueline stumbled to a halt.

And then everything sort of began to make sense.

Anne, who gave a regal nod when she saw Jacqueline, was surrounded by women. There were a dozen or more of them.

About five were dressed in the style of Jane Austen: high-waisted, loose frocks of light material. They had short, cupped sleeves and square bodices, and the skirts nearly brushed the ground. Their hair was pinned up in the back, with long curls that hung from their temples.

The others were dressed like fifties and sixties sexpots: tight, low-cut dresses along with perfect makeup including winged eyeliner, false lashes, and perfectly drawn dark brows. Most wore perfectly styled bouffant hair, sleek and curved, of all lengths and colors. They wore impractical heels—pumps or wedges—and the patterns of their clothing were geometric or splashes of colorful, large flowers.

Jacqueline hurried toward what appeared to be a conglomeration of characters from Jane Austen along with a group of—for lack of a better term—Bond Girls. That was the only thing that made sense.

But what she didn't understand was *why*.

What were they all doing here?

## 15

"**H**ark! We seest thou," said Anne when she caught sight of Jacqueline. She made a regal, sweeping gesture. "We require a place of repose for our ladies and ourself. Have one prepared immediately."

Jacqueline's hackles went up—of course she didn't like being given such peremptory orders. But she caught herself before responding sharply. It would be in everyone's best interest if she could contain Anne and her "ladies" as quickly and completely as possible.

"Of course," she replied, thinking fast. Then she realized the perfect place to stow them. "If you'll follow me this way, madam."

Just as she began to lead them toward the court end of the street, Jacqueline heard someone calling her name. She turned to see Egala rushing along the sidewalk, trying to get her attention.

Great. Just what she needed: a witch she didn't trust connecting with a divorced and beheaded queen who was, apparently, *also* a witch.

"I can't talk now," Jacqueline called. "I'll stop by later."

Egala's eponymously named shop was a block and a half from Three Tomes, and although Jacqueline tried to avoid it as much as possible, she couldn't deny that the purses and hand-bags and totes her distant cousin sold there were not only stunning but practical. Half the reason she didn't go in there was because she was afraid of what she'd spend.

Egala came to a halt on the sidewalk and frowned. "It's important."

"Give me thirty minutes," Jacqueline said. "Don't you have customers to see to?" If Egala's shop was half as busy as her own, she didn't know how the other woman had found the time to slip out and chase her down.

Egala narrowed her eyes, muttering, and just then the small branch from a tree fell, landing right in front of Jacqueline. It fell so close, it brushed leaves through her curls. The branch was too small to have done any damage, but it was the thought that counted in this case.

Jacqueline sent her cousin a disgruntled look and felt a little heat jolt through her as she did so.

Egala clapped a hand to her arm—where the visual dart, no more than a sting, had apparently landed (Jacqueline clearly needed to work on her aim)—and gave her dirty look. Then she turned and started stalking away. She took two steps, then said over her shoulder, "Next time I'll make a bird shit on your head." The weird thing was, she wasn't shouting, but Jacqueline heard her as if she was standing next to her, whispering in her ear.

What a pain.

"This way, madam," she said to Anne, and began to direct her toward the ZAP Ladies' house. She could think of no one better to supervise Anne Boleyn and her ladies-in-waiting—and besides, Jacqueline owed the crones for showing up uninvited this morning.

But when they arrived at the pretty blue house and Jacqueline knocked on the front door, no one answered. Surely they weren't still in her apartment. It had been over two hours!

Jacqueline didn't want to bring the entourage back to Three Tomes for a number of very good reasons, so she instantly came up with Plan B.

"Back here, madam," she said, leaving the porch. "There is a lovely garden anon where you and your ladies may take your rest and enjoy the flowers. I will have refreshments prepared for you in a short while."

Fortunately, it was a beautiful day, and so Anne didn't object as Jacqueline led her around to the back of the house. If she'd hoped she might find Andromeda there, tending her very extensive garden, she was meant to be disappointed.

Still, it was the perfect place to settle the women. There were many places to sit, and Anne immediately commandeered the largest bench for herself and her gown.

Flowers spilled everywhere—roses in full bloom far too early for the season, zinnias, lilacs (too late for the season), celosia, daisies (much too early), lavender, hydrangea, and many, many more. A little brook wound through the area, with two small bridges for crossing. A happy little waterfall tumbled down the side of the eight-foot-high stone wall that enclosed the backyard, and ivy, honeysuckle, and clematis climbed trellises, trees, and the stone wall, and even crawled over one of the little bridges. There were pots overflowing with flowers, rows of neat vegetables, clumps of herbs whose scents wafted through the air, obelisk trellises and arbors and archways... All filled and sprawling with greenery and blossoms and fruit.

It was the most enchanted, colorful, eclectic garden Jacqueline had ever imagined—let alone seen—and it was perfectly representative of Andromeda's personality.

"This *is* a most pleasant place," the queen said with approval

—as if it had been created just for her pleasure. "We shall have a repast anon."

"Yeah, I'll get right on that," Jacqueline muttered. Then she smiled. "Of course, madam. I shall see to it immediately. Please, have your ladies make themselves comfortable. I wonder if you would introduce me to them. I am most desirous of meeting Lady Kitty."

As she spoke, Jacqueline looked over the cluster of women, all of whom had somehow found places to sit—on benches, boulders, tree trunks, rustic swings, and even on a blanket that was somehow on the ground. There were definitely two distinct groups: the Regency-era type in their demure, long, and loose frocks, and the fifties/sixties sexpots.

"I'm Kitty," said one of the women, speaking with a lilting Caribbean accent. She was absolutely beautiful, with honey-tinged, light brown skin and large eyes. Her dark brown hair was styled in a short, sleek bob—extremely *un*natural for a Black woman's hair, but what did one expect from a book written in the fifties? "Why do you want to know?"

"It was my ex-fiancé that you locked in the stocks last night," Jacqueline said.

Kitty grinned, narrowing her eyes with delight. "Was it? Served the man right, didn't it?" She pronounced "man" more like "mon."

"I can't disagree. So, are you...uh..." Jacqueline struggled with how to phrase the question, as she was fairly certain none of the characters who came out of books actually realized they were the creations of a writer. "Do you happen to know a man named James Bond?"

Kitty's eyes narrowed again, but this time with disgust. Her full, peach-tinted lips flattened. "Oh, I know Bond, all right. The love-her-and-leave-her man himself. The seducer of all seducers. We all know him, don't we, ladies?"

The other women from her era nodded and muttered and exchanged women-scorned looks.

"He's an absolute *cad*," said one in a cultured English accent. She was sleek and blond, and wore a skirt suit of ice blue and hot-pink lipstick.

"An utter snake," said another. She was curvy and brunette and wore a short, tight dress with a very low vee and lots of silvery sequins.

"If I could get my hands on him...*again*..." said a third, flexing fingers that looked strong enough to snap a man's neck. She was a tall, Amazonian sort of woman with a perfect hourglass figure.

"Right," said Jacqueline. Who were these women? She didn't know the books or movies well enough to be able to identify a Pussy Galore or a Holly Goodhead.

But hadn't Gerry Dawdle said the tarot-reading character from *Live and Let Die* was named Solitaire?

"Um...is anyone here named Solitaire?" Jacqueline asked. She wondered if Kitty's real name might be Solitaire, even though Jane Seymour, a white woman, had played her in the movie.

This was getting very confusing.

"I know Solitaire," said Kitty. "We were in the same book. She's not here."

"What's your name again?"

"Kitty. Kitty Bushwell," she said with a proud sneer.

Jacqueline flinched a little. Yikes. She had never heard that name before, but it certainly sounded like the sort of name Ian Fleming would have given a Bond Girl.

"And you know James Bond?"

"Like I said, I *know* him," she replied. "I only wish he were here. We all do."

Her comrades nodded vehemently.

"I see." But Jacqueline didn't quite see. She felt as if she were missing some big piece of the puzzle. "And could the rest of you tell me your names as well?"

The women exchanged looks.

"Must we?" said the Amazonian woman.

"*We* are *not* our *names*," replied one of her companions bracingly, and patted her on the hand. It was one who hadn't spoken before, and she had carroty-red hair, sun-kissed golden skin, and the most elegant nose Jacqueline had ever seen. Like the other women, she was very beautiful. "We are strong, independent women who have been turned into nothing but *sexual objects* by men—and one man in particular. And this is how we're going to *take back our own agency*. My name is Puddin' Snatch," she said boldly, as if to challenge anyone who would laugh or recoil—and Jacqueline nearly did both.

*OMG.* She swallowed hard, hoping her expression didn't telegraph the horrified shock she felt.

"You're *right*, Puddin'," said the Amazon stoutly. "This is the first step toward independence and vengeance, isn't it? I'm Misty Mountains." She stood straight, throwing her shoulders back, causing her large breasts to thrust forward.

"I'm Labeea Luscious," said the brunette in the silver sequined dress. "And this is my sister, Muffy." She put her arm around another blonde who resembled her greatly, but was obviously not a twin. Muffy wore a similar short, low-cut dress sequined in pink.

It was all Jacqueline could do to keep a straight face—and her eyes from popping out of her head—as the women stepped forward, introducing themselves. Each was as beautiful as the next, and together, they were as colorful as a rainbow in both physical looks as well as attire.

"Sweetie Comfort."

"Heidi Whole."

"Hoochie Cooter."

"Precious Parts."

"Corky Pop."

"Lola Areola."

"Gloria S. Mount."

"Martina Meetoo."

Jacqueline managed to nod gravely once they were all finished, but Puddin' said, "You don't need to try to hide your reaction. We know. We *loathe* our names. They're terrible and misogynistic and crude. And we hate the way we've been treated by James Bond. Nameless, faceless lays is what we were. And half the time, we didn't even enjoy them, let me tell you. He's not the lover everyone makes him out to be."

"He's certainly not," said Labeea Luscious. "We were just women Bond screwed and left behind as he went on to his next conquest—like Solitaire or Pussy or Holly. At least they were acknowledged in the books."

"So...um...you were in the books? Are all of you from *Live and Let Die?*" Jacqueline asked.

"I'm from *Moonraker*," said Hoochie. "And so are the Luscious sisters."

"I'm from *Dr. No*," Misty Mountains told her.

"*Diamonds Are Forever*," said Puddin'.

"You're all from different books? I don't remember those names. I mean, you..." Jacqueline stammered. She'd *certainly* remember if she'd read or heard about a Puddin' Snatch or a Labeea Luscious.

"We were in the books, sometimes even off-page, but our names were either cut or never included," said Corky Pop.

"I think that's even more insulting," said Muffy Luscious. "We were good enough for James Bond to screw, but not important enough to be named."

"Hmm, yes," was all Jacqueline could say. Her mind was totally blown.

Did authors do that? Put stock "extras" in books and give them names—but only in their imagination? Or off-page? Like the waitress that serves the meal or the shopkeeper who rings up a purchase? Did they all have names in the mind of the writer?

Before she could think what to do next, the queen harrumphed loudly. "And where is this repast you have promised us?" demanded Anne. "Hie thyself off to prepare it at once!"

Jacqueline managed—just barely—not to give her a dirty look. Instead she nodded (she did need to get back to the shop anyway) and said primly, "Your wish is my command, madam. I shall have the repast for you as soon as possible. All of you, please remain here and enjoy the beautiful day in this lovely garden. I'll return shortly."

Giving one last curious look at the Jane Austen characters, Jacqueline left them. She was disappointed that she hadn't had the chance to talk to them and find out who they were—and disappointed that there'd been no sign of Darcy, to be honest—but she had work to do.

Besides, she reminded herself—it wasn't her circus and they weren't her clowns, even if said clowns did come out via her bookshop.

Jacqueline groaned.

That was a lie.

Like it or not, she felt responsible for whatever was going on.

∾

THE COFFEE MASSERMEY had brought Jacqueline was cold by the time she got back to the store and was able to sip it, but she was grateful for the caffeine nevertheless.

There was a steady stream of customers in and out all morning, and Jacqueline was in her glory helping all of them. She was even happier that no books were heard falling from shelves in the back, no one was coming in and asking for hexes or curses, and there was no sign of any other disruptions, including imperious Tudor queens or sexy spy mistresses.

She managed to find the time to text Suzette and ask if one of her helpers could deliver a box of pastries and a jug of coffee to the garden behind the ZAP Ladies' house; that would have to do for the "repast." And she also bounded up two flights of stairs on her newly healed ankle to check whether the crones were still lurking in her apartment.

They weren't, and so she told herself they'd returned to their house and would have discovered the visitors in the garden and everything was fine.

She hoped.

But there was nothing she could do—she had a job to do and a business to run, and she had absolutely no control over what Anne and her cronies did. And, obviously, Nadine and Suzette were in the same boat, for she didn't hear anything from either of them except a confirmation from Suzette that the pastries had been delivered.

It was early afternoon during a much-needed lull when the front door bell jangled. Jacqueline had gone back to the Romance Room to re-shelve books people had been browsing and do a general tidying up, and she poked her head out of the room to see who'd come in.

"Nadine!" Jacqueline was thrilled to see her friend, if a little confused. It was almost three o'clock. "What are you doing here? Don't you have a class right now?"

Nadine had back-to-back classes on Sunday afternoons, from one through four. Jacqueline knew this because Nadine had drummed it into her and Suzette's heads that they absolutely weren't allowed to have exciting, funny, or interesting text threads, make plans, or have anything wild happen at the bookshop (or anywhere) during that time. It was a hard and fast rule.

"I got a sub. Had to take Michaela to the ER because she had a rash we thought might be chicken pox, and of course the doctor's office is closed on Sundays," Nadine said. She looked and sounded a little harried, and Jacqueline couldn't blame her. Spending an hour—probably even longer—sitting in the ER or urgent care was not fun. "Even when they're nineteen, they still want their mommy when they're sick. And to pay the emergency room copay."

"You should have called Gerry to look at it," Jacqueline said.

"I would have, and he would happily have done so, but he was on a run down to Wicks Hollow and wouldn't be back for at least two hours. Michaela was really itchy, and we wanted to make sure it wasn't contagious."

"Well, is it chicken pox?" Jacqueline was still mystified as to why Nadine was here—not that she minded.

"No, thank goodness. Poison ivy. So a Tide soak for her arm and some of that topical stuff that takes away the itching. *Anyway*, I'm here because I've *got* to tell you something that happened while I was at the ER." Her voice had dropped conspiratorially even though no one was around. "Can we go upstairs to your place?"

"I shouldn't. We've been so busy all day. How about the tea room? We can sit in the corner. I'll go find Danvers and she can — Oh, there you are, Mrs. Danvers."

The hair on the back of Jacqueline's neck stood up. *How* did the creepy woman just materialize whenever she wanted her to —*and* didn't want her to?

Nadine practically dragged Jacqueline upstairs. There were a few customers sitting around at tables and on the sofas. Mrs. Hudson was bustling around taking care of them and likely brewing more tea than anyone ever needed.

Nadine led her to a tiny two-seater table by the front window that was away from everyone. "Okay, so guess who was in the ER while we were there."

"I have no idea," Jacqueline said, still mystified.

"Josh."

"Okay...?"

Nadine was looking at her as if she expected her to say something. "Come on, spill, Jacqueline."

"What are you talking about?"

"He was in there, and I *heard* him. You know how it is in the back in the ER—half the rooms are just curtains pulled around a cot. We were in the room next to him; he didn't notice us, I'm sure. He was too busy with...er...his other problem."

"What problem?"

Nadine was still staring at her expectantly. Then she huffed a sigh. "Well, I could hear him—and unfortunately, I'm pretty sure Michaela could too, but she wouldn't say anything if she did."

"What did you hear?"

"He was complaining about his penis," Nadine said in a whisper. "That there was something wrong with it." She leaned forward, her eyes sparkling with mischief. "Fess up. Did you put a hex on him?"

"*No!*" Jacqueline whispered back. "I certainly did not."

"Oh." Nadine huffed and sat back in her chair, eyeing her skeptically. "I was sure you did."

"Of course I didn't!" Jacqueline rolled her eyes. "He probably stuck it in somewhere it didn't belong and got an STD or something. Good thing I had—have—absolutely no interest in that."

"Yeah, I guess." Nadine crossed her arms over her middle.

"He was probably so put out that you cockblocked him last night by inviting us over that he picked up some woman at a bar and drowned his sorrows."

"I don't know and I don't care," said Jacqueline. "But thanks for letting me know. He deserves everything that happens to him. Karma, you know."

"Yep." Nadine grinned. "So, are we still on for pizza tonight? I deserve one—or two—cocktails for spending three hours at the ER *and* having to pay Polly time and a half to cover for me on a Sunday."

"For sure. We've been slammed all day—I'm not complaining—and I've got *tons* of stuff to tell you and Suze."

"I'll bet you do," replied Nadine with a knowing grin. "Just give me the high level. Does Detective Put-His-Massive-Hands-On-Me live up to the hype?"

Jacqueline's face heated. "Let's just say I've got no complaints."

Nadine hooted and gave her a high five. "All right, more later over pizza and drinks. If I scoot now I can do the three-fifteen vinyasa class and not have to pay Polly."

"See ya later tonight."

Jacqueline followed her friend downstairs and found Mrs. Danvers ringing up a customer, with a second one waiting. As she slipped behind the counter and greeted the person waiting, she was reminded that she still didn't know what happened to Anne Boleyn's codex. The one that had been behind this very counter and stolen yesterday.

She should have asked Kitty if she'd taken it, or if she knew where it was. She also should have asked her if she was the one who'd summoned Anne, and why. But she'd been so taken aback and sympathetic to the Bond Girls—hell, they weren't even called Bond *Women*, were they?—that she'd missed her chance.

She hoped they were all still at the ZAP Ladies' house, but she couldn't worry about it now.

The line of customers was three deep when Egala marched into the shop. She sent Jacqueline a very dark look and jabbed a finger at her watch as if to say, *That was a long freaking thirty minutes.*

Jacqueline had completely forgotten that Egala wanted to talk to her. "I'll be with you in a minute," she told her cousin as she began to ring up the second-to-last customer.

Egala parked herself near the counter and began to flip through *A Discovery of Witches*. She sneered, then rolled her eyes, then scoffed, but she was probably three chapters into the book before Jacqueline was finished with her customers.

"I'll be happy to ring that up for you," she told Egala pointedly. "You seem to be enjoying it quite a bit."

"Only because it's ridiculous. Is it *supposed* to be a comedy?" Egala set the book on the counter. "Fine. I'll pay for it."

"What did you want to talk to me about?" asked Jacqueline as she gladly rang up Egala's purchase.

"Have you figured out anything yet? About what's going on?" Egala's eyes were thickly outlined in unflattering black liner, and they darted around warily.

"Not really. Anne Boleyn is here along with a bunch of James Bond's—uh—one-night stands, I guess you'd call them." Egala gave her a WTF look, and Jacqueline shrugged, then said, "Will that be cash or card?"

Egala muttered something and dug in her pocket, then slapped a credit card onto the counter. "I wish you'd take this seriously, Jacqueline. There's something going on, and quite frankly, I'm not sure you're equipped to handle whatever it is." She looked around the shop pointedly, as if to remind Jacqueline that *she* thought she should have been the one to inherit the place instead. "Sending little baby zap-glares at people isn't going to be enough to help you when the shit comes down, because when it does, it's going to come fast and smelly."

She huffed and snatched up the book before Jacqueline could stuff it in a bag.

"Do *you* know what's going on?" Jacqueline retorted.

"Of course I don't, or I wouldn't be down here *asking* you," Egala hissed. "I'd be taking care of it."

"Thank you for your business," Jacqueline told her brightly, but her smile had an edge. "I'll be sure to let you know if anything comes up that I need your help for." She didn't even care that she ended her sentence with a preposition; she was too annoyed. "Oh, one more thing, Egala," she said quickly as the woman started away. "Have you seen a very, very old book with a bright red leather cover?"

"No." Egala turned away, then pivoted back suddenly, her eyes crafty. "What is it? Some sort of spell book? Did you *lose* a spell book, Jacqueline?" Her mouth crinkled up in satisfied disgust, with lines radiating from it like a row of stitches.

"Someone stole it, and there are some pretty ugly curses in it," Jacqueline told her. "Maybe that's what's bothering you."

"Maybe it is. I'll see ya later," Egala trilled, waving as she swept off and out the door...leaving Jacqueline staring after her with a very bad feeling.

## 16

The rest of the afternoon at the bookshop continued to be steady, but not as wildly busy as the morning had been.

Jacqueline was straightening some of the books in the Summer Reading window display when she glanced out onto the street and saw two women dressed in Regency-era clothing strolling along.

She fumbled *The Ranger's Apprentice* but caught it before it fell and tore its dust jacket. She shoved it into place and hurried out into the street.

"Excuse me," she said, approaching the pair of women. She wasn't certain whether they had been sitting in the garden with the others or not; there'd been too many faces to notice. "Would you like to come inside and have some tea?" She gestured to the bookshop door.

"Oh, that would be quite lovely," replied one of them in dulcet English tones. "We've been quite discombobulated, you see, not quite sure where we're going. It would be lovely to sit down and—and take stock." She looked at her friend for confirmation. The friend nodded.

Jacqueline ushered them inside and then up to the tea room. "Did I meet you earlier, sitting in the garden?" she asked.

"A garden? No, I don't believe so," replied the other woman. "We've been... Well, we're a bit lost. We've only just arrived, you see." She looked around as if trying to determine just where she'd arrived.

"Of course," Jacqueline said. "Why don't you sit right here at this table in the corner, and I'll have someone bring you a nice bit of tea."

Mrs. Hudson would be in her glory, serving two very proper and very correct young Englishwomen. They, at least, wouldn't order anything offensive like oat milk or lattes or flat whites.

Jacqueline settled them in the same tucked-away table where she and Nadine had talked a while ago, then went over to Mrs. Hudson and explained the situation. "Please take care of them. They're a bit lost and confused. Maybe you can figure out what's going on. I'm certain they'll talk to you, and I've got things to do downstairs."

"Right, then, of course, luv," said Mrs. Hudson, already sailing over to greet the young ladies.

Satisfied that, at least for the time being, the young women would be occupied, Jacqueline went back downstairs. The front room was empty of customers and Mrs. Danvers for the first time that day, and, heaving a huge sigh, she slid onto the stool they kept behind the counter for such moments of respite.

Was this the first time she'd been off her feet since coming downstairs this morning? There was still half a cup of her coffee, and it was stone cold. She was getting a little hungry, too, and when she looked at the clock, she realized why. It was after three, and all she'd had to eat was half a scone and a few bites of quiche. At this rate, she was going to easily lose that extra ten or fifteen (depending on the day) pounds.

Before she could decide whether to run back up to the tea room, the shop door rattled, then opened.

Massermey came in, and Jacqueline felt a wave of delight suffuse her.

"Miles," she said, sliding off the stool to greet him.

But the expression on his face had her jolting to a halt several steps away.

"Jacqueline," he said. He was using his cop voice, not the sexy, soft-J one. "I need to talk to you for a minute."

Her belly did an ugly, nauseating dip. "Okay."

"Where would you like to talk? Somewhere private?"

"What is going on?" she asked, because even though he was suggesting they go somewhere alone, it wasn't the least bit *suggestive*. It was scary.

He gave an awkward shrug. "I need to talk to you." His eyes were devoid of emotion.

"All right. I guess...the-the back room." She was *not* about to suggest her apartment, although the back room wasn't much better. The last time they'd been there together, he'd kissed her. She suspected that wouldn't be happening today. "Let me see if I can find Mrs. D— Oh, here she is." Once again, her heart gave a startled lurch at the sudden appearance of the housekeeper.

"Yes, ma'am," said Danvers. Was there a bit of *pity* in her eyes? At the very least, her tone was far less impertinent than it usually was. "I'll be happy to watch over the shop while you speak with the detective. Take your time, ma'am. Everything will be kept in good order up here."

Jacqueline's knees were a little weak as she led the way down the corridor to the back of the shop, then cut to the right where a little storage room was tucked away at the end of another short hall. She wasn't certain which was more frightening—Massermey's impersonal approach or Mrs. Danvers's mild and sympathetic manner.

"What is going on, Miles?" she asked.

She had no reason to be worried. She'd done nothing to put that expression on his face. Whatever it was, he was upset over nothing.

"Jacqueline, I've just come from meeting with Raymond Gould. Is there anything you'd like to tell me?"

"No," she said. "I've never met Raymond Gould, and I haven't seen or spoken to his wife since early yesterday morning."

"Are you certain?" His blue gaze delved into hers like little ice picks. There wasn't a trace of warmth or even familiarity in it.

"Miles, did you hear me? I've never met him. What happened? What are you accusing me of?" Now she was getting angry. It was bad enough that Massermey had this impersonal, cop-like attitude when less than twelve hours ago they'd been rolling around in the sheets together—but even worse that he seemed not to *believe* her.

"I met with him at the hospital," Massermey said, his voice still cool and calm. "He claims to have been hexed."

"Hexed?" Jacqueline blinked, suddenly at a loss for words. "H-hexed? What makes him think he's been hexed?"

"Apparently, his wife told him she'd had him hexed," Massermey said flatly. "Did you have anything to do with...uh... it?" For the first time, his voice faltered, and Jacqueline jumped on that fact.

"What's going on? What makes him think it's a hex? And *no*, I did not have anything to do with it, Miles. Whatever it is. I've been so busy here all day I haven't had the chance to breathe."

Massermey scrutinized her for a moment, then sighed. "Look, he's claiming someone put a hex on his...uh...penis. It's— Apparently it's sort of shriveling up—not in the usual way, I mean. Like a grape on a vine. And it's turning a dark kind of blue."

The blood drained from Jacqueline's face. "Oh my God."

"Jacqueline, what the hell is going on here? You said—"

"Listen to me, Miles, because I'm *not* saying this again: *I didn't do anything. At all.* And if you don't believe me, then I don't know what to do. But... Oh, man, you are not going to believe this." She shook her head, blowing out a long exhale of breath.

"Jacqueline, you need to tell me what's going on. Was it one of the ZAP Ladies? I've always thought of them as harmless and a little loony, but if they did something like that, it's basically assault, and—"

"No, no, it's not them. It's... Oh, Miles, I almost wish I *could* tell you it was me."

"Because...?"

"Because the truth is way worse."

He scrubbed a hand over his forehead, dragging it down over his nose and ending at his beard, which he gave a good, hard tug. His eyes were suddenly a little bloodshot, but at least they weren't ice cold anymore. "All right. You'd better tell me."

Jacqueline closed her eyes, exhaled, and then began to speak as she opened them again. "I don't know who's responsible—I have some ideas, but I'm not sure—but I think whatever is happening might be something called the Castratus Curse. And, yes, it's *exactly* what it sounds like—it's way worse than a little revenge hex.

"There was an old book, a codex, that showed up here at the bookshop—I'm not sure how or why—and I was looking through it and saw this...this curse." She went on to describe the three drawings that depicted the curse: the man with the large, erect phallus, the second picture with the phallus shrunken up, and the third picture with the shrunken phallus on the ground.

"That's ridiculous," Massermey said in a weak voice. His hand had jolted slightly toward his crotch, as if in a reflexive move to protect his own genitals. "That's impossible."

Jacqueline shrugged. "You said vampires didn't exist."

"I never *said* they didn't exist, I just never— Whatever, Jacqueline, it doesn't matter. I find it hard to believe that there's a curse that makes a man's dick just die and fall off."

"But you believed I had put a hex on Raymond Gould," she reminded him coolly. Her fingertips were tingling, and she curled them into each other. The last thing she needed was to shoot a spark at a cop. "So which is it, Miles? Hexes and curses or no hexes and curses?"

"I— Oh, hell, Jacqueline, I don't know what the hell to believe. They don't teach us this shit at the annual conferences, you know." His frustration was understandable, but she was still pretty salty over his mistrust of her. "If you say there's such a thing, then I believe it, all right? I'm sorry." He looked at her unwaveringly, and she felt herself softening. After all, she *could* kind of understand his position. "I really am sorry."

"Look, I'm just telling you I saw a codex with that sort of curse described in it. Maybe that's not what's going on...but maybe it is."

"So where's this codex—what is a codex, anyway?—now?"

Jacqueline sighed again. "A codex is an old book, and... someone took it."

He muffled a curse behind the hand that he dragged down over his face again. "Of course." He tugged his beard again, this time so hard his lower eyelids moved.

"I've been trying to find out who took it," she went on when he finally looked at her again.

"So what in the hell am I going to do?" said Massermey.

"It's: what are *we* going to do," Jacqueline told him, and patted his arm lightly. "I'm pretty sure this is out of your league, Detective Massermey. You're going to need help—a different kind of help than what you're used to."

"I'm afraid you might be right. But I still have to do something. Hell, I don't even know where to start."

"Well, if someone put the Castratus Curse on Raymond Gould, then— *Holy shit*." Jacqueline's eyes popped wide. Josh had been at the ER complaining about something wrong with *his* penis. *Oh shit, oh shit, oh shit...* Was this some sort of epidemic?

"What? What is it now?"

"I'm afraid what's happening to Raymond Gould might not be isolated to him." She explained what Nadine had told her about Josh.

Massermey's eyes bugged out. "You've got to be kidding me." Once more with the hand down his face and beard.

"If someone really did put this Castratus Curse on Raymond Gould and Josh, then we need to find out who did it—or at least *how* they did it."

"Is there..." He shook his head, looking utterly miserable and completely at sea. "Is there a way to reverse it? You know, stop it? Like an antidote? I mean, are these guys' dicks really going to fall off?"

"I don't know the answer to any of that, but I know someone who might."

"Who?"

Jacqueline drew in a breath and decided it wasn't the right time to tell him that Anne Boleyn was wandering around Button Cove and that it was her codex that was missing.

"You wouldn't believe me if I told you. Wait," she said, holding up a hand to stave off the demands that were clearly about to spew forth. "Let me do some, uh, research and find out what I can. In the meantime, I think you should talk to Raymond Gould, and probably Josh as well, and try to find out as much as you can about what they did and whom they talked to in the last twenty-four hours.

"I'm pretty sure you have to actually be in the presence of someone to put a curse on them, but I'm not completely certain.

I'll try to find out, but the point is... If someone cursed them, then I'm pretty sure they'd *have* to have met or encountered them in order to do so. They might not have realized they were being cursed, or when or how, but that's the detective work you're going to have to do, Miles."

"All right," he replied bleakly. "I don't know what else to do."

"You could also...er...find out if anyone else is affected." Jacqueline gave him a humorless smile. "Check with the staff at the emergency room."

"Oh God," was all he said.

"Yeah. Welcome to my world," she replied. She turned away, hurrying back down the corridor. He could let himself out.

## 17

M rs. Danvers was just finishing ringing up a customer when Jacqueline came back into the front room. The housekeeper gave her a curious, almost sympathetic look, but then—probably when she saw that Jacqueline wasn't crying or upset—the normal, severe expression returned to her face.

"I suppose you'll be off doing something else now, won't you," Danvers groused as soon as the customer exited the shop, leaving her and Jacqueline alone. "Leaving me to handle it all."

"But you're ever so capable," Jacqueline replied sweetly, but with an edge. She was not in the mood for anyone's bullshit—Massermey's, Danvers's, or Anne Boleyn's. "Anyhow, I do have to speak with the ZAP Ladies, so you're just going to have to buck up and take care of things here. But I really need to find that codex. The old red book that was taken from under the counter yesterday. Are you *certain* you don't have any idea who might have gone behind the counter and taken it? It's very important."

Danvers looked down her nose at her. "It could have been the woman who knocked over the stack of books."

"What woman who knocked over a stack of books?" Jacqueline said. She was pleased with how calm she managed to sound, because inside she was anything but.

"She knocked over the display right there," Danvers said, pointing to the small rack of poetry collections Jacqueline had arranged on a small table in the front. There was a pretty yellow vase sitting next to it, which appeared intact. "*I* had to attend to it because no one else was here." She gave Jacqueline a little sneer. "I suppose she might have gone behind the counter when my back was turned."

"Ya think?" Jacqueline said from between clenched teeth. "What did she look like? What was she wearing?"

"She was rather...promiscuous looking," replied Danvers. "Nothing like my Rebecca, who *always* looked the lady."

Promiscuous looking in Danvers-speak likely meant the woman was a Bond Girl—dressed in short, tight clothing with lots of cleavage and makeup—assuming that the person about whom she was speaking *was* a character from a book.

"Was she from a book?" Jacqueline asked. If anyone would know, it would be Danvers.

The housekeeper sniffed. "I wouldn't want to say, but it is most likely, ma'am."

"What did she look like? Her coloring, I mean, and her clothing?"

"How am I supposed to remember every person who comes into this shop?"

"You remember, all right. Now tell me. It's very important."

Danvers sniffed again. "Very well. She had light brown skin and dark brown hair. Short hair," she sneered, as if it were a crime. "She spoke as if she were from the Caribbean Islands."

That sounded like Kitty Bushwell. "That's very helpful. Thank you. I'm sorry to leave you alone here, but I do have to go down the street."

Danvers sneered and rolled her eyes, but she said nothing. Jacqueline took that as the closest thing she was going to get to acquiescence. Not that the housekeeper had any choice.

Checking to make certain her phone was in her pocket, Jacqueline was just about to leave the shop when Mrs. Hudson appeared at the top of the stairs.

"I think you ought to come up here, dearie," she said.

Jacqueline hesitated, then sighed and hurried up to the tea room. *Please don't let it be another fire in a singing bowl.* "What is it?"

"It's those two," said Sherlock's landlady in an undertone. Her gaze darted to the Regency-era women still sitting in the corner. "They're quite overset. It's all about Mr. Wickham, you see."

"George Wickham?"

"Why, yes, that's the only Mr. Wickham in the book, isn't it?" Mrs. Hudson gave her an arch look, as if she'd caught her—a librarian and booklover—in a rookie mistake.

Jacqueline could have questioned her further, but it probably would have been a lesson in futility. Neither Danvers nor Hudson were capable of giving a straight answer to anything Jacqueline needed to know.

She went over to the young ladies, both of whom looked as if they were barely eighteen. One of them had very pale blond hair and very pale skin. She was attractive in an ethereal, blow-away-in-the-wind sort of way. The other was also blond, but her hair was more of a honey color, and her cheeks had a healthy pink glow.

"I'm sorry I didn't get to introduce myself earlier," Jacqueline said. "I'm Miss Finch." The title "Ms." wouldn't mean anything to women of the early 1800s. "How are you finding your tea?"

"It's quite lovely, thank you, Miss Finch. Oh, and I'm Miss

Miranda Thewlis," said the ethereal woman. "And this is Miss Winifred Broadley."

"Welcome to my bookshop," said Jacqueline. "Erm...you mentioned you were a bit lost when you arrived here. May I help you find your way to somewhere?"

"Oh, well, we're not quite certain how to find out where—where we are supposed to be. We simply were brought here, you see," said Miss Thewlis. Her blue eyes were so light they nearly disappeared into her pale, pale skin. "We were supposed to, er... I believe we had some other acquaintances with whom we were to meet up."

"That's right," said Miss Broadley. "Why, one moment we were talking about th-things"—she glanced at her companion, ducking a little as if she'd done or said something wrong—"and then, all at once, we were here. It was very...unexpected. This is quite an unusual place."

*I'll say.*

"I daresay none of our acquaintances are *here*, at any rate," said Miss Thewlis, looking about the tea room. "And it is such a lovely place," she added, as if to ensure Jacqueline didn't take offense. "It's quite odd, however, that if we walk too far down the road, we begin to feel rather faint."

"Surely it's because we needed tea and something to eat," said Miss Broadley. "And we are very grateful for your hospitality."

But Jacqueline knew better, for the characters who came out of books couldn't go very far away from their own book. So unless they were carrying it with them, the book was likely still here at Three Tomes, and therefore they would have to remain nearby.

"Mrs. Hudson said that you'd been discussing a—er—particular friend of yours," Jacqueline said. She needed answers quickly, and didn't have time to be subtle. "A Mr. George Wickham? Is that whom you were supposed to meet?"

"*Oh.*" Miss Broadley jolted, her eyes wide and a hand covering her mouth. Her cheeks turned pinker. It was as if the verbalizing of George Wickham's name caused the same consternation as the mention of Voldemort in the Harry Potter books.

"Mr. Wickham is *not* a friend of ours," said Miss Thewlis flatly. Two spots of color flared high on her white cheeks. "And we were *not* to meet *him*."

"No, not at all," said Miss Broadley in a stout voice that was nonetheless not believable, for it shook a little at the end.

"I see."

"He's— Why, he's an absolute *cad*," said Miss Thewlis.

"An utter *snake*," agreed Miss Broadley.

It was not lost on Jacqueline that the Bond Girls had used the exact same nouns to describe James Bond, and the hair at the back of her neck began to prickle. She didn't remember a Miss Broadley or a Miss Thewlis from *Pride and Prejudice*...just as she hadn't remembered a Puddin' Snatch or Misty Mountain from any of the Bond books or movies.

Were these two women unnamed, off-page characters as well? If so, that explained the cluster of *other* Regency-era women hanging around with Anne. Were all of them casualties of George Wickham?

"Why, Mr. Wickham nearly *ruined* that young Bennet girl," said Miss Broadley in a low voice. She glanced around as if someone might overhear, but she clearly wanted Jacqueline to have the details. "It was only Miss Darcy's brother who helped fix it all. Still, he's an absolute *scoundrel* of the first order."

"And what about you?" asked Jacqueline, looking at both of the young women. "Did he try to—er—compromise either of you?"

Suddenly Miss Thewlis burst into tears, and Miss Broadley shoved a handkerchief at her. Miss Broadley's own eyes had filled with tears as well.

"How did you know?" she said in a low, muffled voice. "He-he-he's just an *awful, awful man*," she said, extracting another handkerchief from the little pouch that hung from a cord around her wrist. "He deserves *everything* that's going to happen to him."

"What's going to happen to him?" Jacqueline asked. "Is he *here*?"

"I-I don't know," said Miss Broadley. "But I hope s-so. That's why we're here, you see. Isn't that so, Miranda? He-he almost ruined both of us."

"Is there someone who's...rather...in charge of this plan?" Jacqueline found herself slipping into a bit of British speak.

"Oh," said Miss Thewlis. The two young women looked at each other. "Well, perhaps. I mean to say, if there *is* a plan, it would be Miss Carleton in charge, I daresay."

"Yes, Miss Carleton. Miss June Carleton—and we were meant to find her, but we've just been...lost," said Miss Broadley.

"Well, now, ladies, I'm certain she'll show up soon," Jacqueline replied. "Perhaps you ought to just sit here and rest. If you go wandering off, how will Miss Carleton find you? Surely she'll look here when she realizes you are missing."

"Why, that's an excellent thought," said Miss Broadley, obviously relieved. "We'll just sit here and wait."

"And...if you happen to see Mr. Wickham," Jacqueline said, "perhaps you could tell Mrs. Hudson. You needn't speak to him, you know. Just tell her."

"Oh, yes, thank you, Miss Finch," said Miss Thewlis. The flush of high color had receded from her cheeks. "That is a most excellent idea. Neither of us *ever* wish to see or speak to him again."

"Of course not. Well, I must be off, but I'll return as soon as I'm able," Jacqueline said. She left the two women and, on her way out of the tea room, paused to tell Mrs. Hudson to keep them fed and plied with tea, and to let her know if George Wickham showed up.

Now she needed to find Anne Boleyn and Kitty Bushwell and get some answers...and a curse antidote.

❧

JACQUELINE DIDN'T BOTHER to knock on the front door. Instead, she hurried around the back of the ZAP Ladies' house to the garden...and stumbled to a halt.

*Damn. Damn. Damn.*

The garden was empty of Bond Girls, Jane Austen characters, and Queens of England.

She whirled and fairly ran to the front door of the house, pounding up onto the porch. Before she had the chance to knock, the door swung open.

Zwyla stood there, looming in the doorway. "Jacqueline. What's wrong?" She stepped back and let her enter.

"Is—I mean are—Anne Boleyn and a bunch of women from books here?" Jacqueline was panting a little. "I left them in your garden, and now they're gone."

"No, I'm sorry, it's just us chickens," said Zwyla.

Normally such a light and absurd comment from the regal and serious Zwyla would prompt a smile from Jacqueline, but not this time.

"We are so effed," Jacqueline said, just as the curtain to the back rooms fluttered.

"Why, Jacqueline. Come on back here," said Pietra, peeking around the doorway. "Andromeda is mixing some herbal teas, and I've got a nice summer soup on the fire. You can tell us all about what's going on. You look like you've seen a ghost."

"Not a ghost, but a bunch of women who seem to be hellbent on getting revenge on James Bond and George Wickham, and—and some other men here in Button Cove."

Jacqueline followed Pietra through the doorway with Zwyla on her heels. The curtain fluttered back into place behind them.

This room, which Jacqueline suspected was purposely hidden from most visitors, was a lovely little herbary. It reminded her of the cottage where Brother Cadfael worked with his spices and plants and herbs, except that it boasted much more modern conveniences: running water, electric lights, a gas stove. There was, however, a large fireplace that always seemed to be filled with a crackling fire. Today a small black cauldron hung over the flames, and the smells wafting from it were testament to Pietra's adroitness in the kitchen. The soup's aroma made Jacqueline's mouth water. To top it off, on a counter next to the fireplace was a fresh loaf of round bread.

Throughout the herbary, there were shelves lined with everything from beakers to test tubes to crocks to bowls to vials. Herbs hung in bunches from the ceiling and over the long, scarred wooden worktable that always seemed to have the exact number of chairs needed—at the moment, four. Battered, ancient books lined a shelf; knives, scalpels, athames, forks, whisks, sieves, scissors, spoons, and countless other tools hung from hooks or sat in utensil jars for easy access.

Andromeda sat on one side of the table. She had half a dozen bowls containing dried herbs and berries lined up in front of her, and a large mixing bowl next to her. She was obviously measuring and mixing, and then spooning batches into small linen bags that were piled on the table.

"Did any of you see the women in the back garden?" Jacqueline said, plumping herself down onto one of the chairs across from Andi. She explained briefly.

"I'm sorry, but we didn't see anyone. We only just returned from some errands," Zwyla said. "But we—and you—really can't control what they do, you know."

"It's a lesson in futility," said Pietra gravely. "I mean, if we could, Z here would tell Paul Bunyan that she doesn't need a gutted deer or an entire rosebush every time he comes to visit." Her soberness cracked as six dimples danced near her lips.

Jacqueline's brows rose, and she looked at Zwyla, whose cheeks had flushed a little darker. She knew, although she'd never witnessed it, that Paul Bunyan had a serious crush on the elegant crone. She could only imagine Zwyla's reaction to finding a dead deer, prepped for cooking, sprawled on her threshold.

"That's neither here nor there, Pietra," Zwyla said briskly. "Jacqueline, tell us everything new that's happened."

And so Jacqueline did. She started with the apparent Castratus Curse on Raymond Gould, and then mentioned that it had also quite possibly been placed on Josh as well. "I don't know if Anne Boleyn did it last night when she locked him in the stocks at the Ren Faire or not, but I'm going to find out...if I ever find her."

The three crones nodded in agreement, and Jacqueline went on, sharing her biggest worry. "So, doesn't a person have to be present to be cursed? Please tell me that's the case, or we're never going to figure this out. But even more importantly, please tell me there's a way to reverse the curse." She knew she sounded desperate, and also that trying to stop the curse was quite possibly another lesson in futility, but she had to try.

The crones exchanged glances, and the last bit of ease and levity drained from their expressions. That didn't make Jacqueline feel any better.

"It's rare, and it takes immense skill to inflict a curse on someone without being present, but it could happen," Zwyla told her. "Still, as I said, it's rare, so we should work with the assumption that the two men who have been inflicted had to have at least been in the presence of their curser recently. But the good news is, if there's a curse, there must be an antidote. It's the Rule of Balance. Just as evil must be balanced by good. You can't have one without the other."

Jacqueline exhaled a breath. "Well, that is good news. And we do know that Anne Boleyn was with Josh last night, so it seems obvious that she did it. But I don't have any idea *why* she would curse Josh—a random guy.

"And then there's the whole Kitty Bushwell complication— Oh, you don't know about her and the other Bond Girls." She quickly explained the off-page characters who seemed to have erupted in droves from Ian Fleming novels and *Pride and Prejudice*. "And so since *Live and Let Die* is the only book with anything like witchcraft in it—it has voodoo for the backdrop— and with that in mind, it seems fairly logical that Kitty Bushwell was the one who summoned Anne Boleyn and her codex. So maybe *she* is putting the curse on people and not Anne? Or maybe they're working together?"

"Voodoo is a religion," said Zwyla in an annoyed voice. "It's *not* magic; that's a completely false narrative that has been promoted for centuries. Voodoo is a religion that was brought to this hemisphere by the Africans who were kidnapped and shipped here as slaves. Voodoo is *not* witchcraft, and, to be precise, what is often termed voodoo in Jamaica is really called Obeah. And in Haiti, it's Vudou. The touristy thing popular in New Orleans that's called voodoo is just that—a bastardization of the religion to be a touristy thing. The true religion is something far different."

"Yes, yes, I do know that," Jacqueline hastened to say. Her stomach had dropped sharply at the older woman's expression. Zwyla did not look pleased. "I really do know all of that. I didn't mean to imply otherwise. It's just that the book was written in the fifties...and by a white man. And so it's not surprising that misinformation and a false narrative runs rampant in it, and therefore, I thought it would likely also be present in the characters. I'm sorry." She curled her fingers tightly in her lap. She hated disappointing any of the crones, but especially the calm and serious Zwyla.

Zwyla nodded, her expression still a little forbidding. "Yes. I understand. And I agree with your conclusion. You're probably right that Fleming borrowed from common misperceptions about voodooism to create his characters and the book's environment." She gave a little huff, then the tension in her expression eased. "All right, then, now that that's cleared up, let's talk about what we know and figure out how to stop it."

"It seems that either Anne Boleyn or Kitty Bushwell—or both—were with Josh and could have cursed him. But how and why? And when were they with Raymond Gould? Surely someone would have noticed Anne Boleyn prancing down the street in that getup she's wearing," mused Pietra.

"We're going to have to find them and ask them why," Jacqueline said. "And your point is well taken—it should be easy to find Anne, since she's dressed like she is. Anyhow, would the antidote to the curse be *in* the codex, do you think? I couldn't read the text; I only saw the drawings, so I don't know whether there's a recipe for the counter-curse or whatever you call it."

"It might be there," Andromeda said, looking up from her work. "Having the information about the actual curse would be helpful too, for often one can determine the antidote or counter by looking at the recipe itself."

"It seems that Kitty Bushwell took the codex. At least, that's what Danvers thinks. So maybe she's the one doing the cursing and not Anne. We really need to find her—them. All of them. And...I'm still confused about how they—or she—found Raymond and put the curse on *him*. Is he just a random casualty, like Josh? Or is there some reason they picked those two?"

"And are we expecting James Bond and George Wickham to show up here in order to be cursed as well?" said Pietra. She set a small bowl of clear, pale soup in front of Jacqueline along with a hunk of fresh bread. Bits of green—parsley, chive, green onion, maybe tarragon—floated in the broth, along with paper-thin slices of carrot. "Here, dear. Eat something. I bet you haven't sat down all day. And after the night you had..." She quirked a knowing brow.

Jacqueline shook her head, fought off the blush, and sipped the soup. It tasted so bright and fresh, she practically felt the energy surging through her. "This is wonderful. Thank you, Petey. As to your question about George Wickham and James Bond showing up... From what Miss Broadley and Miss Thewlis told me, the possibility is very likely." She had to explain who Miss Broadley and Miss Thewlis were, which she did in between sips of soup.

"So if they somehow manage to get James and George here —or have already done so," Andromeda said thoughtfully, "they're definitely going to inflict them with the Castratus Curse. But would that even *work*? They are, after all, literary characters who have stories in which they participate and books which they come out from. *Can* they be cursed? Injured? Killed? Outside of their books, I mean. And if they are...what does that mean for their stories?"

The four of them looked at each other, then, as one, they all shrugged.

"Only the Universe knows," said Pietra, her eyes glittering

with delight. Apparently, unlike Jacqueline, Petey loved the idea of not knowing the rules.

"Well, even beside that point—and, honestly, does anyone really care whether George Wickham loses his dick?—there are two men in Button Cove who seem to be on their way to losing theirs. At the very least, we have to figure out how to stop it, if we can," Jacqueline said.

"Does Massermey know?" asked Zwyla.

"Oh, he knows," Jacqueline said grimly. "He's the one who told me about it. *Questioned* me."

"He didn't think *you* did it— Oh, that *man*," said Andromeda in disgust. "Did he really?"

"I made it very clear to him that neither I nor any of you are responsible," Jacqueline told them. "I think he believed me. Anyhow, I don't know what to do next."

"I think we need to locate this Kitty Bushwell and her cronies. If not, then we definitely need the codex if we want any chance of reversing the curse," said Zwyla.

"Don't any of you have any, er, skills that might help us locate the codex?" asked Jacqueline hopefully.

"Like a crystal ball?" Pietra said, and began to giggle. If she didn't look so cute with all six of her dimples dancing and her eyes light with humor, Jacqueline would have been really annoyed. "No, none of us have anything like that."

Jacqueline sighed. "Right. I didn't think it would be that easy." She stood. "I guess I'll go back to the shop. Maybe someone will show up there looking for Miss Broadley and Miss Thewlis—or maybe George and James will appear. And I should probably bring Egala up to date. The more heads thinking about this, the better— *Wait*. I just had a crazy idea."

She started to tell them, then stopped herself. Better to try it out first. "I'm going back to the shop to check on something. I might be able to find the codex."

"Let us know, dear," said Andromeda, unconcernedly going back to her tea mixing. "I'm sure everything will work out. And if George Wickham loses his Johnson, well..." She shrugged and flashed Jacqueline a grin. "There are worse things that could happen."

Jacqueline gave a little wave as she hurried off.

*It can't be as easy as that, can it?* she thought as she half jogged down the street back to the bookshop.

Egala had given her a gorgeous leather tote imbued with a charm that made whatever a person said they needed show up right there at the top of the bag. A woman had been talking about stabbing someone with a fork—jokingly—while in Jacqueline's store once, and when she reached into a similarly charmed Egala purse, she pulled out a fork. And Jacqueline had found what she needed inside her tote (and had never put there) when she was fighting off the vampires. Or trying to, anyway.

So *maybe* if she got the tote and said she needed the codex, it would be right there!

It was worth a try, anyway.

Jacqueline burst into the shop and nearly ran into Massermey, who was just leaving.

"Oh, hello, Detective," she said. "Is there any news?"

"A little," he said, giving her a sharp look. "Detective?" he muttered.

She shrugged. "You're working in your official capacity at the moment, aren't you, Detective?" She was not about to let him completely off the hook quite yet. "Is there anything you can tell me?"

"Nothing that sticks out. Both men went about their days normally. Neither of them saw anyone who looked as if they were putting a curse or hex on them. Of course, Josh Wenczel was locked in the stocks by a woman dressed as Anne Boleyn or some other queen last night, so that was out of the ordinary, but I don't see how it could be related to a curse."

Jaqueline kept her mouth shut, but of course it seemed logical that Anne had had something to do with cursing Josh. Although why lock him in the stocks if she was going to make his dick fall off? Wasn't that enough? Had Anne locked him in and Kitty then cursed him?

"Another interesting thing is when Raymond Gould was leaving for work early this morning. As he was pulling down the driveway, he saw a woman standing there, blowing bubbles. He rolled down his car window to talk to her, and she seemed very pleased to see him. She called him James."

Jacqueline's eyes widened. "She called him *James*?"

"That's what he said. She acted like she knew him, but he said he'd never seen her before in his life. She seemed annoyed, but he didn't really think anything of it, even when she blew a bubble in his face." Massermey leaned a little closer, dropping his voice. "Is that how you put a curse on someone? Breathing on them? Snapping bubblegum bubbles in their face?"

Jacqueline shook her head. "I haven't the faintest idea, Detective. I have never put a curse on anyone, nor have I investigated how to do so. But I'll consult with some other, more educated, people and get back to you on that."

He heaved a sigh. "Jacqueline."

"I can't really talk about this right now," she told him firmly, although the soft-J was back when he said her name, and that made her want to soften a little. "I'm trying to find a codex so we can reverse this thing. Is, uh, anyone else complaining of similar symptoms?"

"No. Not so far. I've advised the staff at the emergency room and urgent care centers in the area to notify us immediately if anyone does. What now?"

"I'll get back to you on that," Jacqueline said, and, giving him a little wave, hurried off down the corridor to the back of the shop.

She dashed up two flights of stairs without hesitation, noting with satisfaction that it was a lot easier to do so than it had been when she first took over the shop. Inside her apartment, she snatched up the leather tote bag from Egala, closed her eyes, and said, "I need the codex."

## 18

Jacqueline opened her eyes and looked inside the tote.

There were lots of things in there—her wallet, lipstick, paper napkins, pens, markers, a compact, a book weight for holding pages open, hand lotion, and more...but no old, red, leather-bound codex.

"Damn," she said, and set the tote down on the coffee table. She glanced into the kitchen and considered whether she wanted to chance a cup of coffee and all of its caffeine this late in the day, and decided against it. She'd just have to run on good old adrenalin.

She was just about to head back out of her apartment when she heard a sound coming from behind the kitchen. In the tiny hall, where the pantry and elevator were.

It sounded like someone calling out.

Mystified, Jacqueline investigated. The sound—a low, moaning call—was coming from the elevator.

She pushed the button to open the doors. When they slid open, she was greeted with a most unusual and awful sight.

It took her a moment to realize what she was seeing: Anne Boleyn, tumbled onto the floor of the elevator. Her head was jammed into a corner of the small space, and her broad, heavy, and stiff skirts had fairly wedged her into place. She'd been unable to pull herself upright. Who knew how long she'd been there!

"Madam!" Jacqueline said in horror, even as she choked back a giggle. It was quite the amusing sight, and it was terribly difficult not to laugh.

"Get me out of here!" cried the queen in a hoarse voice. She'd forgotten the royal we again, and Jacqueline could certainly understand why. Anne helplessly moved her arms and legs, looking very much like an upside-down tortoise in ungainly but magnificently decorated Tudor clothing.

"Of course." Jacqueline was already maneuvering her way into the elevator. It was easier said than done, for the gown basically took up the entire space. There was almost nowhere for her to stand that wasn't on Anne's skirts, and she needed to reach the woman's hands in order to help her up. She caught hold of one of them, but couldn't quite reach the other, and there was nowhere for her to stand for leverage. "I might need to get assistance," she said, stifling another giggle.

"Make haste, you fool!" cried the queen, and Jacqueline did not take offense. She'd probably be just as angry and upset if she were in the same position.

"I'll be right back," she said, and hurried away back through the living room and down the hall to the rear staircase and to the tea room. "Mrs. Hudson, I need your help," she said. When the woman gave her a suspicious and irritated look, Jacqueline added in a low voice, "It's Her Majesty. She's—uh—trapped."

"Oh!" Mrs. Hudson nearly dropped the teapot she was drying. "Oh my goodness. What has happened to her?"

Jacqueline didn't take the time to explain; she merely gestured for Sherlock's landlady to follow her. To her surprise, despite Mrs. Hudson's motherly bulk and age, she kept on her heels as she hurried back up to the apartment. Jacqueline had considered, then rejected, the idea of sending the elevator to the second floor and having Mrs. Hudson assist her there—that would be far too mortifying for the queen if someone saw her.

"My stars!" cried Mrs. Hudson when she saw the situation. "Your Majesty! Good heavens! What has happened?" She stood there, wringing her hands and dithering, all the while curtsying multiple times as Anne writhed ineffectually on the floor, shouting desperate commands.

Jacqueline stepped in and gave Mrs. Hudson terse directions, and together they managed to get the queen onto her feet and out of the elevator. The woman's face was beet red from her struggles and fury, and her light brown hair had fallen loose from the confines of its hood, which sagged to one side. The beaded and bejeweled headdress she wore had slipped to the back of her head, and every part of her clothing—ruffles, lace, bodice, sleeves—was twisted and off-kilter.

As soon as she was upright, Anne angrily shook off their grip and marched—albeit a bit unsteadily—away from the elevator and to the blue velvet sofa in Jacqueline's living room.

She sank regally onto the couch and glared at them. "We shall have the woman imprisoned," she said furiously. "Findest that hellwife. Bring her to us. Thou shall throw her into a cell!"

"Now, now, Your Majesty," said Mrs. Hudson, giving a deep and proper curtsy this time. "I'll get you a nice cup of tea, won't I, and some biscuits too, there we are." She glanced at Jacqueline, who nodded in agreement, then hurried back to the elevator to take it to the tea room.

"Where is she?" demanded Anne. "That woman who put us in there? Who *imprisoned* us?"

"I don't know. Who was it?" asked Jacqueline. "Who did such a thing to you?"

"'Twas Lady Kitty," snapped Anne, her bloodshot eyes

narrow with fury. "I'll—*we'll*—have that hellwife beheaded! How *dare* she put her hands on us?"

"Kitty Bushwell—the woman who was with you last night when you put the man in the stocks?" Jacqueline said.

"Aye, 'twas her, it was." Anne looked as if she were about to cry, and Jacqueline couldn't blame her. Even though the sight had been amusing, the situation was horrifying. "She pushed us into the magic room."

"Why did she do such a thing?"

"She insisted we go back from whence we come, and verily, we would *not* go to have our head removed from our neck! Nay! 'Tis far nicer here, and the magic is quite powerful."

*Oh shit.* "Well, we'll talk about the, uh, going back later," Jacqueline said. What would happen if Anne Boleyn didn't return to her history book? Would she cease to exist?

Jacqueline knew from previous experience that if a literary character didn't return to their book regularly (or ever), they and their story disappeared from the collective consciousness. It had almost happened when Cinderella refused to return to her Grimm fairy tale because she had no interest in marrying the prince.

But what would happen to a real person of history? Surely they wouldn't disappear from history, since there was ample evidence of their actual existence...

But then again, Jacqueline didn't make the rules, nor did she even begin to understand them. One thing she did know: *she* did not want Anne Boleyn hanging around her bookshop for the foreseeable future. Or ever.

"Why did Kitty want you to go back?" she asked.

Anne's expression was dark with fury. "The woman hath taken all that she wanted from us."

"What did she want?"

"The spell book," Anne replied, then looked around worriedly. She lowered her voice further. "And our knowledge."

"It's no worry, madam, no one can hear you," Jacqueline told her.

"She tricked us," Anne added in a louder voice. "And now she means to..." She clamped her lips closed.

"What is she going to do?"

"We are not aware," replied Anne, "of the perfidy they intend to inflict."

"They?"

But Anne clammed up. Jacqueline squelched her frustration and stood. She wanted to get the ZAP Ladies here as soon as possible to talk to Anne. Without the codex, they couldn't study the curse. But the queen would surely have the knowledge about a counter-curse, and if anyone could get her to talk, it would be Zwyla. Anne might even be compelled to tell them what Kitty Bushwell and the others had planned.

"I do hope you'll stay in this chamber now," Jacqueline told her. "And not leave."

"Mayhaps." Anne lifted her chin stubbornly.

Jacqueline shrugged. "It doesn't matter to me whether you go back into your book and get your head chopped off...but you'll certainly be safer if you remain in this chamber."

Anne glared at her but remained silent.

"Very well. I have one more question for you. Which of you cursed the man in the stocks last night? You or Kitty? And *why*?"

But Anne remained silent, with her lips pursed tightly and that stubborn chin thrust forward.

Just then, Mrs. Hudson arrived with the promised tea tray. Jacqueline took the opportunity to escape. She looked at the time and saw it was already nearly five o'clock—closing time on a Sunday, even in the summer. She'd be free to work on this problem without distractions.

Again she was reminded that she had no way to contact the ZAP Ladies other than walking down to their house or hope that they would show up at the shop. That was going to have to change, she thought, seriously annoyed, as she bounded down the steps to the tea room. She was going to interrogate Misses Thewlis and Broadley again and try to get more information from them.

Just then, her phone chimed with a text. She pulled it out and saw a message from Massermey.

*The shriveling is getting seriously worse. Do you have any news? Something's going to fall off soon.*

Jacqueline sighed and looked out the window and down the street at the blue Victorian, willing the ZAP Ladies to get their butts down here and help.

She responded: *Working on it. Any other victims?*

*Not so far,* he said.

Well, there was that, at least.

Jacqueline was torn between going over to talk to the Jane Austen characters and running down the street to collect the ZAP Ladies when she heard the trio come in through the shop's front door. It was unmistakably Pietra, Andromeda, and Zwyla —they clattered, chattered, rattled—and for once, Jacqueline was elated by their arrival.

She ran down the stairs, noted that there weren't any customers hanging about, and quickly explained what had happened with Anne—and that she hadn't found the codex.

"She was trapped in the elevator?" Pietra's eyes danced with humor.

"She'd fallen and couldn't get up?" added a snickering Andromeda, quoting an old television ad.

"Like an upside-down tortoise," Jacqueline told them, managing to keep a straight face. "Completely helpless. I have no idea how long she'd been there, but don't you think she can tell you about a counter-curse? She hasn't been very forth-coming with me, but surely she knows."

"We'll get the information out of her," said Zwyla grimly. "You try to find out what the hell is going on and whether there's going to be anyone else cursed."

"Massermey just told me the, uh, shriveling is getting much worse and something might be falling off soon," Jacqueline said. "Work fast."

"You ought to have him bring the two of them here," Andromeda said. "I might be able to stay or slow the progress while we figure out what's going on."

"Okay, great. I'll tell him." Jacqueline whipped off a text to Massermey with the information and then, not waiting for a reply, fired off another text to the thread she shared with Nadine and Suzette. It was Sunday night, their normal pizza night at Nadine's, but Jacqueline knew she wasn't going to be able to make it.

The ZAP Ladies had disappeared, presumably to go up to the apartment and speak with Anne, and it was just about time to close the shop. Mrs. Danvers wasn't around, and Jacqueline tiptoed to the front door to turn the sign to CLOSED.

But just then, a pair of women came into view from down the sidewalk and headed right toward the bookshop door. Jacqueline recognized the one in the lead as Jessie Gould, and her companion as one of the others who'd been requesting hexes on their exes.

Jacqueline stepped back so they could enter. "Hello, ladies. We're closing in ten minutes, but feel free to come on in and look around."

She didn't have the chance to wonder whether Jessie was aware her husband had been cursed, for the woman gave her an elated smile. She surged toward Jacqueline as if she was about to hug her, but Jacqueline evaded the move, and instead Jessie caught her by the arms.

"You're absolutely amazing," Jessie said in a low voice. Her eyes were bright and danced with pleasure. "Thank you for sending that woman—or whoever she was—to help me! The hex is *perfect*, and Ray is completely freaked out. Tell me, will it last for a while?"

"And can you please do mine too?" said her companion. Jacqueline recognized her as the one who'd bragged about booty calls with her ex down in Wicks Hollow, but still wanted to put a hex on him. "I've got a clipping of his hair. Does it matter what part of his body it came from?"

Jacqueline ignored the booty-call woman's question and focused on Jessie. "I didn't send anyone to you. It wasn't me. And I am afraid what your husband is experiencing isn't just a little revenge or humiliation hex. It's a very serious curse."

"Well, it serves him right. Wait—you didn't tell that woman to help me?" Jessie looked closely at Jacqueline. "But she came up to me on the street and said she could help. I just assumed you'd told her about me."

"I didn't tell anyone," Jacqueline said firmly. "What exactly happened when she came up to you on the street?"

Jessie frowned then shrugged. "I don't know why it matters. She did what I asked, and now Ray is being taught a serious lesson. He deserves everything he gets." She cackled happily.

"This is more complicated than you think," Jacqueline said sharply. "It could be a matter of life and death and not just a little inconvenient, humiliating hex. I really need to know what happened. I don't want anyone else around your husband to get hurt."

"What do you mean, around him? Get hurt? It's just a little hex on his dick—how can it hurt anyone else except Fergie

Valentine? *I'm* sure as hell not getting near it anymore." Jessie was skeptical, but Jacqueline saw the concern in her eyes.

"Like I said, it's not just a little hex. It's a serious curse, and curses can sometimes extend into the family and then go on for generations." Jacqueline had no reason to believe this was the case with the Castratus Curse, but she wasn't above exaggerating in order to get Jessie's cooperation.

"The family? Like my *sons*? What have you done?" Jessie's expression turned to shock.

"I told you, *I* didn't do anything. But I'm trying to stop whatever is happening. Please tell me how you met up with this woman, and maybe we—my friends and I"—Jacqueline nodded at Suzette and Nadine, who'd just slipped in through the bookshop's door, yay!—"can fix things."

Jessie swallowed hard and, after a moment, nodded. "All right, fine. I definitely don't want anything to happen to Travis and Joey—my sons. I...uh, I was coming back to see you yesterday, late. It took me a while, but I got a fingernail clipping from Ray and wanted to bring it to you for the hex. You said you needed it in order to do the spell." She frowned. "But now that I think about it, I didn't actually give it to the woman, either. I think I still have it. How did she put a hex on Ray without having something personal of his?" She fixed a suspicious look on Jacqueline.

"I told you—it's not a hex. It's a curse, and they're very different from hexes. They're far more serious and they work differently. They're longer-lasting, sometimes permanent, and they can spread through families," Jacqueline added as a pointed reminder, uncaring whether it was technically true or not. "How did the woman—did you get her name?—know that you wanted a hex on your husband?"

"I'm not sure." Jessie looked confused. "I really don't know. I got to the bookshop and it was closed, and Suki was here with me—" She glanced at Booty Call.

"I think she must have overheard us talking," said Suki. "We were standing on the street, and Jessie wasn't happy that the bookshop was closed and she was, you know, saying a few things. Kind of upset? And this woman just came up and said, 'You want to get back at your ex? I can help with that.' I guess we just assumed you'd sent her."

"Well, I didn't. And I want to make that perfectly clear," Jacqueline said flatly. "So what happened then? Did you take her to your husband?"

"No, I didn't do that. I didn't want to be around when it happened. But I did show her his picture and told her where she could find him. Of course he's got his mug plastered all over every ad for Gould Motors in the entire cove. All I had to do was show her a picture of his recent billboard." She rolled her eyes. "It was weird, though, when I showed her what he looked like. She kind of freaked out and called him James. I told her his name was Ray, but she didn't seem to care."

"Yeah, that was when she got kind of mean," Suki said. "Almost as if it was *her* husband she was going to hex. She was really worked up. Maybe she knew him from before, Jess?"

"Or maybe he *reminded* her of someone she knew," Jacqueline said drily. It had happened recently that a character from a book had "recognized" a person from real life as looking exactly like someone from their book. Very surreal, and very confusing for the person who resembled the character. And as to whether they actually *were* the character in question was a mystery. "We definitely need to find this woman and get her to reverse that curse before it gets more serious. What did she look like? How was she dressed? Was she with anyone else?"

Jacqueline was aware that Nadine and Suzette were standing

there listening to everything. She had confidence they'd catch up with what was going on; her friends were hella smart.

Suki and Jessie's ensuing description of the woman was obviously of Kitty Bushwell, and according to them, she had two other women with her. One of them was attired "normally, though kind of dressy," as Suki put it, and the other was outfitted "like she was in *Persuasion* or something."

"All right, thanks. Have you seen them since?" Jacqueline asked.

"No, I don't think so," Jessie said. "But I haven't even been over on this side of town."

Jacqueline suppressed a sigh. How could it be that difficult to find a group of women dressed like Jane Austen acolytes? "All right. Thank you. If you see them, can you please text me right away?" She gave both of them her number then flipped the OPEN sign on the shop door to CLOSED. "I'll keep you posted," she said, opening the door in a firm indication that it was time for them to leave. She also wanted them gone before Massermey arrived with Raymond Gould and Josh; she wasn't certain what would happen between the two Goulds if they encountered each other.

"Oh, wait, I just thought of something," said Suki, pausing on the threshold. "I think one of the women said something about 'couldn't it wait until tomorrow when we do it?' when the leader—Kitty, I think was her name—said she'd help Jessie."

Jacqueline paused in the act of closing the door. "She said something about *tomorrow*?"

"Yes. I got the impression there's something happening tomorrow," Suki said. "I don't know what, though."

"Did she say anything else that might help us figure out what they have planned?"

"I think she was talking about the Memorial Day parade,"

Jessie said. "I got the impression they were going to be in the parade, or come to the parade, and that's what she meant."

"The parade," Jacqueline mused. "All right, thank you for that information. Please contact me if you think of anything else at all, or if you see any of those women."

"Are you sure this is a curse and not just a little hex?" asked Jessie, her fingers curled around the edge of the door so Jacqueline couldn't close it. "And that you have to stop it? Ray really deserves the worst, you know."

"But Travis and Joey don't," Jacqueline said briskly. "We have to reverse it to save them—and everyone else—but I will bet your husband's learned his lesson anyway." That seemed to satisfy Jessie, and she relinquished the door so Jacqueline could finally close and lock it.

She turned to Nadine and Suzette, about to fill in whatever details they needed, when she saw Mrs. Danvers coming from the back of the shop. Behind her was Massermey, Josh, and a third man who was presumably Raymond Gould.

Jacqueline was still feeling a little frosty toward Massermey, so she just gave him a little wave and said, "Andromeda is up in my flat. Go on up." Then she turned back to Nadine and Suzette.

"All right, what's up?" Nadine demanded, tugging Jacqueline away and toward the front of the shop.

"Well, you heard most of it, but it seems like Kitty Bushwell—"

"No, no, I mean with you and Massermey!"

"Yeah, that was a pretty cold greeting you gave him," Suzette said in her low, dry voice. "After all, didn't you just screw each other's brains out last night?"

Jacqueline's face went dark, hot red. "Suzette!" she hissed.

"Well, that's basically what you told me," Nadine replied. "And I, of course, told Suze."

"Of course you did." Jacqueline rolled her eyes, then gave a very high-level and brief explanation of why she was feeling salty toward Massermey.

"The poor guy." Nadine, as usual, had a soft spot for the detective. "He probably doesn't know which end is up. He doesn't want to believe in the witchery stuff, but he's seeing evidence of it and so now is worried that you're way more powerful than he ever imagined."

"Not to mention him wondering if you could put that sort of curse on *him* if he pisses you off enough," Suzette added.

"Okay, whatever. My love life is not at issue here," Jacqueline said, still in that low voice. "Let's focus on the real problems. We've got a castration curse happening, a bunch of random characters running around Button Cove, and it really seems like they've got something planned for tomorrow." She glanced at the ceiling. "I was just going to go up there and talk to two of the women from *Pride and Prejudice.* Maybe I can get more information out of them."

"On it," said Nadine, already starting for the stairs.

When Jacqueline got to the top of the steps, she discovered that not only were Miss Thewlis and Miss Broadley sitting in the tea room, but they had been joined by several other women—all dressed either in Regency-era garb or mid-last-century sexpot fashion.

Their low buzz of conversation faded when Jacqueline and her friends came into view.

"Well, well, well," Jacqueline said, feeling a cross between relief and shock. "I'm very glad to see that you're all here. Now, I need to know what's going on."

## 19

J acqueline looked around at the group of women. There were at least two dozen of them, and, she assumed, each of them had been a casualty of either George Wickham or James Bond.

But so far there hadn't been a sign of either caddish literary character (even though it seemed that Ray Gould resembled the spy), so what on earth were they doing here?

That was when Jacqueline realized she didn't see Kitty Bushwell. "Where's Kitty?" she asked.

One of them—she thought it was Gloria S. Mount—shrugged. "We don't know. She left us here."

"She's the one in charge," said Puddin' Snatch.

"Who are all these people?" muttered Nadine, reminding Jacqueline that she hadn't told them about the Bond Girls and the group of women from *Pride and Prejudice*.

"These ladies," said Jacqueline grandly, "are either casualties of George Wickham or cast-off lovers of James Bond from a number of different books. Ladies, if you could introduce yourselves to my friends here?"

Jacqueline didn't catch all the names of the Jane Austen types—they were all Miss something or other (and some with hyphenations, all sounding very stuffy and British)—although she noted which one was Miss Carleton because Miss Thewlis had named her as the ringleader, at least from their world.

Nadine and Suzette listened silently with bugged-out eyes and struggling poker faces as the Bond Girls stoically introduced themselves.

"Puddin' Snatch."

"Gloria S. Mount.

"Precious Parts."

"Sweetie Comfort."

"Heidi Whole."

"Hoochie Cooter."

"Corky Pop."

"Lola Areola."

"Muffy Luscious."

"Labeea Luscious."

"Martina Meetoo."

"Misty Mountains."

"Oh my God," Suzette said under her breath.

"Those poor things," Nadine muttered.

"They're off-page lovers of Double-Oh-Seven," Jacqueline told them. "Not named in the books, but there nevertheless. Loved and left, wronged by their man, et cetera, et cetera."

"Wow," said Nadine.

"So, what are you all doing here? Is this some sort of broken hearts club?" Suzette, never one to mince words, said.

"*Broken hearts?* Hell no," said one of the Bond Girls. "We're not broken. We're *angry*."

"And we're here for revenge," said Miss Carleton.

"Revenge on exactly who?" Nadine said.

"Whom," Jacqueline muttered, causing her friend to give her a death glare. Jacqueline winked and sent her an air kiss.

"Why, on Mr. Wickham, of course," said Miss Carleton, who clearly *was* the leader of the Jane Austenites.

"And James Bond," said Heidi Whole. "*Especially* James Bond."

"Are they here? Bond and Wickham?" asked Jacqueline.

There was a sort of collective shrug that went around the group of women, and they looked at each other.

"They're supposed to be here, I believe," said Miss Carleton. "By tomorrow, when we're going to—" But she was quickly and vehemently shushed by Misty Mountains.

"What is happening tomorrow?" Jacqueline demanded.

No one answered.

She put on her best firm, prim, judgy librarian look and said, "Look, I know about the curse. I'm guessing you're planning to put the curse on Wickham and Bond sometime tomorrow—and I'm also guessing you know *exactly* what it's supposed to do to them. But what you might not know is that there have already been two innocent—well, relatively innocent...well, not at *all* innocent, but also not Bond or Wickham—men who have been cursed."

The women looked around at each other with expressions in varying degrees of smugness, surprise, confusion, and determination. But none of them said anything.

"This curse has been inflicted on two men who haven't done anything to you," Jacqueline said, driving home the point. "And we need to reverse it—"

"Perhaps they've done nothing to *us*, but they're not at all innocent of being cads," Miss Carleton said, lifting a prim nose. "The curse only works on men who've been untrue or were otherwise awful to their wives or beaux. Thus, if the curse has taken effect, they clearly deserved it. Anyone who deserves it would be afflicted."

Jacqueline blinked. Was that true? Was the curse only effective on someone who'd been a dick (to put it in modern terms, not understated Regency-era terms) to their girlfriend, wife, fiancée, et cetera?

"It's still not right," Jacqueline said, albeit a little weakly. She wasn't certain she even had an argument against their position. After all, Josh and Ray *had* inflicted much pain on their supposed loved ones.

"Aside from that, the wife of one of them *wanted* the curse put on him," said Miss Carleton, again lifting her nose haughtily. "I was there and I heard her say it." She frowned a little. "Miss Bushwell seemed to know who he was, though."

"All right, leaving that argument aside, I need to know what you all have planned for tomorrow," Jacqueline said.

"We don't have to tell you," said Misty Mountains. She'd pulled herself to her full height and loomed over Jacqueline.

Jacqueline was reminded that not only was Misty Mountains built like an Amazon, but all of the Bond Girls had been in spy novels, and a good number of the ones she knew about had been bad-asses in their own right. In other words, she was likely facing a group of smart, brave, take-no-prisoners women...which also meant that Ray, Josh, and anyone else who got in their way —including George Wickham and Bond himself—were in for a hell of a fight.

"Look, all I want to know is whether any, uh, anyone else besides Mr. Wickham and James Bond are going to be affected by your plan. Whatever it is."

Once again, she was met with blank stares and shrugs from the group of women. Their response, though unspoken, was clearly: *Not your business, and you can't stop us.*

The problem was, Jacqueline was beginning to believe that was true.

～

"WHAT ARE WE GOING TO DO?" asked Nadine.

The three of them had squeezed into the elevator to Jacqueline's flat to find out whether the ZAP Ladies had had any luck with Anne Boleyn and learning the counter-curse.

"I don't know. Maybe Anne will tell us what's going on," Jacqueline said. "She clammed up before, but maybe the ZAP Ladies have worn her down. God knows they know how to do that."

"And how *does* Anne Boleyn actually fit into this plot, anyway?" Suzette said as the elevator doors slid open.

Jacqueline shrugged and spread her hands. "I think she was only the tool to get the codex with the curse. Anne told me Kitty wanted to send her back, so apparently she doesn't need to be here for whatever they have planned tomorrow."

"I want to know how these people from different books know each other," Nadine complained.

"You and me both," said Jacqueline as they piled out of the elevator and into her compact kitchen. "And how Kitty Bushwell even knew Anne Boleyn *had* a codex."

The flat was silent and empty, and for a moment, Jacqueline was ready to freak out again. *Where did they all go?*

But then she saw the note: *Took everyone back home. Easier to work there. Making progress. —ZAP*

"Okay, whew," she said, and collapsed on the sofa, delighted not to have to deal with any of that for the moment. "The ZAP Ladies have taken Anne and the two cursed guys back to their house so they can try to find a way to counteract the curse. That means I—we—have a few moments of quiet." She looked at Nadine and Suzette, who'd also taken seats. "Even so, I should stick around here, just in case. I'm going to have to miss pizza night."

"Hell no you won't," said Suzette. "Nadine and I already decided we'll do it here. I just need to run across the street and grab the stuff."

"You are a goddess," Jacqueline said with great feeling and a wave of affection for her friends. They really were the best. "Both of you. Goddesses. Thank you."

"I'll get the wine," Nadine said, and she and Suzette rose from the seats they'd only just taken. "We'll be back!"

As the door closed behind them, Jacqueline realized this was the first time she'd been alone in more than thirty-six hours. As a person who'd lived solo for more than thirty years, and one whose favorite activities were gardening and reading, she was not used to being around people all the time. Having them in her space, in her head, messing up her day, insisting she *talk* to them or interact with them or whatever. She smiled ruefully to herself. And now she was a shopkeeper? Boy, did the Universe like to laugh.

That wasn't to say she didn't enjoy her time with Massermey (she most certainly *did* and, despite her exasperation with him, expected she'd continue to do so), and that her two friends hadn't become important parts of her life. It was just that Jacqueline craved alone time. Especially when things were crazy like they were now, with characters coming out of books and mobbing up to wreak some sort of revenge on two *other* literary characters...who weren't even here.

She closed her eyes for a moment and reveled in the quiet and solitude, tipping her head back against the sofa. But even then, she couldn't turn off her brain.

Two sets of characters—minor characters, who'd never been seen on the pages of their books!—were here in order to get revenge on two very roguish, rakish, deceitful men. And somehow they—or one of them—had summoned Anne Boleyn, an *historical* figure, who may or may not have been (but clearly was) a witch to help them do so.

It hardly made sense, and Jacqueline *liked* things to make sense. She was a voracious reader, and when books and stories and movies didn't make sense, it bothered her greatly.

But this was real life...and real life rarely made sense. It was rarely tied up neatly like a fantasy novel (when good always triumphed over evil) or a murder mystery (when the killer was always caught and brought to justice) or a romance (where the main characters somehow found happiness together—at least for a while).

And yet...*was* this real life? How could it be real life when it was peppered with characters pouring willy-nilly out of books? Books they hadn't even really been *in*!

She shook her head and opened her eyes, staring into the distance. *What am I missing? What are they going to do?*

Her attention fell on the painting that hung above the fireplace, directly across from her, the gloaming image of a gnarled cedar, arching gracefully over the scene at dusk. As always, Jacqueline noticed new and different things in the picture. It was as if she was watching a trail-cam trained on a quiet and beautiful glen at twilight, with critters coming and going...stars winking in and out...constellations appearing and then fading... the moon at varying degrees of fullness.

She was reminded of the white raven that flew into the picture earlier and helped her put the pieces together that the codex belonged to Anne Boleyn. And now, as Jacqueline stared at the painting, her vision became unfocused. The scene became a gentle blur, and she felt relaxed...thoughtful... meditative.

*What am I missing?*

She was still sitting there, in a trancelike state and unseeing, when she heard the sounds of her friends returning. Jacqueline blinked and came back to herself, and her focus landed on the painting once more.

There was something different in the serene, twilit glen. Movement in the corner.

Jacqueline rose and went closer, keeping her eyes focused on the scene, ignoring the sounds of Nadine and Suzette clomping from the back door of the apartment...

Bubbles.

Those were bubbles floating up gently from the corner of the painting. *In* the painting. As she watched, they wafted, tumbled, danced, landed on leaves and branches, on the shell of a snail, on the wing of a dragonfly, on the curve of a chipmunk's ear...and popped. Little, glassy spheres, exploding with tiny bursts of color from the moon- and star-cast above them.

Bubbles.

"Bubbles," Jacqueline said to Nadine and Suzette.

"Huh?" said Nadine.

"Yes...?" prompted Suzette.

Jacqueline rubbed her forehead, pressing away the tension that had gathered between her brows. "Somehow I think there are bubbles involved. Josh mentioned there being bubbles—you know, like the soap bubbles kids blow with those little wands?—when he was at the Ren Faire getting locked up in the stocks. Massermey said something about the woman who cursed Ray Gould blowing a bubble in his face—like a bubblegum bubble. But what if it was a *soap* bubble?"

"Interesting. So there were bubbles at both scenes," said Nadine as she began pouring glasses of wine.

"I didn't put it together until now," Jacqueline said, glancing at the painting again. The bubbles were no longer there, but they had done their job, firing up her brain. "I need to ask

Massermey—or Ray—whether it was a bubblegum bubble or a soap bubble. Because maybe that's the way they're putting the curse on the men."

"It sure would seem innocuous," commented Suzette, rolling out the pizza dough. Jacqueline appreciated that her friends made themselves at home; it required her to do less work. "A soap bubble floating through the air wouldn't faze anyone. And then, what, it pops in their face or lands on them and pops, and that's how they get the curse?"

Jacqueline was nodding. "Maybe. It sounds feasible to me."

"So they're going to do something at the parade tomorrow with bubbles," said Nadine, handing out glasses of wine to her friends.

"Something to do with the parade," Jacqueline mused. "That's what Suki said. And I definitely got the impression from the ladies that whatever it is, it's going to be more than just Bond and Wickham."

"Same here. They're definitely out for blood, and I don't think they care who gets caught in it," said Nadine.

"Well, lots of people are going to be at the parade," said Suzette. "The route is always packed with people. They start claiming their spots an hour before it even starts, putting down their lawn chairs and strollers and blankets. It doesn't come down Camellia, but it crosses it right at the end of the block. Really close by."

"And there are always lots of men in the parade," said Nadine. "Not being sexist, but, you know, police and firefighters and, of course, since it's Memorial Day, veterans and people in the armed forces. Largely male."

"Didn't Suki say one of them wanted to 'wait until tomorrow when they do it' and one of the Wickham women said 'anyone who deserves it would be afflicted'?" said Nadine thoughtfully. "That sounded kind of...broad."

"You don't think... Surely they're not just going to willy-nilly curse every man around, do you?" said Jacqueline, horrified at the thought.

They stared at each other.

That, somehow, seemed *exactly* what they—the Bond Girls and the Jane Austen acolytes—were going to do.

## 20

J acqueline rushed out of her flat down the stairs to the tea room. She didn't want to wait for the elevator. She wanted answers *now*.

But when she burst through the door and started down the hall from the back of the building, she realized the tea room was empty and silent.

The mobbed-up characters, as she'd begun to think of them, had gone.

Of course they'd gone.

Swearing vehemently, Jacqueline turned and started back from the way she'd come. She passed by the New Age Room, and something compelled her to look inside.

As soon as she got close, she caught a faint whiff of something burning. *Again?*

She stepped inside and, though it was dim because the lights were off, immediately realized the room was still occupied. It took her only a moment to recognize Kitty Bushwell and Miss Carleton.

They both looked up as Jacqueline hurried toward them,

where they were sitting in the back on the floor on poufs. Just as, she assumed, they—or at least Kitty—had done before.

"What's going on here?" Jacqueline said.

Kitty rose to her feet, and Jacqueline saw what she'd been doing. There, on the floor, was the Henry VIII biography from which Anne Boleyn had presumably come. Next to it was a small singing bowl with the last bit of ashes in it.

"We're just finishing up," said Kitty, giving her an arch smile. Miss Carleton also rose.

"What is going on here?" Jacqueline demanded again, although she had a suspicion she knew *exactly* what had happened. "Did you send Anne Boleyn back?"

Miss Carleton gave a genteel shrug. "We didn't need her anymore. And she was becoming rather demanding...as one would expect from a queen. But she was exceedingly helpful."

*Damn.* If Anne had been sent back, the ZAP Ladies wouldn't be able to get the information about reversing the curse.

"I think it's time both of you—and your friends—went back as well," Jacqueline said firmly. "You've had your fun. Two innocent men are cursed—"

"Innocent? Neither of those men are innocent," snapped Kitty. "James has always been a careless, emotionless, unfeeling bastard who takes what he wants and then moves on to the next victim—and George... Well, he ruined many innocent lives as well. And even once he married Miss Bennet, he didn't keep his willie in his pants."

Miss Carleton nodded, and Jacqueline saw her blinking rapidly as if to hold back tears.

"Neither James nor George are here," Jacqueline said. "The men you cursed are... Well, while they're not exactly guiltless, they're not who you think they are. They're not James Bond and George Wickham."

"If the curse stuck, they're guilty as hell," Kitty said flatly.

"And James *is* here. I saw him this morning, and it *was* him, and I was happy to curse that bastard. George was the one I put in the stocks so Anne could show me how to put the curse on him."

"I couldn't *bear* to see Mr. Wickham again," said Miss Carleton. "Even to put the curse on him. I s-saw him here, coming out of your shop. I didn't know what to do. I was— I couldn't face him. And so Miss Bushwell did it for me. For *all* of us."

"But we're not finished, Miss Finch," said Kitty with a sly smile. "There are plenty of other men who deserve to be so afflicted."

The hair on the back of Jacqueline's neck rose. "Like who?"

"Countless men," said Kitty. There was an unholy gleam in her eyes, and Jacqueline absolutely did not like the way her smile tipped up to one side...like a sneer. "As I said, the curse only afflicts those who deserve it. Who have done wrong to their women. If a man is innocent, it wouldn't affect him in the least." She laughed. "It'll be easy to tell the bastards and the snakes and the cheats. Their Johnsons will be raining to the ground in an epidemic."

The prickle got worse, and now Jacqueline felt a little surge of panic. "But what's your definition of 'done wrong'?" she asked.

"Well, Miss Finch, I suppose that's in the eye of the beholder —or the woman, shall I say." Kitty's eyes narrowed with delight. "We—all of us," she said, gesturing to the space at large and presumably referring to her fellow Bond Girls and *Pride and Prejudice* characters, "are tired of being used and objectified by men, especially when they promise us love and respect and fidelity...and then do the exact opposite. We're going to have our revenge on as many men as we can—for *you*. It's for you, Miss Finch, and every other woman who's been wronged. They deserve it. They deserve it all."

"No," said Jacqueline. "You can't do that. Surely some of

them have regretted their mistakes," she said, thinking of Josh and his apology.

Kitty and Miss Carleton exchange glances and laughed. "I do believe you believe that," said Miss Carleton. "But George will never have full remorse. He might tell you otherwise, but he's still a cad."

"But surely there are others who might regret their actions," Jacqueline said.

"It matters not," said Miss Carleton. "Once a cad, once a snake, *always* a cad and a snake. Men don't change their stripes just because they get caught," she said fiercely. "They don't suddenly become honest, true husbands and lovers if they've treated their women as chattel. Talked to them as if they're stupid. Control them. Abuse them."

"Indeed not," agreed Kitty. "A man who lies or cheats or abuses his woman, or dumps her or flirts with other women or any of that... It's just as bad. It's wrong. And they're all going to pay."

"How? How are you going to make them pay?" Jacqueline asked. How the *hell* was she going to stop these women? More importantly, how could she get them back into their books?

"You'll see," said Kitty with that arch smile.

"It's going to be at the parade," Jacqueline said. "You're going to do something at the parade. Something with bubbles, aren't you? Well, we're going to stop—"

"How did you know that?" Kitty's eyes flashed angrily. "Maybe we ought to send *her* to Tudor England," she said, looking at Miss Carleton. "Get her out of the way."

Jacqueline froze. Could they *do* that? Holy crap, if they could get Anne Boleyn out of the book, then could they put *her*, Jacqueline, *in* there too? Jacqueline had been taken into a book once before (it was an experience she did not want to repeat, even though she hadn't encountered a dragon, an ogre, or an evil witch), and so she knew it was possible—but she'd been *pulled* in by a character, not sent there by one.

Suddenly, Miss Carleton was holding the Henry VIII biography and Kitty had snatched up the singing bowl. She was beginning to murmur something, focused on the bowl. Miss Carleton opened the book and tore off part of a page, giving it to Kitty.

Jacqueline was so stunned that she didn't immediately react. It wasn't until Kitty pulled a lighter from the pocket of her tight, low-cut suit dress and lit the page that fear swarmed over Jacqueline.

She felt it explode through her: fear, anger, determination. A surge of energy burned from her belly through her limbs, to her hands, and suddenly blazed out from the tips of her fingers.

She actually *saw* as well as *felt* the light, the sparks, the blast of whatever it was that cut through the air like a blue streak of lightning. Kitty and Miss Carleton lost their grips on the book and singing bowl. They flew off the ground, spun, and then, as Jacqueline watched in shock and horror, the two women spiraled wildly, sucked into a sort of cyclonic gust that went smaller and smaller...spinning right into the Henry VIII book.

Everything was still. Jacqueline's heart pounded in her ears and she couldn't catch her breath. She was gasping and breathing in a sort of high-pitched keen.

The singing bowl had clattered to the ground and was still ringing quietly. The page from the book smoldered, and she stomped on it to put out the bit of flame.

The book sat on the floor, closed.

And no one was there but Jacqueline.

## 21

J acqueline backed out of the New Age Room, then thought
again and went back to snatch up the Henry VIII book.

She was still panting and her hands were shaking when
she came out into the tea room. It was still silent and empty.

She stared at the book, gripping it in both hands. There was
a sizzle of heat and energy emanating from it. Maybe even the
slight tinge of smoke. But nothing more. And even now, that
sizzle was fading.

She turned and tottered back to the elevator that would take
her upstairs. She didn't trust her knees on the steps.

"What took you so— Jacqueline, what's wrong? What
happened?" Nadine said as Jacqueline walked in from the
elevator.

The kitchen smelled like amazing pizza, and suddenly she
was *starving*.

"I..." Jacqueline began. She dropped the book onto the
counter, snagged a glass of wine—not even sure whose it was—
and took two big gulps. The wine burned her throat and she
barely kept from coughing. Her eyes watered with effort as her
two friends stared at her.

When she collected herself, she said, "I'm...pretty sure I just sent Kitty Bushwell and Miss Carleton to—uh—Tudor England."

Nadine and Suzette gaped at her, but before she could explain further, there was a loud ruckus in the back hall of the flat.

Jacqueline knew without looking that it was the ZAP Ladies, and when they rushed into view, she saw that Egala was with them.

"Is everything all right?" said Zwyla. Despite their hurry, she didn't appear the least bit rushed. Even so, her gaze fastened on Jacqueline.

"We felt it," said Pietra. "All of us," she added, looking at Egala. "The upset in the field of energy. It was sudden and violent and a little out of control."

Andromeda came forward and snatched one of Jacqueline's hands. "Aha," she said. "It *was* her." She held up Jacqueline's hand for everyone to see.

For the first time, Jacqueline noticed her fingers were tinged blue. "Oh."

"Tell us what happened," said Zwyla.

"I think I sent Miss Carleton and Kitty Bushwell back into this book," Jacqueline replied, pointing to the Henry VIII book. "They were trying to send *me* there. And...and something just happened. The next thing I knew, I was shooting sparks or lightning or something at them, and they were gone."

She looked around. The ZAP Ladies and Egala were nodding, and Nadine and Suzette were gawking.

"Sounds about right," said Egala. "You were threatened, and you reversed their intent on them. A little more effective than those tiny sparks you've been shooting." She looked down her nose at Jacqueline. "I knew I'd been feeling something in the air."

Jacqueline glanced at Zwyla, who'd recently admonished her for needing better control of her...whatever it was. Magic. Emotions. Crone-ness.

Zwyla gave her a spare nod. "We'll work on that. It seems your natural defense mechanism helped you in this case. You're fortunate it didn't backfire."

"I wasn't *trying* to do anything," Jacqueline said. "I just... It just happened." She looked at her fingers again. The blue seemed to be fading. She hoped.

"So...exactly *what* happened?" Suzette said. "And, by the way, pizza's ready for anyone who wants some."

Egala was the first to make her way over to the table where Suzette was cutting the pies, but Pietra was right behind her.

Jacqueline told them all how the group of vengeful women had not been in the tea room when she arrived, but that she'd discovered Kitty and Miss Carleton in the New Age Room. "They've sent back Anne, I think," she said, looking at the ZAP Ladies.

"Yes, she's gone," said Andromeda.

Jacqueline grimaced, but Zwyla said, "We got what we needed before she went. She... Let's just say she was intimidated by our—er—magic in this new world. Not to mention, the three of us are a formidable team. Anyhow, she told us what we needed to know. Raymond Gould and Josh Wenczel have been put in a special sleep that will keep the curse from progressing while Andromeda mixes up the cure. She had just begun when we realized something had happened here and knew we'd better check on things." Zwyla gave Jacqueline a small smile.

"Right. Well, I found Kitty and Miss Carleton in the New Age Room, and when I confronted them and tried to get them to see reason, they decided they were going to send *me* into the book. The next thing I knew..." Jacqueline held up her hands, fingers spread, and looked at them. "They were gone."

"Well done," said Pietra with her dimpled smile. "Now that the ringleaders are gone, hopefully things will settle down."

"Do you think the other vengeful ladies have left as well?" asked Nadine. "Or are they still lurking about, waiting to blow bubbles on everyone tomorrow at the parade?"

Jacqueline shook her head. "I have no idea. I suppose we're just going to have to wait and see what happens tomorrow." She sighed and reached for a piece of pizza. Margherita with extra buffalo mozzarella. *Yum.*

"So you think that they're going to show up and just blow bubbles at everyone? And all these random men are going to be cursed?" said Suzette.

"I get the feeling that's the plan. Although with the two ring-leaders gone, maybe the others won't follow through," Jacqueline said. "Maybe they *can't*, don't have the ability, you know? But the thing that worries me is, just in case they can, the way Kitty and Miss Carleton were talking, it sounds like *every* man is at risk. What they said was something like they were going to have revenge on as many men as they could for every woman who's been wronged. That's what worries me. I asked them what they meant by 'wronged,' and Kitty said something like 'it's in the eye of the beholder—or the woman'."

"So what they mean is, if a woman was hurt by a man, or angered by something he did, then he wronged her? That's... gonna be a *lot* of men," said Nadine.

"Exactly. And here's the other thing—what if it's something like, the guy broke up with her, you know, openly and cleanly without doing anything wrong other that realizing the relation-ship wasn't working and therefore *wronged* her, even though he wasn't being a dick? He just wanted to break up?"

"Or what if the woman was the one who was the problem and the guy just wanted out?" said Suzette.

"The eye of the beholder," said Egala. "That's pretty broad."

"Exactly my point. Any man who got divorced could be considered to have wronged his wife," said Jacqueline. She shivered a little because she didn't really know why Massermey had gotten divorced. He said it was partly due to his job—could that be considered "wronging" his wife in the eye of the beholder?

"Yikes," whispered Nadine. "I have no idea what happened in Gerry's past relationships, but...there could be some 'wronged' women there." She and Jacqueline exchanged meaningful, worried looks.

"Exactly. This could be really bad."

"It might not even happen," said Pietra.

"But it might," said Zwyla. She didn't look happy.

"Well, I'd best get back and fix up that antidote," said Andromeda. "And maybe I ought to make a *really* big batch."

"It's going to be all right," said Zwyla, rising. "Pizza was excellent, Suzette," she said, even though Jacqueline hadn't even seen her eating a piece. "Even better than Petey's. You don't put nearly enough cheese on it," she said as her friend began to protest.

"I thought you were cutting back on dairy," said Pietra as she and her friends swept out of the flat. Egala gave Jacqueline one last grudging look (maybe she was realizing that she really couldn't mess with her) and followed them.

For a moment, Jacqueline wondered about her distant cousin—was she lonely? Did she have any friends or anyone to go home to?—and then remembered how Egala had tried to wrest the shop away from her when she'd first arrived here, and how she'd cursed the purse of one of Jacqueline's friends in order to chase her away from Button Cove. And she decided that, at least for tonight, she wasn't going to worry about the woman. After all, she *had* made a tree branch fall on her.

Instead, she ate more pizza, drank more wine, and hung out with her besties.

Tomorrow and whatever it brought would come soon enough.

## 22

As Suzette had promised, the walkways lining the parade route were crammed with people—along with strollers, wagons, lawn chairs, dogs, bicycles, and scooters—by nine thirty the next morning.

It was a beautiful day—perfect for a parade and for the kickoff of summer. Warm but not hot, clear blue skies, mild breeze, absolutely perfect.

Jacqueline almost wished there was a tornado or thunderstorm coming in so the parade would be canceled.

Three Tomes was normally closed on Mondays, but Jacqueline had decided to be open this morning because of the parade. She was glad she'd done so, because the tea room had done a brisk business with customers wanting go-cups and pastries. She saw just as many people coming in and out of Sweet Devotion across the street. It was definitely good for business, if not for her stress.

How many of these men—innocent or not—were in danger of being castrated by a curse?

She'd checked the tea room multiple times and seen no sign of any of the vengeful ladies, as she'd come to think of them.

Maybe nothing would happen. Maybe they'd all gone back into their books and everything was over.

But she'd also gone into the genre rooms where the books had originally fallen. No books were on the floor, which was the usual signal that the characters had gone back from whence they'd come.

So she was on pins and needles, waiting to see what would happen.

It was just before ten, and Jacqueline was about to leave Mrs. Danvers in charge of the store so she could go to the parade, when Massermey came in.

"Good morning, Jacqueline," he said. He was carrying two go-cups with the logo of her favorite coffee place, Better Grounds, emblazoned on them. "Hi. Um...have you had your coffee yet?" He offered one of the cups with a tentative smile.

"Thank you, Miles," she replied, and saw his shoulders shift with relief at her use of his first name. She took the coffee gratefully.

"Everything...uh...all right?" he asked. "Here, I mean? At the shop. I was over at the blue house just now, and Zwyla said that Ray and Josh would be fully recovered in a few hours. They just need to wake up from their sleep. She also said they won't remember anything."

"That's probably for the better, don't you think?"

"Absolutely." He was still searching her with his gaze. "Look, Jacqueline, I'm really sorry I upset you yesterday. I was just... doing my job. I had to ask, but I probably could have done a better job with how I did it. It wasn't good."

"It wasn't, but I understand. I really do. I'm still kind of annoyed, not gonna lie, but I'm sure I'll get over it. But listen, I really think you ought to stay away from the parade today," she said. "Just in case."

"Just in case what?"

*Oh shit.* She just realized *he* didn't know what was going on.

His eyes narrowed suspiciously. "What's going on, Jacqueline?"

She heaved a sigh. "All right, I'll tell you, but you have to promise not to not believe me." She frowned; had that made sense? She plunged on. "Anyway, there's a chance that the Castratus Curse is going to be, um, *spread*, I guess is the word, around at the parade today. And, well..." She gave him a wry smile. "I kind of wouldn't want you to get cursed."

His cheeks flushed a little, but he got a stern look. "I'm law enforcement. I can't just hide away if there's going to be some sort of—what, attack?" He didn't seem too confident of his word use. "How're they going to spread it?"

"Bubbles. Soap bubbles, like the kind little kids blow through those little wands."

Comprehension followed by tension, then disbelief, spread over his face. "Seriously?"

"Yeah. It's going to be a mess if they manage it. Are there any floats with bubble machines?" she asked, suddenly struck by the thought. How perfect that would be for the vengeful ladies' purposes!

He frowned. "Maybe. I think Yankee Laundry has a float—that would be an obvious one to have soap bubbles. I'd better go check. Um...if they are, what should I do? Since this sort of thing is not exactly my realm?"

"Let me know right away, but try to stop it from sending out bubbles if you can. And don't let them touch you!" Jacqueline said, equally unsure of what she should do, but at least she was better equipped than he was. She glanced at her hands. The blue on her fingers was almost gone. But she also knew that whatever had brought it there was still inside her and could be summoned if need be. "The parade's about to start."

"I will. I know. Um...see you later?" He was definitely asking rather than stating, and she nodded.

"Yes." At least, she hoped so.

They both left at the same time, Jacqueline heading to the end of the block where the parade would pass by, and Massermey hoofing it out while on his phone, obviously trying to find out where the Yankee Laundry float was and if it had bubbles.

Nadine waved from across the street and sent Jacqueline a worried look. She remained there, and Suzette slipped out from her bakery to join her. They waved and made motions indicating they planned to stake out that area.

To her surprise, Jacqueline saw the ZAP Ladies standing down by the crosswalk, across the street from her. And Egala was on the other side. Of the four corners at the intersection of Camellia and the parade route, they had three of them covered —no, Zwyla was now crossing the street to position herself on the empty corner. And here was Andromeda, coming to stand next to Jacqueline.

Jacqueline refused to be insulted that the witches felt she needed backup. She did. She had no freaking idea what was going to happen, and what she would do if it did.

The parade was coming. People thronged everywhere. Jacqueline scanned the crowd, watching for any sign of a Bond Girl or a Jane Austenite, or soap bubbles.

Then she spotted a child a few yards away, blowing bubbles. Jacqueline's heart leapt and she grabbed Andromeda's arm, pointing.

They exchanged glances and started toward the child.

Surely the vengeful ladies wouldn't give cursed bubbles to a child...?

Andromeda and Jacqueline pushed their way through the crowd to the little girl with her bubbles, with Jacqueline hoping her companion would be able to tell whether the bubbles carried the Castratus Curse or not—and especially before they landed on any men.

They saw another child with bubbles further down the street, and then Jacqueline noticed the glint of more bubbles across the way. Had the vengeful ladies somehow distributed bubble bottles to the children of Button Cove, and were letting them do their dirty work?

*Crap, crap, crap.* That would be really bad.

The parade was upon them, led by the local high school's marching band. It was *loud.* Cheers and shouts, the thuds of drums and the "hut" calls from the drum major, filled the air, and then suddenly the band began to play "America the Beautiful."

And then Jacqueline saw it. Behind the band, the swath of glittering, pearlescent orbs streaming from a chimney-like projection on a float.

"Andi!"

But Andromeda had already seen it. Jacqueline expected her to start running toward it, but instead, Andi simply stood there. She closed her eyes, took a deep breath, and began to murmur.

Her hands rose slowly, gracefully, as if she were trying to raise or catch some invisible, airy element. Her fingers were spread, and Jacqueline felt something move in the air.

She looked back at the float. Bubbles, *streaming* from the chimney (she couldn't even tell what the float was *for*), filling the air. *Holy shit.* Any moment now, they'd start wafting down, drifting onto the spectators and parade participants, bursting and letting loose their curse onto hundreds of unsuspecting men.

Helpless and frustrated, Jacqueline looked over. To her surprise, she saw that Zwyla was also standing on her corner, eyes closed, shoulders straight and tall, face lifted to the sky, lips moving soundlessly.

What were they doing?

A quick look told her Pietra and even Egala were doing something similar...and then, all at once, the rain came.

From out of nowhere, from a clear blue sky, a light gray cloud had appeared, filling the area above the parade...and it seemed to unzip all at once, releasing a sudden downpour.

Jacqueline gasped and smiled—here was the weather she'd hoped for, albeit a little late. Then she gasped again, this time with full comprehension.

For not only was the rain pouring down causing people to cover themselves and duck into shelter, away from the bubbles, but the rain pelted the bubbles, destroying them as fast as they came from the float and bursting them high in the air.

The sudden wet destroyed the soap bubbles as water always would, rendering them—and presumably the curse—harmless.

Her hair was streaming down into her eyes, and everyone else was wet and heading for shelter. She looked at Andi, and was not at all surprised to see that she somehow remained completely dry.

Someone came up behind her, touching her shoulder, and she turned. It was Massermey, water dripping down his face, glittering in his beard.

He looked at her, then at Andi, then at the rain...and then he shrugged and spread his hands.

"I'm not even gonna ask."

## 23

"So can we assume the vengeful ladies are all gone?" Nadine asked.

It was much later that day. Danvers had allowed Jacqueline to close the shop at five ("It's a holiday, of course you should close at five, ma'am") and Nadine, Suzette, and the ZAP Ladies had gathered in Jacqueline's apartment.

They were expecting Gerry Dawdle and Massermey in a short while.

"I am working with that assumption," Jacqueline told her, nursing the martini she'd decided to have tonight. She figured she needed something *very* strong. "When I came back into the shop after the parade, I found *Pride and Prejudice* and *Moonraker* on the floor. Both were closed, which has always meant the characters have gone back. Danvers told me she'd picked up several other books in that room too," Jacqueline added. "I'm guessing since the ringleaders are gone, the rest of them went back to wherever they came from."

"Glad to hear it," said Nadine. "And the cursed ones—have they fully recovered?" She looked at the ZAP Ladies.

"Back to normal, and with not an iota of memory of what

happened," said Pietra. "Seems sort of a shame that they couldn't have the reminder of their unscrupulous ways, though."

Zwyla shook her head. "It's better that way. The fewer who understand, the better. We've also...let's say *chatted* with Mrs. Gould and her friend Suki. So all is well there."

"So how *do* you think that all happened?" said Suzette. "Kitty summoning Anne and then all of the other vengeful ladies showing up?"

Jacqueline looked at the ZAP Ladies, but as usual, none of them seemed willing to spill the tea—verbal *or* herbal. So she put out her own theory.

"Here's my thought. Anne Boleyn is obviously a real person, so Kitty Bushwell could certainly have known about her, and if she's any sort of witch—which she must be—she might have known that Anne was too. And Kitty, being around in the fifties, was surely aware of *Pride and Prejudice* and George Wickham's perfidy. He's one of the most notoriously rakish sort of villains in literature, so maybe Kitty just wanted to get revenge on him too. Who knows. Maybe *Pride and Prejudice* was her favorite novel? Anyway, I'm just guessing the other women came out of the books too because, well, you know what they say about women scorned."

Everyone chuckled and made noises of agreement.

"That makes as much sense as anything, and I'm hoping none of them are ever going to be around again to ask," said Suzette. She shifted a plate of macarons in the middle of the table to draw everyone's attention to it.

"Here's to that," said Nadine, lifting her glass for a toast.

They all clinked glasses, and Jacqueline settled back in her chair with a raspberry macaron. Suzette was really outdoing herself.

"So Kitty and Miss Carleton got sent to Tudor England?"

said Nadine. "Aren't you afraid they'll come back out and stir up trouble again?"

Jacqueline gave her a wry smile. "I *suspect* that Anne Boleyn might very well have ensured they never leave. It wouldn't surprise me in the least if she had them thrown in the dungeon after what Kitty tried to do to her—or even have them beheaded. Anne is not a woman to be crossed, and don't forget that they left her upended in an elevator for who knows how long. She would want vengeance of her own, I'm sure.

"I was looking through that history book a little while ago, and there's a picture—a drawing—of several women being taken off to a prison. Two of them are definitely not dressed in Tudor-era clothing." She grinned and looked at Pietra, whose eyes gleamed with delight. Jacqueline took that as confirmation she was right.

"But I still have one question," said Suzette. "It's the same one. What in the hell did Josh Wenczel have to do with all of this?"

"And *why* did those women think he was George Wickham and Ray Gould was James Bond?" said Nadine.

"I've been giving this a lot of thought," Jacqueline said, casting a look at Zwyla. "I think it's simple. When we read a book, each of us has our own idea of what the characters look like. And it's probably even different from the author's vision— even if the character is fully described. So that means that a character can look like *anyone*. And so, who knows? Maybe Josh *was* someone's George Wickham—he certainly was Miss Carleton's image of him. And same with Ray Gould looking like Bond." She glanced at Zwyla again and *thought* she saw an imperceptible nod.

"That makes complete sense," said Nadine. "I love it! Now I can sleep at night."

"But I *still* want to know why Josh was involved," said Suzette.

Jacqueline shrugged. "I've got nothing. No idea. Random synchronicity? Small-world syndrome? Chance?"

She glanced at the ZAP Ladies. They all had poker faces. As usual.

"I have an idea," said Nadine. "I think you sort of summoned him. In a way. Not *consciously*, though. What I mean is, you ran into him at *Six*—which, can I point out the connection to Anne Boleyn once again?—and something happened to crisscross those two elements in this woo-woo world of yours.

"And even though you were over him and probably had hardly thought about him for years—especially since Massermey came on the scene—suddenly he's there in your head *juxtaposed* with *Six* and Henry VIII...and there you have it. It sort of maybe made it all happen. Like—as you said—a sort of synchronicity." She dusted her hands together as if to punctuate her words. "After all," she added, "we all know you've got *some* sort of serious woo-woo shit going on."

Jacqueline laughed. "I suppose that could explain it—as much as anything could. Works for me."

"And me," said Suzette.

"Well, I'm still *pissed*," said Pietra, refilling her wine glass for the second time.

"You're certainly on your way to being so," muttered Andromeda. Petey made a face at her and took a big drink of her wine.

"Why are you pissed?" said Jacqueline.

"Why, because—what?—a dozen characters came out of *Pride and Prejudice*, and not one of them was Fitzwilliam Darcy!"

And no one—absolutely no one—disagreed.

~

# A NOTE FROM THE AUTHOR

Thank you so much for reading about Jacqueline's adventures with the Three Tomes Bookshop! I have the most fun writing these books because they are so very different from everything else I write. (Check out my website colleengleason.com for *everything* I've written!)

I wanted to mention that every book that is mentioned or alluded to in this series is a real book, and if they sound interesting or intriguing to you, I encourage you to look them up and enjoy! The exception to this is the mentions of Darby Wright and her beautifully illustrated fairy tales—Darby is a fictional character who will appear in the seventh Wicks Hollow book, tentatively titled *Sinister Symphony*, when I get to it (not sure if it'll be 2024 or 2025...hopefully not any later than that!).

Also, I wanted to make clear that the names of all of the Bond Girls who actually appear in *Hexes, Exes and Codexes* are fictional and were *not* ever created by Ian Fleming. (They were, in fact, created during a wine- and bourbon-fueled brainstorming session with several of my friends, with most of the credit going to my friend Phillip Devon for coming up with the best—ie, most horrific—ones.) However, since Mr. Fleming did create Pussy Galore and Holly Goodhead, I don't feel the least bit uncomfortable with presenting these other names as fictional possibilities—nor am I at all shy about the opinions of his misogynism presented by Suzette, Nadine, Jacqueline and the fictional Bond Girls in this book.

Thank you again for reading, and please consider subscribing to my newsletter (you can find the link on my website) in order to stay in the know about book signing events, new releases, give aways, and cover reveals!

Colleen Gleason
    February 2024

Prefer not to get messages in your email?
Sign up for SMS/Text messages and help keep your inbox clear!

Just type in 38470 for the phone number,
and then type COLLEEN in the message space!

.

# ABOUT THE AUTHOR

**Colleen Gleason** is an award-winning, New York Times and USA Today best-selling author. She's written more than forty novels in a variety of genres—truly, something for everyone!

She loves to hear from readers, so feel free to find her online.

～

Get SMS/Text alerts for any
**New Releases** or **Promotions!**

Text: **COLLEEN** to **38470**

(You will only receive a single message when Colleen has a new release or title on sale. *We promise.*)

～

If you would like SMS/Text alerts for any **Events** or book signings Colleen is attending,
Text: **MEET** to **38470**

～

Subscribe to Colleen's non-spam newsletter for other updates, news, sneak peeks, and special offers!
http://cgbks.com/news

*Connect with Colleen online:*
www.colleengleason.com
books@colleengleason.com

# ALSO BY COLLEEN GLEASON

*A Lily on the Heath*

**The Envy Chronicles**

*Beyond the Night*

*Embrace the Night*

*Abandon the Night*

*Night Beckons*

*Night Forbidden*

*Night Resurrected*

*Tempted by the Night* (only available to newsletter subscribers; sign up here: http://cgbks.com/news)

∿

**The Lincoln's White House Mystery Series**

(writing as C. M. Gleason)

*Murder in the Lincoln White House*

*Murder in the Oval Library*

*Murder at the Capitol*

**The Marina Alexander Adventure Novels**

(writing as C. M. Gleason)

*Siberian Treasure*

*Amazon Roulette*

*Sanskrit Cipher*

∿

**The Phyllida Bright Mysteries**

(writing as Colleen Cambridge)

*Murder at Mallowan Hall* (Oct 2021)

Milton Keynes UK
Ingram Content Group UK Ltd.
UKHW010837220224
438295UK00004B/169